BURY THE PAST

A FRENCH QUARTER MYSTERY

JEN PITTS

For My Family
Whether we're family by blood, marriage, or choice, I am
thankful to have you in my life

AUTHOR'S NOTE

While many of the places and events in this book are real, many are not. I hope you will enjoy visiting the real places as well as the fictional ones I created. Hurricane Katrina unfortunately was a real storm, but Hurricane Geoffrey, at the time of publication, was not an actual storm.

CONTENTS

1

"Ruby, it's too early to burn sage." I opened my front door to find musty scented smoke mixing with the humid New Orleans air.

"Samantha, the spirits are restless. I must clear away all the negativity." Ruby stood in the middle of the courtyard, waving a bundle of sage. "And that includes you."

I rolled my eyes as I called for my black cat, Nubi. Ruby Virtue had been my next-door neighbor for four months, but we still weren't what I considered friends. Our cats, however, were buddies with their daily jaunts around the neighborhood and sun-basking sessions in our apartment building's courtyard.

This morning Ruby and I looked like we belonged to the same coven, with our fluttering bathrobes and black cats racing toward us. Ruby's lilac chiffon robe with a matching headscarf was more theatrical than my utilitarian white cotton robe, although my cat-shaped slippers added a bit of whimsy, but not witch chic, to my ensemble. They also protected my feet as Nubi pounced and attacked my slippers. Ruby's cats, Cleopatra and Nefertiti, sat calmly by their human but watched Nubi's every move. I bet they wanted to join in on his fun.

I picked up Nubi after he nicked my ankle. "It's also too hot. I can't believe it's this warm already."

"Heat and evil spirits are just part of New Orleans." Ruby grasped the purple crystal around her neck. "You should know that by now."

Yes, I knew that. At least about the heat. It was early summer and the humidity permeated the air at 7 a.m. I would need to crank up the air conditioning when I got to work. Lagniappe Books would fill with heat and customers as soon as I opened the store. As the new co-owner of the shop, I was managing alone today. My best friend and business partner, Andrew Ballard, taught a class at Tulane University every Friday.

"But why are you out here?" I asked. "I don't think I've ever seen you up this early."

"True, I'm not a morning person, but the Goddess of Good called to me. I picked up my sage and headed right out here to find the negativity." She adjusted her headscarf with her ring-laden fingers. "And you."

My spiritualist neighbor was not my favorite person with her constant admonishments about the trouble that followed me or that I supposedly invited in. While I found myself in sticky situations on occasion — OK, on a lot of occasions — I still didn't know why I irritated her so much.

"Then I'll head back inside with Nubi and my newspaper before you stink up the whole French Quarter with your herbs." Before I took a step, the sound of the front gate startled me. It must have done the same to Ruby as she dropped her sage and stared at the two people entering our courtyard.

Although I considered them friends, by their solemn

faces and brisk walk, I could tell Rob and Christine were here on business. As homicide detectives for the New Orleans Police Department, Rob Armstrong and Christine Gammon handled many of the murder cases in the French Quarter. I squeezed Nubi tighter as I prayed they weren't here to see me.

Ruby was praying too, although I could never make out the words when she chanted to her Goddess of Good. Her prayers went unanswered this time.

"Miss Ruby, I'm glad you're already awake this morning," Rob said. He lived above our apartments with his fiancée and my other best friend, Sissy Covington, so he was aware of Ruby's habits. After a few run-ins with her, Rob now crept down the stairs when he left at odd hours, which wasn't easy with his body-building physique and size fourteen shoes. "We need you to look at something."

Christine took out a small plastic bag from the pocket of her gray blazer. "Miss Virtue, do you recognize this bracelet?" She showed Ruby a tarnished silver bracelet with specks of dirt encrusted on the five charms dangling from it.

Ruby was so entranced looking at the jewelry while Rob and Christine stared at her, so I put Nubi on the ground and stepped closer. It was a chunky bracelet, and the charms were a microphone, a key, a book, a cat, and a heart with a V engraved on both sides.

"Miss Ruby, do you recognize this?" Rob asked.

"Of course I do. I bought it for my daughter, Verity." She reached out for it, but Rob gently clasped her hand in midair and held it.

"Miss Ruby, I'm sorry, but we found it with human remains here in the French Quarter."

"Where is she?" Ruby's voice cracked. "When did she get here?"

"Ma'am, why do you ask when she got here?" Christine put the bracelet away and took out her notepad and pen.

"She left twenty-six years ago when she was seventeen years old." Ruby closed her eyes and wrapped her arms tightly around her body.

"You have a daughter?" I gasped. She had never mentioned a child, or any family, to me or anyone else in our building. "Where has she been?"

Ruby's eyes flew open. "I have no idea where my daughter has been. Did she come back to New Orleans just to die?"

"Miss Virtue, the body we found is a skeleton of a young woman." Christine put away her notebook. "If it's your daughter, she never left the French Quarter. In fact, she never left this street."

2

"Down the street?" Ruby's bracelets rattled as her hands shook. "Was it the Delmar building?"

"Yes, the body was discovered in the courtyard of the Delmar Apartments. Have you been there?" Rob said.

"Verity's *friend* lived there." The venom in Ruby's voice made it clear she didn't consider that person a friend.

"Who was that?" Christine asked.

"Myles Delmar, Junior," she said. "His father owns the building."

"Actually, the younger Myles owns it," Rob said. "Or at least he did until two months ago. He sold it, but he's still living there."

Ruby started walking to the courtyard gate, but Christine quickly stepped in front of her. "Miss Virtue, I realize you're upset, but you can't just go after Myles Delmar."

"I wasn't." Ruby crossed her arms. "I want to see my daughter."

"Now, Miss Ruby, that's not a good idea..." Rob stopped speaking when Ruby put her hands up like she was a traffic cop signaling a car to stop. She turned her head from one detective to the other, giving them an intense stare that I'd never seen her use. And I had endured many of her reprimands.

Rob and Christine raised their eyebrows at each other, communicating in a manner only they understood. They had been partners for over five years and handled many high-profile cases. While they'd dealt with all kinds of people, Ruby appeared to be unique.

"Miss Virtue, we're not ready for you yet," Christine said. "If it is your daughter, you don't want to see her that way."

"You have her bracelet, but I need to look at the body. I need to see her." Ruby put her hands down by her side and grasped the ends of the frayed belt of her robe. "If her spirit is there, I must help her cross over."

I witnessed Ruby contacting the spirits once at a haunted hotel. While her methods were melodramatic with her chanting, candle burning, and the clutching of crystals, I had no doubt she believed she was speaking with ghosts.

Rob and Christine didn't change expressions or say anything, so Ruby tried another tactic.

"I am well acquainted with the residents of the Delmar Apartments from twenty-six years ago. Myles Delmar, Junior was a liar back then and I cannot imagine that he has changed." Ruby stood tall and jutted her chin at the detectives. "You'll want objective information about him and the other residents. I can give you that."

This time I was included in Rob and Christine's unspoken dialogue as we all raised our eyebrows. I'd never heard an objective word come from Ruby's mouth.

She apparently caught our expressions, so Ruby tried another approach. "Perhaps objective is the wrong word.

But between my spiritual gifts and earthly knowledge, I can be of help to you."

Rob and Christine might not believe in Ruby's spiritual abilities, but they decided she would be useful. They nodded at each other, and then Rob gestured toward Ruby's front door. "Miss Ruby, as soon as you get ready, we will escort you to Delmar Apartments," Rob said.

"Thank you." Ruby went to her front door, but turned before she entered her apartment. "Samantha, I need you to accompany me."

"Me?" I was surprised by the detectives' decision to let Ruby come with them, but I was flabbergasted she wanted me to join her.

"Yes." Ruby blinked rapidly and looked directly at me. For a moment, I thought she was communicating with me non-verbally, but when a single tear fell down her face, I understood she was trying to be strong. "Please, Samantha."

I looked at the detectives. Knowing my history with Ruby, they appeared as shocked as I was. But they nodded, so I said, "Of course I'll come with you."

"We'll wait outside on the sidewalk for you both," Rob said.

He and Christine left the courtyard and after Ruby's cats entered her apartment, she closed her door. I picked up Nubi, who was waiting at my doorstep with his nose twitching. "Well, Nubi, Ruby wants my help. Has hell frozen over?"

Nubi meowed, jumped out of my arms, and dashed into our home. Was that a yes or a no? I hurried to get dressed so I could join Ruby and find out.

3

"**R**uby has a daughter? And she's dead?" The disbelief in Andrew's voice resonated through the phone. I had called him to tell him I might have to open the shop later than usual.

"I'm just as shocked as you are." As I spoke to him on the phone, I threw on a black shirtdress. "But I'm more surprised she asked me to come with her."

"Ruby is quite aware of your sleuthing prowess. But you need to be careful. You don't know the circumstances of her daughter's death, and I can't bear for you to be in a murderer's sights again."

I had been involved with several mysteries and murders since I'd moved to New Orleans four months ago. Ruby acted as if she had no interest in the lives of her neighbors. Occasionally though, she let on that she kept up on the news and gossip about the nine other residents of Thibodeaux Mansion.

"You think she wants me there for my detective skills?" I slid my feet into a pair of espadrille sandals and put my hair up in a ponytail. "That makes more sense than her wanting me there for emotional support."

"Whatever the case, Ruby needs someone at a time like this, and you are the one she wants. Treat it as an honor rather than a duty." Before he went to teach his class at Tulane, Andrew promised to place a note on the shop's door that we'd open late and insisted I call him later with an update. After we hung up, I grabbed my little blue backpack and rushed out of my apartment. Nubi followed me out. He joined Cleopatra and Nefertiti, who waited on top of the brick wall in the back of the courtyard.

"There you are." Ruby stood by her door with a large white leather bag in her hands. She had changed, but her outfit wasn't much different from her morning clothes. She wore a deep blue silk dress with a matching scarf around her neck and another one around her head. There was a sadness in her green eyes, but also a look of determination. Her hands were steady as she strode to the courtyard gate.

I glanced back at our cats, who watched Ruby intently. They appeared concerned about Ruby even if she acted as if she was fine. I nodded at them, hoping they understood I would take care of her — as much as she would let me.

Rob and Christine stopped talking when we met them on the sidewalk.

"Are you sure you still want to do this, Miss Ruby?" Rob asked. "We can speak at the police station instead."

"I appreciate your concern, Rob, but I will be fine." Ruby turned to Christine. "Detective, I don't know your name."

"I apologize for not introducing myself, Miss Virtue," Christine said. "I assumed you knew who I was from Rob. I'm Christine Gammon."

"Christine? Not Tina?" Ruby tilted her head. "The spirit

of an elderly woman behind you keeps calling you that name. She says she's very proud of you."

I arched my neck to peek around Christine as if I could see the ghost. I couldn't and neither could Rob, judging by the shaking of his head. Christine didn't turn, but she said evenly, "Good to hear. I didn't think my grandmother would have approved of me being a police officer."

"No, she wasn't talking about your job. She's proud that you renovated her house, and that you took out that awful green wallpaper in the powder room," Ruby said. "She insists it was your grandfather who put it up all cattywampus, not her."

"Thank you kindly, Miss Virtue. Shall we go to Delmar Apartments?" Christine's face was expressionless, but she touched her gold crucifix necklace before she began walking.

Rob joined Christine, and they proceeded down the street without speaking. Ruby and I followed them silently, too. Was Ruby trying to convince the detectives of her spiritual abilities so they wouldn't change their mind? Perhaps it distracted her from what she was going to face.

Nothing says crime scene like police tape, stone-faced officers, and crowds of curious people. The plastic yellow tape added color to the sun-bleached brick four-story building. Shutters would have given some warmth to the exterior, but only four out of what should have been eight shutters framed the windows. The original black color peeked out from behind the peeling white paint on the wrought-iron balconies on the second and third floors. The only intact architectural details left were the half-crescent windows above the two French doors on the ground floor.

As we had walked to Delmar Apartments, Rob had explained that Myles had sold the building to an out-of-town investor who was renovating the property himself. Luke Ward had a background in construction but not in handling New Orleans tenants. The residents hampered his attempt to update the apartments by limiting his access and even "misplacing" supplies that were delivered. Luke decided to outwit the residents by restoring the courtyard first without giving them notice. When he and one of his employees moved the non-working garden water fountain early this morning, they discovered the skeleton.

"How did they know the body was from this century?" I had asked. "I read about coffins found underneath buildings in the French Quarter."

"You must mean St. Peter's Street Cemetery," Rob had explained. "It was the first cemetery in New Orleans. In the 1700s, when the Spanish ruled the city, the government built a new cemetery, St. Louis No. 1. They didn't move the coffins."

"That's horrible. Did the owner assume he found a body from the old cemetery?" I had shuddered.

"At first, but the guy working with him said they were too far from St. Peter's cemetery," Rob had said.

"And when they saw the charm bracelet, they realized this was a recent burial," Christine had said. "Thankfully, they called us instead of covering it up."

We stayed with Christine outside the building while Rob walked inside to see if the crime scene investigators were ready.

"Detective Gammon, how did you know the bracelet belonged to Verity?" Ruby asked.

"Myles Delmar recognized it," she said. "Apparently the other tenants did, too."

"They looked at the body?" I said.

Christine frowned. "Mr. Ward claims he tried to keep the residents away from the grave, but they crowded around it. He insisted they touched nothing."

I wouldn't have stayed away from a skeleton buried in my courtyard, either. "So they saw the bracelet, and they all recognized it was Verity's?"

"Yes, except Mr. Ward and his employee," Christine said.

"Everyone in that building knew Verity. I had the bracelet made especially for her. Every charm represented a facet of her life." Ruby pointed at the mailboxes on the wall. "It appears everybody is still here from twenty-six years ago. Except for apartment four."

"Everyone is still here?" I asked, although I wasn't that surprised. My search for an apartment in New Orleans was tough until I met my landlady at her cafe. I discovered quickly that good apartments didn't turnover quickly, especially in popular neighborhoods like the French Quarter.

"Yes, except apartment four, as Miss Virtue noted. That renter died five months ago, and the unit stayed empty until the new owner took it over as an office," Christine said. "Do you remember who lived there when your daughter disappeared?"

"Sandra Lewis. She was a singer who toured with a band throughout the country." Ruby clutched her necklace. "She was out of town that week, so she was no help."

By Ruby's grim face, I had a feeling other people were of no help either.

Christine took out her notebook and flipped to a page. "Yes, Miss Lewis rented number four until her death."

"There are two Delmars here then? The mailboxes for apartments two and three have that name on them," I said.

"Myles' father occupied unit three. He was also out of town that week — probably with Sandra Lewis." Ruby said. "Myles Junior lived in the second-floor apartment."

Christine read through her notes and explained that Myles Delmar, Senior, passed away three years ago and Myles moved into his father's apartment. His ex-wife lives in apartment two, which they shared until their divorce. Delores Riggins still rented unit five.

"Was Delores in town when Verity disappeared?" I asked.

"Yes, but she turned her hearing aids off every night at eight so she wouldn't hear the noise in the courtyard." Ruby then smiled briefly. "Verity said Delores took them out so she wouldn't hear her cat meowing."

"I assume you know Sutton O'Berry in apartment one," Christine said to Ruby. "He's in your line of work."

Ruby's nostrils flared when Christine said the man's name. "He is most definitely not in my line of work."

Rob came out of the doorway before I could ask about Sutton O'Berry. "We're ready for you in the courtyard. Are you sure you still want to look at the remains, Miss Ruby?"

"Yes." Ruby's voice relayed her exasperation. There was no stopping her.

We followed Rob through a long hallway that led to the back of the main building. To our left was a two-story outbuilding, probably a former slave quarters, that housed apartments four and five. The courtyard itself was a small square-shaped patio made even smaller by the number of police officers and investigators filling the area. More yellow crime scene tape cordoned off two-thirds of the courtyard. A dismantled fountain lay next to the construction supplies, a rusted bicycle missing its front wheel, and a cracked claw-foot bathtub. Along with the wilted plants in dirty terracotta pots, these broken items just added to the atmosphere of abandonment and decay in Delmar Apartments.

Rob turned around and put his arms out to stop us. "The investigators should be able to take a break for you to see…"

"The grave," Ruby interrupted. "I appreciate your delicate handling of me, but I am fine."

"Hey, Rob, we need ten more minutes," a crime scene investigator called out.

Ruby closed her eyes and sighed. "I'll wait."

The detectives stepped over to speak to an anxious-looking man wearing a green polo shirt and a yellow baseball cap embroidered with Ward Construction. Ruby and I stood together, both of us staring at the gravesite.

"Ruby, I gather you looked for Verity on your own, but did you go to the police?" I asked.

"Of course I did!" she snapped, but then lowered her eyes. "How seriously do you think they took the disappearance of a local psychic's daughter? They laughed and said, 'You're the psychic. Can't you figure out where she is?' I never went to the police again. I scraped up enough money to hire a private investigator, but he found nothing. It was as if she fell off the face of the earth."

"I'm so sorry no one took you seriously. Please don't take this the wrong way, but did you ever sense her spirit? As if she had passed away?"

"That's actually a valid question. My fellow spiritualists ask that frequently." She fluffed the scarf around her neck. "No, I never found her in the spirit world. She could have been hiding from me, but I tried for so long and so hard that I was positive she was alive." She stared back at the makeshift grave. "Until today."

Ruby's breathing labored as she gazed at the grave. I gave her a moment before I spoke. Dealing with a missing child for over twenty-six years and then discovering she was buried down the street all this time was unimaginable. When her breathing returned to normal, I asked, "Do you feel her here now?"

Did unearthing a body bring forth their spirit? I had no idea how any of this worked.

"No, but she could have moved on. Not everyone stays where they left this world."

"I'm sorry, Ruby, this must be difficult to think Verity has been here all these years."

"If it is Verity, it will be painful." Ruby lifted her head and clutched her purse tightly. "But I need to confirm my daughter is in that courtyard before I believe she is dead."

How would Ruby verify it was her daughter? Did she need to perform a spiritual ritual? The detectives made it clear the body was a skeleton, so how would Ruby see it was Verity? Did she believe, since she couldn't find her daughter's spirit, that it wasn't her?

Perhaps she just needed to be closer to the skeleton. Or did Verity want to be left alone — even from her mother?

"Let's go inside the owner's office." Christine walked over to us while Rob stayed with the investigators. "I have some questions for you, Miss Virtue, while we wait."

From Ruby's heavy sigh, she appeared as frustrated as I was. We followed Christine into the apartment-turned-office. By the stacks of boxes marked tile and two new toilets, the apartment also appeared to be a storage unit. Four folding chairs stood in the far corner near the kitchen, but neither Ruby nor I sat. It wasn't only the layer of dirt on the seats that kept me standing; a loud voice was in another room. The closed door muffled his words.

"Fine. I'll call my lawyer and you can talk to him instead." A red-faced, sweaty man swung open the door, stomped out, but halted. "Ruby? What are you doing here?"

"I am here to see if this body belongs to my daughter, Myles." Ruby glared back at the man. "I always said you had something to do with her disappearance."

"I had nothing to do with her death." Myles wiped his brow with his hand. He wore faded blue striped pajama bottoms, a frayed and tight white t-shirt, and no shoes. His short brown hair was greasy and stuck up every which way. The bags under his eyes deepened as he stared back at Ruby.

"We'll just see." Ruby looked him up and down as if she was searching for evidence. "I heard you don't own the building anymore. And you are divorced as well. Everything slips out of your hands."

"I could say the same about you." Miles snickered. "Oh, wait, there's no could. I *can* say the same about you. Verity disappeared right from under your crooked nose."

I gasped. Although Ruby wasn't holding back, I couldn't fathom someone mocking the mother of a murdered teenager. Then again, Ruby insinuated Myles had something to do with Verity's death.

Instead of verbally or physically attacking Myles, Ruby surprised me by standing perfectly still and closing her eyes. She murmured under her breath so I couldn't understand what she was saying, but the low pitch and the rapid speed of her words sent shivers down my spine.

Myles paled as Ruby's chants grew louder. He stepped

back and shook a finger at her. "Enough of your witchcraft, Ruby. I'll have you arrested again."

He rushed out of the apartment, followed by the detective whom he had been in the other room with earlier. Ruby opened her eyes. "Good. He fears me and he should. If he killed Verity, I will make sure he pays in this world and the great beyond."

Christine smiled slightly and then put on her serious face and voice. "Miss Virtue, would you care to explain what Mr. Delmar meant by having you arrested again?"

"Oh, that?" Ruby shrugged. "It was nothing."

"I can look it up or you can tell me what happened." Christine took out her notepad and pen.

"Fine. The morning after Verity went missing, I confronted Myles out there." Ruby pointed to the courtyard. "We had what I considered a spirited discussion, but the insipid man, actually boy as he was only nineteen, got scared. He called the police and had me arrested for trespassing."

"You were arrested?" The image of Ruby with handcuffs encircling her wrists covered in chiffon came to mind, but I kept my amusement to myself.

"Briefly. Myles' father had the charges dropped immediately." Ruby crossed her arms. "He knew I was not a threat. I read his tarot cards often and channeled his mother for him, so he understood my intentions were good."

A police officer entered the apartment. "They're ready for you, Detective Gammon."

"Let's go," Ruby barked as she brushed past Christine, her scarf fluttering behind her.

"She has nerves of steel," Christine said to me before she picked up her pace to catch up to Ruby.

I quickly followed them. Ruby was tough, but I wondered if her bravado was an act.

4

The chatter and movement stopped when Ruby strode into the courtyard. From the crime scene investigators to the police officers to the detectives, every person stood still. At first I assumed they were watching Ruby only out of curiosity. But as she stepped up to the edge of the grave, officers took off their hats, a handful of people closed their eyes, and a few even made the sign of the cross. The respect shown to her moved me to tears. While it was just another day at work for the police, they must have understood how overwhelming and shocking viewing the body might be for the mother of the victim.

Rob and I stood on either side of Ruby. Christine waited next to me, fiddling with her pen and notepad. I gathered she was eager to talk to Ruby, but she didn't speak. I wanted to offer some words of comfort, but I couldn't think of anything Ruby would want to hear.

Finally, Ruby spoke. "Verity's spirit isn't here. I need more time to see if I can reach her." She squeezed her eyes shut and once again chanted under her breath.

While waiting for Ruby to finish her ritual, I studied the

skeleton. Well, as much as I could from a distance. Wooden stakes and white tape formed a circle around the gravesite. The body lay in the fetal position in the center of the marked-off area. It had been buried about three feet down. Bricks were off to the side, so it appeared the bricks and the fountain were placed on top of her. Someone went to a lot of trouble to hide the remains.

The round four-foot base of the fountain leaned up against the brick wall. The second tier of the fountain was slightly smaller, and it was propped up next to the base. On the other side of it was the third tier, which was the tier the water would come up when it was working. It was a column with a basin in the middle with a decorative piece shaped similar to a bishop chess piece. I hadn't realized that fountains came in parts. It made sense, since it was easier to move in pieces. Even so, the bottom tier must have been at least one hundred pounds. I couldn't imagine someone moving it by themselves.

I stepped away from Ruby to get a better look at them when Christine whispered, "The owner and one of his workers moved the fountain this morning, hoping the tenants wouldn't bother them. They took up the bricks and started digging, and that's when they found the remains."

"Why were they moving it in the first place?" I asked.

"The owner wants to make the water fountain work with a dedicated waterline," Christine said. "It'd just be easier to fill it with a hose, but fortunately for us, he wanted that pipe."

Fortunately for Ruby, too, assuming this was Verity.

"That is not Verity." Ruby's eyes flew open and her body relaxed. "There is no sign of her."

"But Miss Ruby, her bracelet was in there," Rob said

gently. "Of course we'll test for any DNA and we'll review your daughter's medical records."

"You can check them now." Ruby opened her bag and took out a faded and creased manila envelope. "I have her dental records. And I also have the x-ray from when she fractured her wrist from falling off the stage after singing at a talent show."

Christine accepted the envelope from Ruby and walked over to the coroner. Rob joined them and the three of them huddled together, poring over the documents. Ruby and I weren't the only ones staring at the detectives. Everyone in the courtyard focused on the coroner. I even saw Myles Delmar peering down from the third-floor window. He pulled the curtains after we made eye contact.

It didn't take long for the coroner to say, "This person's wrist shows no sign of any fracture as shown on the x-ray. The skeleton is not Verity Virtue."

"But I thought you said the victim had a broken bone," Rob replied.

"Yes, but not the wrist."

Christine furrowed her brow. "What is fractured?"

The coroner tilted his head toward Ruby. "Perhaps we should discuss this later. I'm sure this is exhausting for Miss Virtue."

"I am perfectly fine to receive the news." She put her hands on her hips. "Especially if these remains are not my child."

"Her skull is fractured," an investigator said. "Not her wrist."

"Mitchell, be quiet," snapped the coroner. Obviously, he didn't want this information out and by Rob's and Christine's stern faces, neither did they. At least now we knew this wasn't Verity. But who was she?

5

"Would you two mind waiting over there?" Rob pointed to a bistro table next to the staircase that led to the second floor of the two-story outbuilding. "We'll be with you in a minute."

I followed Ruby to the table. Her face was blank. "Are you OK, Ruby?"

"Yes," she snapped, but then she softened her voice. "Excuse my tone. I'm confused. For just a moment, I thought it was Verity. But it wasn't her and I still don't know where she is. I might never find her."

If this was anybody else, I would have hugged her. I took a chance and put my hand on hers. "I am so sorry. Knowing and not knowing are both difficult in their own ways."

"That is true, but this is nothing new for me. The unknown and grief are just part of my life." She looked down at the table. "Anyone who hasn't known this pain fears it. Friends and acquaintances act as if they'll catch my affliction."

"Ruby, you're not alone."

She raised her head and stared at me, her expression

one of doubt. After what she'd been through, I understood her aloofness better. "Well, I'm back to where I started from."

"No, you're not." I removed my hand and took out the notebook and pen I always carried with me. "You've learned where Verity's charm bracelet was for several years. It's a start."

"You'll investigate Verity's disappearance?" Ruby's head wrap fell down her forehead, and she pushed it back, exposing a few locks of silver hair.

"I assumed that's why you wanted me here." I crossed my hands on top of my notebook. Did Ruby want me here for moral support instead of my investigation, or as some called it, snooping skills?

"Yes, yes, that's why I asked you here." Ruby turned her head to stare at the gravesite. "You will look into Verity's disappearance even though the remains aren't her?"

"Of course. This is just the break you needed to find your daughter." I flipped to a blank page and clicked my pen. "Let's start from the beginning."

"Oh, my goodness, that is you!" A voice clamored from the now open door of the first-floor apartment in the main building.

Ruby had her back to the door. She didn't turn around as she sneered, "Charlatan."

"Fake." The male equivalent of Ruby exited the apartment. He wasn't wearing a long dress, but he had layers of scarves and a turquoise necklace around his neck. His white linen shirt was unbuttoned to his belly button, and his jeans hung low on his narrow hips.

He took a seat at the table next to Ruby. "Nice to see you, too. Although I am sorry about the circumstances. I can't believe Verity has been here all these years."

"Actually, it isn't Verity," I said.

"But it was Verity's bracelet." The man blinked profusely and ran a hand through his curly brown hair streaked with gray.

"Yes, it was her bracelet, but that's not her body in that grave in *your* courtyard." Ruby glared at the man.

"It's not my courtyard. Everyone uses it. I don't like your insinuation." The man turned to me. "Excuse me, but I don't know you. Ruby doesn't have friends, so who are you?"

"I'm Samantha Richardson, Ruby's neighbor. And you are?"

"I'm Sutton O'Berry, of course." He fluffed his scarfs and smiled wide enough for me to see most of his nicotine-stained teeth. "You must be new to New Orleans if you don't recognize me."

"Samantha isn't a psychic like you, Sutton." Ruby punctuated each word with biting sarcasm. "But you should have known that with your gift."

Sutton stood up and bowed toward me. "I am a brilliant psychic and I would love to read for you." He took a business card and handed it to me. It said Sutton O'Berry, Psychic, Tarot Card Reader, and Your Guide to the Spiritual World. There was no address, just a phone number.

"Thank you." I put the card in my backpack. "So, Sutton, tell us what happened this morning. I heard the new owner tried to remove the fountain before anyone caught him."

"That Luke Ward has no respect for old things," Sutton huffed.

"Like you?" The color was coming back to Ruby's face. Apparently, belittling a fellow spiritualist made her feel better.

"I am not old." Sutton turned to me and winked. "I am

aging like a fine wine as opposed to you, Ruby. You look and smell like vinegar."

"You used that line twenty-six years ago, Sutton. Can't you think of anything new?" Ruby said.

While it was like a tennis match listening to the two of them insult each other, we needed to get back to the issue at hand. "So, Sutton, you said Luke Ward has no respect for the building. Is he trying to change things?" Sutton nodded, so I continued. "Is there any reason you and the other tenants don't want him changing things? Filling the water fountain seems harmless to me."

"Perhaps, but what will be next? He might paint the brick, which would be devastating in its own right, but what if he picks some garish color? What if he renovates the apartments and removes the fireplaces, the original fixtures?"

"I agree keeping as much of the original building as possible is important, but making upgrades doesn't seem like a bad thing," I said.

"You're worried he's going to raise the rent when he fixes this place up, aren't you?" Ruby asked.

"No. I helped Delmar Senior with spiritual issues, so I have a ninety-nine-year lease."

"Really?" Ruby shook her head. "He must have been desperate to go to you."

"No, he finally realized he needed a real psychic, not a fairground fortune teller like you." He turned his back to her. "Don't let her read your cards, young lady. She will just mislead you."

Ruby snorted, and Sutton turned around to her. Before he said anything, I interjected, "Sutton, let's talk about this morning. Did you wake up when you heard them working?"

"No, I'm a heavy sleeper. It wasn't until Myles banged on

my door and called my phone that I realized something was wrong." Sutton dropped his smile and his voice. "I came out to see the skeleton. Luke's worker picked up the bracelet from the grave and I recognized it instantly."

"You knew Verity well?" I asked. "You were sure it was her bracelet after all this time?"

"She was here almost every day. Not to visit me; I was too old for her to have any romantic inclinations," Sutton insisted.

By Ruby's glare and Sutton's sheepish grin, I doubted either of them believed Sutton wasn't interested in Verity. By the faint lines around his eyes, I guessed he was in his mid-fifties, which would have made him about thirty when Verity disappeared.

"She was here to see Myles?" I asked.

"Yes, she and Nicole hung out with him since he was closer in age to them," Sutton said.

Ruby pushed back her chair and rushed over to Christine and Rob. "Detectives, I know who is in that grave."

Sutton and I followed her. Everyone in the courtyard turned to watch Ruby.

"Miss Ruby, who is it?" Rob asked.

"If the bracelet wasn't taken from Verity, there is only one other person she would give it to." Ruby cleared her throat. "It must be Nicole McBride."

6

___

"It's Nicole?" Sutton grabbed Ruby's arm. "She's been here all this time?"

"It must be her." Ruby shook off Sutton's hand. "Who else would wear Verity's bracelet?"

"Who is Nicole?" Rob asked before I did.

"Nicole McBride is Verity's best friend. I should have realized it might be her. Let me try to reach her now." Once again, Ruby closed her eyes and chanted. I expected Sutton to join her, not as her friend or colleague, but to show her up. Instead, he wrung his hands as he stared toward the grave.

"Is she any relation to Momo McBride?" I asked.

I met Myrtle "Momo" McBride a month ago when I helped my friend, Beau Boudreaux, with his hotel, which was next to her townhouse. She was a true New Orleans character with her love of good bourbon, her feisty nature, and her just as feisty cat, Lady Clementine.

"Yes, she's Momo's niece," Sutton said.

"Nicole is actually Momo's grandniece," Ruby said. Her eyes flew open, and she looked at Rob and Christine. "She and Verity were close friends. Someone must telephone Myrtle. She might not have heard about this."

There was no need to call Momo. A police officer walked up to Christine and whispered to her. She said, "Yes, bring her back."

We all turned to the hallway that led from the courtyard to the street. Momo didn't look as polished as usual. Her pink silk blouse was misbuttoned and her matching pants were wrinkled. Even her thick-lensed glasses were smudged. But her stride was purposeful and strong until she saw Ruby. She stopped a few feet from her and her face fell. Ruby grasped her crystal necklace but didn't greet Momo.

"Sammy, you're here?" Momo walked over to me, ignoring Ruby. She clutched my hand, and I cradled it, hoping it would help her stop shaking.

"Hi, Momo, I came here with Ruby. We're neighbors."

"I forgot," Momo said. "But why are you two here?"

I looked at Ruby to let her answer, but she just stared at the ground.

"They found a bracelet with the body and we believed it belonged to Verity Virtue," Christine answered. "Did you know Verity?"

"It's Verity?" Momo stepped toward the grave, but Rob gently put a hand on her shoulder. "Is Nicole with her?"

"Miss McBride, we have only established one set of remains so far, but it is not Verity Virtue," Rob said. "I take it you also have a missing relative?"

"Nicole is my grandniece. She stayed with me when she was seventeen," Momo explained. "She and Ruby's daughter disappeared at the same time. Verity is still missing, isn't she?"

Ruby looked up at Momo. "Yes, but her bracelet was discovered here this morning."

Momo's eyes widened. "Verity always wore that charm bracelet. Nicole wanted one just like it."

"Nicole is the only person Verity would have given it to." Ruby's voice faltered. "I can't find Verity's spirit here. Or Nicole."

"Hogwash," Momo sputtered. "You can trust all that ghost mumbo-jumbo you want, but I believe in science." She opened her purse and took out a manilla envelope just like Ruby's. "Here are Nicole's dental and medical records. And in the baggie is her toothbrush."

Christine accepted the envelope from Momo. "Miss McBride, let's talk over at the table."

Momo followed Christine, but gazed back at me. "Sammy, come see me tomorrow, please."

"I will."

A subdued Momo sat down at the table with Christine. If Ruby was right, Nicole was in that grave. Momo would know what happened to her grandniece, but Ruby was still in the dark about Verity.

"If you're done with me, I'm going home," Ruby said.

"Yes, Miss Ruby, that would be fine. We'll come by later with some follow-up questions," Rob said.

"Would you like me to escort you out, ladies?" Sutton asked. I'd forgotten he was there since he hadn't said a word after Momo entered the courtyard. "The press are outside, so I can assist you in getting around them."

By the gleam in his eye when he said press, I doubted he would help us avoid the media, but take advantage of the free publicity. Ruby appeared to feel the same way.

"We are perfectly fine on our own, Sutton," Ruby said.

"Thank you for the offer." I smiled at Sutton. While I believed his intentions were self-serving, I wanted to talk to him later about the building, its tenants, and Verity and Nicole. "Is there another exit out besides the front gate?"

"You're welcome to go through my place." Sutton offered. Ruby shook her head. I agreed, since his front door opened right out to the crowds waiting outside. It wasn't any better than going out the courtyard gate.

"Thank you, but I'll walk the ladies out," Rob said. "I'll talk to the media to distract them so Miss Ruby and Sammy can leave without notice. Mr. O'Berry, please wait in your apartment until my partner and I come to speak with you."

Ruby looked relieved, while Sutton frowned. He made the "call me" gesture at me before he closed his door. I didn't want a psychic reading, but I wanted to talk to him later. His reaction to Nicole's name and his proximity to the crime scene made him a prime suspect.

Rob's appearance at the entrance to the building distracted the crowd, so I guided Ruby down the street quickly. When we were a block away, we slowed our pace.

"Ruby, tell me about Verity's disappearance," I said after we passed a tour group listening to a guide lecture on the history of French Quarter architecture. It felt like the right time to discuss the past. Ruby's slumped shoulders and strained face told me she didn't feel the same way, but if she wanted me to help, she needed to cooperate. "I understand this is difficult, but I need to know what happened."

"Yes, you do. I want you to hear the facts from me." She sighed. "Verity and I moved to New Orleans about six months before she disappeared. She had a hard time adjusting since we had always lived in rural areas."

"Where did you move from?"

"That's not important." Ruby's forehead wrinkled. "She

did not return to any of the places we lived in before. I checked."

I let this go for now, as I didn't want her to shut down and not talk. "OK. Why did she have a hard time living here?"

"Honestly, I was surprised that she didn't like New Orleans right away," Ruby said. "She is smart and funny, but she always had her head in a book or was singing a song by herself. I hoped being in a neighborhood with artists, writers, and musicians would inspire her to explore her natural gifts."

"So Verity is an artistic person?"

"No, I mean her abilities in the spiritual world. Verity could be just as good as me, even better, if she worked on her spiritual powers."

Pressure to become a psychic seemed like a solid reason for Verity to run away.

"She didn't want to follow in your footsteps," I said. "Could that be why she left?"

"No, of course not." Ruby huffed. "I admit I hoped she'd join the family business, but I would have supported her in any other worthwhile vocation."

By Ruby's lackluster declaration, Verity's choice of another path would not have made Ruby happy.

"What did her friends say?"

"Nicole was her best friend, and the only other people she spent time with were Myles and his neighbors." A muscle twitched in her jaw. "She and Nicole were fascinated with that boy."

"Did either of them date him?" Perhaps he was a kinder man twenty-six years ago, but with the little interaction I had with him this morning, I doubted it.

"No. Nicole and Verity were both seventeen when they

met the 19-year-old Myles. He already had a girlfriend, Tabitha Calloway, but that didn't stop them from hanging around in the courtyard with them and Sutton."

"And Sutton was definitely too old to date them," I said. "Or so he claimed."

"Exactly." Ruby nodded. "Verity spent most of her free time with Nicole and with Myles and Tabitha."

"I can't imagine his girlfriend liked that."

"Tabitha seemed to like them as far as I could tell. She was the same age as Myles, so she wouldn't have considered them competition."

I put Tabitha on my list of suspects. I didn't agree that a nineteen-year-old wouldn't dismiss the younger girls as rivals, especially if they spent that much time at Myles' home. And why did Sutton hang around with the teenagers?

"OK, Ruby, now tell me about the day she disappeared." I braced myself for her resistance. She had a pained expression on her face, and I assumed she would say she was too exhausted to talk any longer. But she surprised me.

Ruby immediately told me the entire story, starting with the fight she and Verity had that night. They argued about everything: school, chores, the weather.

"You fought over the weather?"

"Yes, I'd tell her it was raining and she would say I was wrong." Ruby scoffed. "She didn't listen to anything I said."

"Was that argument worse than usual?"

"I didn't think so. We just stopped talking, and we had dinner." Ruby smiled. "She loves my chicken fried steak."

After Verity finished eating, she went to meet Nicole, taking her backpack, which wasn't unusual. She told Ruby she was spending the night with Nicole, which they did often. Ruby then left the very apartment she still lived in to see a client for a reading.

"I meant to call Momo to make sure the girls were at her house, but I fell asleep as soon as I got home." She frowned. "My session had been unusually draining, and I assumed if there was a problem, Momo would have called me."

Instead, Momo phoned the next morning, asking if Nicole and Verity were with her. The girls told her they were staying at Verity's house. Ruby assumed they must have been out with Myles all night.

"And that's when you went to confront Myles." I understood why Ruby rushed directly to the apartment building.

"I did. Myles and his girlfriend were still in their pajamas when I banged on his door." Ruby's face turned red. "They claimed the girls left around ten the night before. We ended up in the courtyard where Sutton came and agreed with them."

"But you didn't believe any of them, did you?"

"No. They're all liars," she said.

"Everyone assumed they had run off together except you and Momo?"

"Yes. They were rambunctious and moody teenagers, but they wouldn't just leave without a note." Ruby's eyes watered. "All these years, I hoped they would come home. But Nicole never left."

Nicole didn't, but what about Verity? Could Verity have had something to do with Nicole's death? Was Ruby ready for that possibility?

7

<hr>

While I needed more information on Nicole and Verity's relationship and their lives in the French Quarter, I had to wait. We arrived at our apartment's courtyard and found a group of concerned neighbors. The news about the skeleton had already made it around the neighborhood.

"Oh, Ruby, I am so sorry!" Libby Tyler, Thibodeaux Mansion's landlord and mother figure to all rushed over and hugged her. "We didn't know you had a daughter."

Ruby extricated herself from Libby's embrace. William, Libby's husband, said, "We are terribly sorry for your loss, Ruby."

"Sammy's already on the case, right?" Neal Bennett wore one of the green t-shirts from his business, New Orleans Past and Present Tours, and blue cargo shorts. His tennis shoes were in his hands as if he has just rushed down the stairs from his second-floor apartment. "She'll get this figured out for you."

"Sammy will help you, Miss Ruby." Connor Tyler, my boyfriend, put his arm around me and I rested against him.

The emotional ups and downs of the morning were more tiring than I had realized once Connor's comforting body was next to mine. He bent down and whispered in my ear, "You're going to end up with a badge at this rate."

I elbowed him and whispered back, "Shh, I can do more without a badge."

"Tru dat." Connor winked.

"Yes, Samantha came with me, but the remains weren't my daughter's," Ruby said.

"Oh, thank goodness, but what a shock!" Libby put her hands to her face. "Who was it then?"

Ruby looked at me, so I answered, "It might be Nicole McBride, Momo's grandniece."

"I didn't know two women went missing in the Quarter, and one of them your daughter Miss Ruby." William's normally serious face grew more so at the news. "When was this?"

Once again, Ruby glanced at me and then started toward her apartment. Before she unlocked her door, Libby rushed up to her. "Let me help you."

"I just need to rest," Ruby said. "I will call Papa later, and I am sure he will come over."

Papa Gede would definitely rush over as soon as she called. He and Ruby were good friends. Actually, I believed they were more than that. I met Papa when Andrew's book on the Voodoo ritual, the Gates to Guinee, sparked a murder spree in the French Quarter. Besides his help in solving the case, Papa gave me his friendship and spiritual protection in the form of a gris-gris bag. While I couldn't offer him spiritual protection, I gave him my friendship and bags of beignets.

"Yes, but you also need a strong cup of tea and a shoulder to cry on," Libby said. "I'm a mother and my heart is breaking for you. You've had a shock this morning and I hate to say more bad news could be coming. Let me get you settled, even if you don't want to talk."

Ruby stared as if she didn't understand the words. Libby finished unlocking Ruby's door and opened it. "Shall we go in now?" Much to everyone's surprise, Ruby nodded and held the door open for Libby.

The group of BB dolls sitting on a chair inside Ruby's apartment caught my eye. I had a doll like them and I learned they were originally sold in the French Market. I noted them the first week I moved into the building and wondered if Ruby had grandchildren. Now I realized the dolls must be Verity's. She must have never given up on her daughter.

After Ruby closed her door, Neal, Connor, and William made me explain the entire story, starting with Rob and Christine coming into the courtyard and ending with the revelation that the remains weren't Verity's. They had only heard that a body might be related to Ruby.

"I wondered how you ended up going to the Delmar Apartments," Neal said. "Ruby asking for help must be a first."

"She has always kept to herself," William said. "Libby and I assumed there was a reason for her aloofness, but I never imagined she had lost a child."

"No, I can't say I would have guessed that either." Connor put his arm around his father's shoulders. William had to look up to see into his son's face. While Connor resembled his mother more with his brown hair, artistic abilities, and warm smile, he was also his father's son. William and Connor shared a dry sense of humor, the love of crawfish étouffée, and a compassionate nature.

"It must have been a terrible loss for her," William said. "You don't have to be a parent to imagine her pain."

"I get why Ruby is the way she is," Neal said. "But I still can't believe she asked you for something, Sammy."

"I'm not surprised. Ruby acts like she doesn't care about her neighbors, but she does." William said. "But in her own way. She notices what we do, so she knows Sammy is a good investigator — an amateur one, of course." William smiled at me. "You're what Ruby needs right now."

"Dad, do you think Ruby's daughter's disappearance is the reason you and mom had to honor her lease?" Connor asked. When his parents bought the building fifteen years ago, one term of their purchase was they let Ruby rent her apartment indefinitely at its under-market rate. Libby and William wanted Thibodeaux Mansion badly enough that they agreed to those terms.

"Most likely," William said. "I know Randall Boyd was a client of Ruby's, so they had a personal connection."

"He must have felt sorry for her," Neal said. "And I bet a cheap apartment made it easier to deal with the memories of her daughter."

"Or Ruby could have been waiting for Verity to come home," I said.

On that somber note, William and Neal left the courtyard to go to their respective offices. Connor followed me into my place as I finished getting ready for work. While I was dressed, I hadn't put on any make-up or brushed my hair before I left with Ruby.

"You're pretty without makeup." Connor kissed me when I joined him in my kitchen, which really was a pass through to my bedroom. My apartment had a decent sized living room and a galley kitchen. I used it mostly for brewing coffee and reheating prepared food from my favorite neighborhood grocery.

"Complimenting me and making me coffee. My, my, you are a keeper." I accepted the travel mug from Connor and took a sip. "You even put the right amount of creamer in it. Now I have to keep you."

"Yes, I added that hideous fake stuff you like." Connor wrinkled his nose as he put away the creamer in my fridge.

"Sorry, but I won't change my sugar-free creamer for anyone." I stood up on my tiptoes to throw my arms around him. "Not even for you."

"I guess I need to try harder to convince you that cream and sugar are better." Connor hugged me back and then handed me a brown paper bag. "Here's your lightly toasted bagel with veggie cream cheese. I would have made you a sandwich, but you're out of bread. Actually, you're out of just about everything."

"I need to go shopping, but not today. My schedule is already off kilter after going out with Ruby." I grabbed my backpack, coffee and lunch, and we left my apartment.

"That was kind of you to go with her, considering how she talks to you." Connor walked me to the courtyard gate. "But I understand now why she is the way she is."

"As rude as she can be, I couldn't say no when she asked for help."

"You're sweet to everyone." Connor reached out and brushed the stray hair from my face. "But we all know you can't say no to a mystery."

I kissed him goodbye and headed to work. While I tried to be nice to everyone, Connor was definitely right. I never said no to a mystery — even if it involved my cranky neighbor.

8

____

A line of tourists was standing outside Lagniappe Books when I arrived at 10:30 a.m., and by their empty coffee cups and anxious faces, they wanted to shop right away. I had planned to restock the shelves and send out an email newsletter before opening, but I didn't want to lose any potential sales.

It was the right choice as I had steady business all morning. When Andrew asked me to be his business partner, I worried I wouldn't sell as many books as he did. He picked out the right book for whoever came through the door. Rarely did anyone leave the shop without making a purchase. My skills were improving; I tried to replicate Andrew's method of asking open-ended questions, giving the customer time to answer, and then putting the book in their hands. Sometimes I got it wrong. Once, a quiet old lady said she enjoyed historical fiction, but she really meant historical romance with the emphasis on romance.

The crowds thinned out around 1 p.m. when most people went to lunch. My bagel was still in my bag, but before I could eat it, my cousin Jasper St. Martin came through the door.

"Hey, Sammy. I hope you haven't had lunch yet." He raised a sack from Central Grocery. "I heard about your morning and figured you needed food."

"You're my favorite cousin." I headed to the seating area in the back of the store, my favorite spot in the shop. Andrew furnished it as a sitting room with a burgundy loveseat, two matching chairs, and a low marble topped coffee table. Andrew designed Lagniappe Books more like a library, which he felt made customers more comfortable.

"I'm your only cousin." He laughed and set the bag down on the table.

It was true; he was my only cousin and actually only one of four living people (including me) in my biological family alive. Jasper's mother, my Aunt Charlene, had been married to my birth father's younger brother.

The other person was my brother, known to me as Joey, but as Samuel to my birth family. At least I assumed he was still among the living. Over the last few months he had mailed me letters and postcards, but I hadn't received any in three weeks.

Jasper's laughter ended as he reached into the pocket of his cargo shorts. "But you're not my only cousin. And it seems he's closer than before."

He handed me a postcard from St. Louis Cemetery. I turned it over to see familiar handwriting. "Funny how death changes our lives. Enjoy the French Quarter," I read and then stared up into Jasper's concerned face. "My brother knows you live here."

"How could he?" Jasper plopped down onto a chair. Fortunately, it was sturdier than it looked. Not that he was heavy, but he was tall and "solid as a rock," as his mother liked to say. "It's not like I announced it in the newspaper."

"Are you sure Aunt Charlene didn't?" I joked, hoping it would hide my fear. This was the first time Joey had sent anyone besides me a message. Why would he do that? He never threatened me and he hadn't done so in Jasper's postcard, but I doubted Joey was just saying hello. He wanted us to know he was keeping tabs on us. But for what reason?

"Huntley has a local paper, and they did an article about Scarlett." Jasper sighed. "I didn't read it, but Momma probably moaned about losing her other baby to New Orleans."

No one could blame his mother for worrying about her son moving after her daughter had been murdered in the French Quarter. But no matter where or when had Jasper moved away, she would have lamented over her only living child leaving her.

"I bet that's how he found out." I took a gulp of my sweet tea.

"I don't believe that and neither do you." Jasper crossed his arms. "I can see in your eyes you're worried."

I opened up the bag of food so Jasper couldn't see my face. Taking out our sandwiches and chips and arranging them on the table gave me the time I needed to pull myself together. "Jasper, Joey could have come into town and mailed the postcard and left. I think he just likes me, and now you, to know that he's still around."

"But he has never done anything without a reason," Jasper said. "It might be a stupid reason, but he always has a plan. Or he comes up with one on the fly. His messages mean something."

"They could just be his way of letting us know he's OK. Maybe its way of saying he's sorry for what he's done."

"Considering everything he's done to you, Sammy, you're

giving him a lot more credit than I do." Jasper shook his head. "These postcards are a reminder that he's out there and we shouldn't forget about him. We can't forget about him and what he did."

"Could you have ever imagined he would do what he did? Did you ever think he'd become a killer?" I asked.

"If you'd asked me before he found out my father knew you were alive, I'd have said no. When he found out, he snapped. I was sure he'd be happy you were alive, but the truth changed him."

"And then he found out I remembered nothing, and he snapped again." I blinked back the tears as I recalled the pain my brother caused when I came to New Orleans.

"None of that was your fault. You aren't responsible for what he did." Jasper jumped up and sat next to me on the love seat. He put his arm around me and I let the tears flow down my cheeks.

"I know, but I just wish I could make things right for all of us." I wiped my face with a napkin from the table. Actually I wanted to make things right for Joey, too. I couldn't change what happened to him, but if he turned himself into the police, it would make a judge and jury look more favorably on him. Being on the run must be difficult and lonely for someone has family oriented and friendly as Joey.

I also didn't want this fear of him returning and hurting my family and friends any more. Especially as Jasper rubbed the crescent moon scar on the right side of his face. He hadn't done that since he'd moved here.

As much as I wanted to lie to keep Jasper from worrying, I was honest. "Jasper, we don't know what Joey is up to, so all we can do is be cautious. Keep an eye out for him as I'm sure you've been doing already."

"I have been. Anything else I should do?"

"Take the postcard to Rob and Christine at the police station after you leave here. If they're not there, make sure to leave it for them. The front desk is used to me dropping them off." I smiled half-heartedly.

"I will. What else?"

"Just try not to worry. The police are searching for him and our friends are keeping an eye on our apartment building and us."

"I'll try not to. Eating one of these will distract me." He stopped rubbing his scar and picked up his sandwich.

We ate our muffulettas in companionable silence. I loved everything I'd eaten so far in New Orleans, but this sandwich was my favorite. The salty olive salad, the layers of meat and cheese, and the crisp bread that held it all together made this the best sandwich I'd ever had.

"How was the hotel this morning?" I wiped off the crumbs off my dress. Since Jasper had moved here, he was taking odd jobs. His father had discouraged him from going to college, but even at thirty-two, it was still Jasper's dream. He planned to earn enough money so he wouldn't have to work as much when he started school.

"Fine. Just a few tweaks to the air conditioning units and hanging up some new towel bars in the rooms."

My friend, Beau Boudreaux, bought Hotel Jeanne last month and immediately began putting his own stamp on the business.

"Did Beau ask you if you saw any ghosts?" I asked.

"He did." Jasper smiled half-heartedly. "He hoped Scarlett would appear to me, but she didn't."

After his sister, Scarlett, was murdered at the hotel, Ruby couldn't find her spirit there. Scarlett and I didn't get along when she was alive, so I didn't feel the need to connect with her as a ghost.

"If there is an afterlife, Scarlett is getting her nails done and then dancing all night." He sighed. "Momma misses her so much. I do, too, I have to admit. Even if she was a pain."

The way he talked about her with his mother made me realize that although he had a difficult childhood between his sister's meanness and his father's cruelty, he still loved them both. Would I ever feel like that about my brother? Can you forgive someone who was a murderer?

9

Fortunately, my afternoon was as busy as the morning so I didn't have time to worry about my brother. After lunch, Jasper helped me restock the shelves and recommended several books to customers.

"Thanks for making that big sale," I said after a couple from California purchased all the books Jasper suggested.

"They just liked my accent." Jasper laughed. "But those history books are helping me in my tour guide preparation, so I thought they'd like them."

Becoming a part-time tour guide was another one of Jasper's odd jobs. Neal had lost two guides in the past few months and really needed the help.

"How is the training going with Neal?" I asked. "Does he quiz you at home, too?"

Jasper had moved into Neal's empty bedroom, but only after Neal warned him. Before he let Jasper take the room, he had said, "Not to be flip, but my first roommate was murdered. My second was a murderer."

"Sounds like you've had both sides of the coin, so to speak, as far as roommates go. I should be safe," Jasper had said. He and Neal had looked at each other with what I considered an understanding of the loss they both had experienced. But there was also a feeling of hope between them.

"No, he doesn't quiz me at home, but he's eager for me to start. But now Beau wants me to do more work at the hotel, too," Jasper said.

"What else does he want you to do?"

"Once he heard I have construction experience, he asked if I could remodel the attic to add two more guest rooms." Jasper shook his head. "I worked on construction sites back home, but I can't do anything that complicated."

"That seems like a job better suited to a construction firm."

"It is. And bathrooms are difficult. Once your brother and I worked on a motel being built in Huntley. It was a pain installing toilets and showers."

"So you and Joey worked together?"

"Sometimes we did. He and I both did a bunch of different jobs. He's more of a jack-of-all-trades than me."

Jasper shared a few stories about working with Joey. My brother picked up new skills quickly so he was in demand on construction sites and he would get Jasper hired on, too. Joey joked around as they worked to make the day go by quickly. If anyone tried to pick on Jasper, Joey always protected his younger cousin.

But my brother became bored easily so once he finished a job, he went looking for the next one. Besides construction work, Joey had been a bartender, used car salesman, and a blackjack dealer. "He got the casino job even though he'd never played the game." Jasper laughed. "He was just so likable and smart."

With that, Jasper had to leave to meet Neal. I hugged

him goodbye and reminded him to go by the police station with the postcard. I believed we would both have Joey on our minds the rest of the day. Where was he?

10

While my brother didn't come out and say it, I was now certain he was in New Orleans.

"Get off my mail, Nubi." My cat gave me a sharp meow, but jumped off my coffee table and onto the loveseat next to me. "Don't give me that cranky look unless you're going to pay these bills."

Nubi ignored me and curled up into a tight ball and promptly fell asleep by the looks of his twitching whiskers. Oh, to be a cat without a care in the world. I shuffled through my mail, and amongst my bills and magazines was a postcard.

Jasper wasn't the only one to get a message from my brother. The front of the postcard featured Jackson Square. On the back it said,

Don't let Charlene bother you and tell Jasper to stop rubbing that scar of his. And make Andrew give you a raise. That window display has you written all over it. Looks like you got the job you always wanted.

I didn't need the New Orleans postmark to prove Joey was in town and still here. Three days ago, I set up a new mystery-themed display. I snapped pictures of it, but hadn't uploaded it to the shop's social media accounts. Unless someone else had posted a photo of the window, my brother was here. And apparently keeping an eye on me.

"No, I'm fine, Sissy," I said to her on my phone, but I opened my front door to find her standing there. I ended the call and ushered her inside. "You didn't need to come down here."

I called Sissy to see if, by some miracle, Rob was home. The sooner the postcard was out of my house, the better. I gave everything my brother sent me to the police, but so far it hadn't helped them locate him. Even so, I didn't want any reminders of him in my home.

"Of course I did!" Sissy showed me a bottle of wine. "You called as I was changing from my work clothes, so I just had time to throw on a shirt and shoes and grab this chilled bottle that we both need."

That explained Sissy's purple LSU t-shirt and blue scrub pants. Her blond hair was still in a tight ponytail, but she wore rhinestone-studded flip flops on her perfectly pink manicured toes. Normally when she came home from her job as a nurse at the hospital, she threw on a t-shirt and shorts if she wasn't going out anywhere.

"You could have changed. I would have survived that long." I opened the wine bottle and poured two glasses.

"You claimed you were OK, but that postcard must have spooked you. Especially after this morning." She took her glass and sat on the loveseat. "Just turn up your air conditioning so I don't sweat to death in these pants."

"I can do that since you brought wine." I sat next to her and handed her the postcard from the coffee table.

"Yep, I'd say your brother is in town, but to do what? Do you think he's going to try to hurt you again?"

I took a gulp of my wine before I answered, "No, but I'm not sure what he really wants."

"Well, he's not here to talk about the weather! Come on, Sammy, Joey is obviously not of sound mind."

"Is that your expert opinion?" I raised my eyebrows.

"Ha, my work and life experience definitely make me qualified to say he's crazy." Sissy laughed, but then her face became serious. "You need to tell Rob about it right now. Text him a picture."

"I'll give it to him in the morning. Since he's not home, he must be busy with the skeleton down the street," I said.

"He is, but he and Christine will want to see this right away." She took my wine glass away from me. "No more wine until you message him."

"Fine." By Sissy's firm grasp on my glass, I wouldn't get it back until I texted Rob. It wasn't that I didn't think Joey's latest postcard wasn't serious; I just didn't want to deal with it. The thought of him looking in the window of Lagniappe Books when I could have been just on the other side of the glass made me shiver. When his postcards came from other cities, I let myself believe he wouldn't come back to town. It appeared I was wrong.

I snapped a photo of the postcard and texted it to Rob along with a declaration that I was OK and Sissy was keeping me company. Rob was a detective but also my friend and he would worry. It was the right thing to do and for now I could put my brother out of my mind. "That's done. Let's talk about something else."

"I'll agree to that since you've messaged Rob. Should we

talk about this morning?" Sissy handed my glass to me. "I got the basics from Rob, but tell me everything you learned. Starting with how Ruby asked you to come with her."

I filled her in on the day's events. She nodded along, so I suspected she had already heard most of the news from Rob.

"OK, that's my version, so what did Rob say? I'm sure you wheedled a little info from your fiancé."

"Who, me?" Sissy batted her long eyelashes. "Well, yes, perhaps I used my Southern charm to entice him to share some information."

"Of course you did." I laughed. "But he won't tell you too much. He is a good detective, after all."

"He is." She sighed. "But I wrangled a bit of dirt you don't have yet."

"Tell me!"

"Now, girl, don't get your panties in a wad, I'll tell you." Sissy grinned and motioned for me to drink my wine. "Honestly, it's not a lot, but I learned that the construction worker that dug up the body has disappeared."

"He's gone? Didn't the police keep him there?"

"The guy took off before they showed up. The owner of the building said his employee said he would wait for the cops outside, but he left."

"That's suspicious." I put down my now empty wine glass. "What did Luke Ward say about the man?"

"You know the owner's name? Of course you do. Nothing gets past you." Sissy grinned. "He has no idea why this guy disappeared."

"Maybe he was working illegally or had warrants out." I grabbed my notebook out of my backpack and made notes. "What is his name?"

"Raymond West, but Rob didn't find anyone with that

name that matched Luke's description of the man. Luke admitted he was paying him under the table so he didn't check his ID or get a social security number."

"Raymond West?" I stopped writing and looked at Sissy. "Are you sure?"

"Yes, why?"

"That's the name of Miss Marple's nephew in Agatha Christie's books." I tapped my pen against my lips.

"Now, Sammy, Raymond West must be a common name." Sissy refilled our glasses. "You think the guy picked it out for a reason? Assuming it's not his real name."

"It might be nothing, but it just struck me as odd." I decided not to share my suspicions that Joey could be the missing Raymond West. It sounded a bit crazy even to me. "You're probably right. OK, tell me more."

Sissy had no more details, so we talked about our own theories. We agreed that whoever buried the body must live there. Who else would have the time to move the fountain, dig a hole, place the body in it, and then put everything back as if nothing happened?

I planned to focus on the tenants of Delmar Apartments and also the disappearing construction worker. Even if he wasn't my brother he could have seen something important. And I needed all the information I could get.

11

Before Sissy left my apartment, she checked my pepper spray keychain. While I appreciated her concern for my safety, I didn't want my brother's possible return to New Orleans to change my life. I promised to be careful, but I wouldn't hide either.

Before I crawled into bed, Rob called to say he received my information about my brother's postcard. He also confirmed that the skeleton under the fountain was Nicole McBride, Momo's grandniece.

The next morning on our way to open the shop I told Andrew about my brother's postcards to me and Jasper. I didn't want to for fear he would send me home or worse, insist I leave town, but he didn't.

"Sissy, phoned me last night and told me," he said. "But thank you for telling me yourself."

"She did?" I frowned. "She didn't think I'd tell you, did she?"

"Samantha, don't be upset." Andrew put his arm around me. "Sissy called me because she wondered if we should offer to put an alarm system in your apartment. She's worried, but she also knows you're determined not to put your life on hold until your brother is captured."

"That's true. I can't wait until he's found, but I promise I will be careful." We reached the shop and I took my key out of my backpack. "And I need everyone I love to do the same. He hasn't mentioned anyone else, but just keep an eye out."

"We are and we will, my dear." Andrew followed me and locked the door behind us. "And now, let's talk about today's schedule. You must go see Momo as soon as we move these boxes to the office."

"I can't leave. We have so much to do." I protested.

"I just need help moving the boxes, but Momo needs you for moral support," he said. " We can catch up this afternoon. Take as long as you need with our dear friend. I insist."

I hated to leave Andrew with all the work, but I did want to get to Momo as soon as possible. We put away yesterday's late delivery and I rushed out of the store. I picked up a bouquet and headed to Momo's house.

I barely managed not to gasp when Momo opened her door. Instead of her hair braided and then wrapped around her head as usual, it hung down like unraveled balls of gray yarn. She held a half-burnt cigarette in a shaky hand. Her eyes were puffy and her face was blank. All the passion Momo usually showed was gone.

Even her cat, Lady Clementine, appeared despondent. She flopped at Momo's feet and gave a plaintive meow. I wanted to pick her up and cradle her in my arms, but Momo needed attending to first.

"Hi, Momo, I don't mean to bother you."

"I know I look horrible, but trust me, I feel worse." She half-heartedly smiled and opened her door wider. "And you remembered I asked you to come by. Thank you for coming to see me and for the flowers. I could use a friendly face."

I stepped inside, breathing in the stale air. Momo walked toward the staircase with Lady Clementine and I following behind. She led us out to her balcony on the second floor and motioned for me to sit at the wrought-iron table.

"I've just been sitting here with my coffee. Would you like some?" Momo poured a cup before I answered. She placed the china cup in front of me along with a blueberry scone. While she obviously was hurting, Momo's good manners trumped her melancholy.

"Are you by yourself?" I assumed Momo's family would be with her, or at the very least, her friends.

"Nicole's father will be here in a few days. Her mother passed away years ago. I always felt it was heartache — just like our Lovelorn Ghost." She looked over at Hotel Jeanne where the ghost story of a brokenhearted woman had brought Momo and me together.

"How about your friends?" I asked.

"Casseroles are stacked up in my refrigerator from my friends and neighbors. They've all come by, but they don't stay. Grief scares people; they act like it's contagious."

"Ruby said the same thing."

"Did she now?" Momo gave me a weak smile. "That might be the first thing we've ever agreed upon."

"So you and Ruby have known each other for a while, then?"

"We met when Nicole and Verity became friends." Momo explained Nicole moved in with her at the beginning of her junior year of high school. Her father decided that moving his daughter out of New York and away from her boy troubles was the best option for Nicole. She and Verity met Myles Delmar in the neighborhood. He introduced them to his girlfriend, Tabby Calloway, and his neighbor, Sutton O'Berry.

"Nicole was friends with them, but Verity was her best friend." Momo reached into her pants pocket and pulled out a creased photo. The teenagers could have been sisters with their long brown hair and delicate features. They wore matching jeans and black t-shirts as they sat at a table at Cafe du Monde. "It's one of the few photos of them together. People didn't take those selfie things like they do now."

"They look happy." Their smiles were big, as if they were caught laughing.

"They were. They didn't smile much. They were always trying to be tough teenagers. But I said, 'Smile, or I'll eat all the beignets.' So they did." Momo took off her thick-lensed glasses to wipe the tears spilling from her eyes. "I miss them both terribly."

"I'm so sorry, Momo."

"Thank you, Sammy, but I don't need your condolences."

"Oh, I didn't mean to offend you." Momo's stark words surprised me so much I sat back in my chair.

"You didn't. I'm sorry, that came out wrong." Momo leaned over the table and grasped my hand. "I appreciate your sympathies, but what I really need is your help."

"Of course." I squeezed her hand gently. "Anything I can do, I will."

"I hoped you'd say that." Momo smiled. "You're a good woman. I'd like to think Nicole would have grown up to be like you."

"Thank you, Momo."

"It's the truth, so let me tell you what I need." She let go of my hand. "I need you to find out what happened to Nicole. Yes, the police are working on it. But you see things a bit differently and people will talk to you more than the detectives. No matter how attractive Detectives Armstrong and Gammon are."

"They're good detectives, and they're taking this case very seriously," I said. "But I'm happy to check on things. Ruby asked me to do the same."

The coffee cup in Momo's hand fell onto its saucer with a thud. Neither piece of china broke, but the bottom of the cup had a large chip on it. "Ruby Virtue actually asked for help? Hell has frozen over."

"I was surprised, too." I giggled. "But I'm happy to help both of you."

"Yes, I'd like to know what happened to Verity, too." Momo poured some cream into a saucer for Lady Clementine. The Siamese cat lapped up her treat. When she finished, the cat jumped up into Momo's lap.

"Will you tell me about the night Nicole and Verity disappeared? Ruby said the girls claimed to be sleeping over at each other's homes."

"The girls did that all the time. They carried these huge backpacks with that had a few sets of clothes so they could stay at Ruby's home or mine. I believe they did carry text books in there since the bags were so heavy." Momo laughed softly. "Nicole and Verity both got good grades. They were smart girls."

"Why did you call Ruby that morning then?"

"I called to see if Nicole would be home for lunch. I had a craving for catfish, but I don't like to fry it just for myself." Momo's shoulders drooped. "That's when Ruby and I realized we didn't know where the girls had been all night."

"So their disappearance wasn't noticed until you called Ruby in the morning."

"It is the biggest regret of my life, Sammy." With shaky hands, Momo petted Lady Clementine. "And I've lived a long life. Yes, I assumed they were at Ruby's house. I should have checked, but I had no reason to. Nicole had never given me any cause to worry."

Momo looked off into the distance and I had a feeling she was thinking what I was thinking — that she hadn't known what trouble Nicole might have been in.

"Did you believe that Myles Delmar had something to do with the girls' disappearance like Ruby did?" I asked.

"No, I didn't. Myles was an arrogant boy, but he didn't have any backbone. He couldn't have engineered the girls' disappearance." Momo squeezed her eyes shut. "Or killed them."

But someone killed Nicole. And Verity was still missing.

12

T hanks to a quick stop at Frankie's Groceries for sweet tea and roast beef po' boy sandwiches, I learned some new information.

"Oh, Sammy, I heard you were with Ruby Virtue and saw the skeleton!" Frankie Fortuna squeezed me after I walked into her store. Good food and the latest neighborhood gossip were always available here. "Are you OK? I can't believe poor Nicole has been here all these years. Momo is devastated."

"I'm fine. I'm worried about Momo, though. She's a strong woman, but her grandniece's death has hit her hard."

"You've already seen her?" Frankie stood on a step stool to take down a box of Zapp's Chips. I knew better than to offer to help her. While she was petite and elderly, Frankie made it clear she could do things for herself.

"I just left her. She's putting up a brave front."

"That's how she was when Nicole went missing." She placed the box on the sales counter and then handed me two bags of chips. "Now, I'm a big supporter of the police, but it makes me angry that they didn't take Nicole and Verity's disappearance seriously. They just called them runaways."

"Ruby told me. That must have been so hard for Momo and Ruby."

Frankie wiped her hands on her apron. "It was. All the businesses put up posters and kept an eye out for the girls, but they were just gone."

"Until yesterday," I said. "This must have been weighing on Momo for the last twenty-six years."

"She's a strong Southern woman, but we all need help now and then," Frankie said.

"All women do." I smiled.

"You're right. I'll go to Momo as soon as Frank gets back. He's delivering lunch to the police at Delmar Apartments."

"Delivering food, but picking up some information, too, I bet."

Frankie put her hands on her hips. "Information? You think he's there to get the latest gossip?"

"Don't act like you're offended." I grasped Frankie's hands and gave them a squeeze. "You're going to grill your grandson as soon as he gets back."

"You know me too well." Frankie's eyes crinkled as she laughed. "But I already have some clues for you now. If you're interested."

"You know me too well." I smiled. "Fill me in."

As Frankie made po' boy sandwiches, she told me an officer came in earlier. After coffee and freshly baked chocolate chip cookies, he said no other body was found in the courtyard.

"So Verity wasn't there, but they discovered an angel buried with the poor child." Frankie handed me my sandwiches.

"An angel?"

"Yes, a small angel statue about this big." Frankie put her hands in the air as if she was holding a one foot statue. "He said it looked like the one outside his family's tomb in Metairie."

"Why in the world would someone leave a statue under Nicole's body?"

Frankie shook her head. "It's as if the murderer wanted to give the poor child some comfort."

A statue offered little consolation for having been killed. Frankie gave the murderer the benefit of the doubt, but I didn't. I needed to find out more about that angel.

"Keep me posted, Sammy, when you learn more or solve this mystery." Frankie hugged me again after ringing up my purchases.

"I was going to say the same to you."

"Oh, no, I just pick up on things. You're our neighborhood sleuth." She laughed as she shut the door behind me. "But you better get back to the shop to give Andrew his lunch. And the latest news."

I headed back to Lagniappe Books, but now I had another type of work to do: investigating.

13

Andrew and I batted ideas back and forth over the new information I learned from Frankie all afternoon. He read the newspapers and I searched online for any information about a statue found with Nicole's body. It wasn't mentioned anywhere. The only new information we gleaned was that the Delmar family were well-known in the local antique business but rumored to have fallen under hard times.

In between customers, we talked about what might have happened to Verity. We hoped she was alive somewhere, but most likely she was dead. Or worse, what if she had something to do with Nicole's murder and went on the run?

Verity was on my mind as I walked home after work. Andrew had invited me to join him and Beau for drinks at the Carousel Bar at the Hotel Monteleone. But I begged off as I wanted to go by the Delmar Apartments. I doubted I could get inside the courtyard, but I should be able to peek through the gate.

Sure enough, a policeman guarded the building. By his dour expression and folded arms, I gathered he was in no mood to chat. A day-old crime scene still drew curious folks, but they passed by quickly with just a stare from the officer. Only two other people stood by the building's gate and lucky for me, I had met one of them.

"Hi, Sutton!" I walked up to him and smiled. "Remember me? I was here yesterday with Ruby Virtue."

"How could I forget you? Your aura is as red as your hair." Sutton reached out his hand and I assumed he wanted to shake hands. Instead, he kissed the top of my hand. "Such a delight to see you again, Samantha."

"You're too kind." I restrained myself from wiping my damp hand on my pants. "Excuse me, I didn't mean to interrupt."

"I was just leaving." The woman looked me up and down, her eyes resting on my green belt with a fleur-de-lis buckle. "But if you're interested in that belt in other colors come to my shop, The Graceful Girl Boutique, on Magazine Street."

"Thanks," I said to the back of her head as she walked away from us. She flipped her long auburn hair over her broad shoulders. Between her muscular arms and shoulders, the woman must be an athlete. And with her serious attitude, she didn't seem like a client of Sutton's.

"Don't mind Tabby. She's constantly pushing her store. And she's always brusque. Which is a shame. She used to be so carefree."

"Is she a friend?"

"Oh, yes, we've known each other for decades. Tabby lives in the building."

"Is she Myles' ex-wife?"

"Aren't you up on all the people in the Delmar Apartments?" He stepped closer. "Why the interest?"

"You can't help but be curious when there's a murder on

your street." I smiled but took a half-step backward. Apparently, Sutton didn't know about my involvement in a few mysteries. I would use this to my advantage. "Would you like to grab coffee and chat about what happened here? If it's not too upsetting for you, that is."

Sutton puffed out his chest. "My dear, while I am devastated over dear sweet Nicole, I am perfectly fine to talk about it. But let's skip coffee and have a drink."

"A drink is fine. It'll be my treat. We can go to The Gas Light." I started toward Decatur Street, but Sutton hesitated.

"It's not my preferred drinking establishment, but if you insist."

I insisted. While Sutton appeared friendly, I didn't trust him. It wasn't his profession as a psychic that made me wary of him. Since moving to New Orleans, I'd met spiritualists of all kinds, and most of them were sincere in their beliefs. And while I wasn't sure of Ruby's abilities, I appreciated how seriously she took her profession. If she called Sutton a charlatan, I would be cautious of him.

When we entered The Gas Light, my concerns were validated. Sutton kept his head down as he strode toward the back of the room, but he didn't get far.

"What on God's green earth are you doing here?" Terry, one of the bar regulars and my friend, grabbed Sutton's arm with his paint-splattered hand.

"I am here to have a drink with this lovely young woman." Sutton shook off Terry and frowned.

"You ain't trying to use this as your office again, are you?" Terry pointed his beer bottle at him. "Remember what happened last time?"

Sutton's face turned red, and he opened and closed his mouth twice before he said, "That was like twenty years ago, Terry! How can you remember that with all the beers you inhale?"

He cocked his head toward the two empty bottles by Terry's right hand.

"Pshaw, that's nothing. No one forgets the fool who tries to run his business from a bar."

"I was just in between spaces," Sutton sputtered. "I can't help if some of my clientele like to drink while I read their cards."

Sutton stomped off to a table under a flickering gaslight.

"Sammy, are you friends with this guy?" Terry asked, scowling after him.

"We met yesterday. We have a mutual acquaintance." I leaned down to kiss Terry on the cheek and whispered in his ear. "What should I watch out for with Sutton?"

He looked at me and grinned. "Don't give him any money and take nothing he says as truth. Let your neighbor, Ruby, read your cards instead."

I stood up and nodded. So Terry knew Ruby? I wondered if he had used Ruby's services.

Sutton fidgeted with his scarf as I sat down. "Is Terry your friend, or did he just harass me for fun?"

"He's a friend. I met him when I first moved to the Quarter." I turned to find Rose Habert, bartender extraordinaire and another friend, standing next to me. "Hi, Rose. Have you recovered from your trip to Alabama?"

"Almost. Neal's family is as crazy as he is. Their idea of relaxing is waterskiing and line-dancing." Rose grinned. "They figured out pretty quickly that I hadn't done either before. Here are the bruises to prove it."

Rose pulled up her jeans to reveal a bandage around her left ankle and a bruise on the right ankle.

"Wow! You really do like Neal." I laughed along with Rose. She and Neal had been dating for three months. While they seemed like an odd couple with Rose's quiet but firm manner and Neal's boisterous and energetic nature, they were a perfect pair.

"We'll see how much Neal likes me when we visit my family." She grinned. "If he can play poker all night while roasting a pig, he'll do just fine."

Sutton interrupted. "I am dying of thirst. I saw you behind the bar, so I assume you're the bartender. Can I order now?"

Rose gave him the tight smile she used on drunk and/or rude patrons. "Yes. What can I get you, Sutton?"

"Wonderful! You recognize me. Have I read your cards? I'm sure I'd recall a woman like you."

Sutton would have remembered Rose as she stood out, even in this eclectic neighborhood. She favored cardigans in soft colors, which contrasted with the doubled-pierced eyebrows. And Rose thought the same. "Yes, you would remember me. Terry told me who you are."

"Of course." Sutton grimaced. "If you'd like me to read your cards after I read Samantha's cards..."

"You ain't charging either one of them!" Terry shouted.

"How did he hear me from over here?" Sutton craned his neck to look over at a grinning Terry. "This place is so loud."

"Terry keeps an eye on everyone in here," Rose said. "I'm not interested in tarot cards. Sammy, what can I bring you?"

"I'd love a Pimm's Cup. Sutton, what would you like?"

"A Ramos Gin Fizz." Sutton leaned across the table toward Rose. "I'm sure you are aware you must shake the drink at least five minutes."

I bit my lip so I wouldn't laugh out loud. While considered a classic New Orleans cocktail, most bars in town, especially ones that catered to locals, didn't serve Ramos Gin Fizzes. Some ingredients were commonplace in many bars: gin, simple syrup, club soda, and lemon and lime juice. But I doubted The Gas Light or any "dive" bars had cream, orange flower water, and egg whites.

"You'll have a Sazerac." Rose headed back to the bar, but winked at me before she left.

"Thankfully, I do like Sazeracs. I hope she uses the best whiskey for it."

"She will." I scooted my chair a little closer to Sutton, hoping it would get his attention. I lowered my voice and said, "Now, Sutton, have you recovered from yesterday? What a day it must have been for you."

"Oh, yes, I was busy from morning to night!" Sutton's face lit up, and he babbled on for a good ten minutes about how devastated and distraught he was yesterday. And how he could barely concentrate. And the media knocked on his door constantly. He even kept talking when Rose dropped off our drinks. His continuous chatter confirmed my theory that if I made the situation about him, he would ramble.

"Did you go to the police station?" I asked when Sutton finally took a gulp of his cocktail. "They must have so many questions since Nicole was buried right outside your door."

Sutton coughed and put his glass down on the table with a thud. "Yes, the police had a lot of questions. Unfortunately, I didn't have any answers for them. I don't know how or why pretty little Nicole ended up dead in the courtyard."

"Oh, I assumed you might have some inside information." I sighed and looked around the room, hoping if I acted bored, Sutton would take the bait.

He did.

"My dear, I'm sure I do. Just ask away." Sutton propped his elbows on the table and rested his chin in his hands.

"Did they find another body in the courtyard?" I took a sip of my drink.

"No, no one else. Poor Verity is still missing."

That wasn't news to me, but at least I knew he told the truth about somethings.

"Perhaps they'll find her alive somewhere," I said. "Did they discover anything else with Nicole?"

"Besides Verity's charm bracelet? I don't think so." Sutton took his chin off his hands and shook his head. "Why? What have you heard?"

"Nothing. I assumed the bracelet wasn't the only thing in there."

Did the police officer make the statue story up just to give Frankie a bit of gossip for coffee and a cookie? Or were the detectives keeping that information to themselves? I dropped that line of questioning with Sutton.

"You saw it? The bracelet, I mean," I asked.

Sutton shuddered. "I did. That construction worker had it in his hand, but wouldn't let anyone touch it. But we all realized it was Verity's. It was a delightful piece of jewelry, considering Ruby picked it out."

"What happened after everyone recognized it?"

"Luke rushed back and said the police were coming. He took the bracelet from Roy or Ray. I can't recall his name to save my life. Ray or Roy ran outside to wait for the cops. Luke shooed us away like we were dogs sniffing for bones."

Sutton put a hand up to his mouth. "That's the wrong comparison. Luke didn't understand how shocked we were to see Verity dead in our courtyard."

"And then it turned out to be Nicole," I said soothingly. "How did you meet the girls?"

"I met them through Myles. They came to visit him all the time." He fished the orange peel out of his glass and chewed on it. "It broke my heart when they ran away, but it wasn't surprising."

"Why's that? Momo and Ruby were shocked Verity and Nicole left town without a word."

"Mothers, or in Momo's case, great-aunts, aren't always aware of what their young-ins are doing."

"That doesn't sound good."

"Oh, I don't mean to imply anything." He dropped the orange peel back into his glass. "They just liked to hang out with Myles and Tabby and drink beer and listen to music in the courtyard."

"Is that all?" I turned around in my chair to make eye contact with Rose at the bar. She nodded toward a server who was bringing two drinks our way. How many cocktails would I need to buy Sutton to get the truth out of him? He took a sip of his second drink and leaned in to talk to me. I breathed in through my mouth as his nicotine and whiskey breath overwhelmed me.

"Well, that group was tight. They always whispered in the courtyard and stayed out very late."

"What were they up to?" For Momo's and Ruby's sakes, I hoped the girls weren't into something illegal. "Did other people hang out with them?"

"You're wondering if they sold drugs? I did, too, for a bit. But I watched over them and saw nothing like that happening."

"What did you see happening?"

"Besides the partying, they came in and out at all kinds of hours. But listen, Sammy, as a well-renowned psychic, I checked through the spiritual world and made sure they were not doing anything that would disrupt my living space."

I choked down my laughter since I wanted to keep Sutton talking. Whatever checking through the spiritual world meant, he obviously didn't do it well, since Nicole had been buried outside his door. "That's good. But do you think whatever they did together caused Verity and Nicole to leave?"

"Oh, no, I'm sure they just partied as teenagers do. Myles and Tabby were devastated when they disappeared."

I sipped my drink as Sutton shared how Myles' father offered a $10,000 reward for any information on the missing girls. Tabby and Myles put posters up around the Quarter and even went to neighboring cities looking for them. "Or at least that's what they told me they did," Sutton said after he took a breath from rattling on. "I'm sure they did. They were good kids, too."

"Are they good adults?"

Sutton let out a raspy laugh. "Now that's my favorite question that you've asked. Myles grew up trying to be like his daddy, but he's failed. He has no head for money. Or women. He lost Tabby and Delmar Apartments last year."

"They live in the same building, so the divorce must have been amicable."

"Is any divorce amicable?" Sutton smiled. "Mine wasn't, but that was years ago. I'm single now. How about you, Sammy?"

"No divorces in my past." I edged my seat back. "But I am dating someone."

"Of course you are." Sutton sighed. "Are you ready for your reading?"

I nodded and finished my drink. While I had little faith

in Sutton's abilities, the goosebumps that rose on my arms made me doubt that this would be all fun and games.

14

———

I wasn't paying Sutton for the reading, but he pulled out all the stops. And by that, I meant theatrics. He took out a deck of dog-eared tarot cards from his right-hand vest pocket. The back of the cards were a deep purple with a gold eye in the center. Sutton fanned the deck across the table, slowly blew on them, and stacked them in a tight pile.

"The cards are ready. Please shuffle them and return them to me, Sammy."

I shuffled the cards and placed them in Sutton's outstretched hand. He fanned them out once again.

"Now, pick three cards with your left hand. Don't look at them. Give them to me face down."

"Here you go." I picked from the left, right, and middle of the cards and handed them to Sutton.

"Tonight I'll do a past, present, and future reading." He placed them in a row, face down. "Relax your mind and heart, and we'll let the cards tell us what you need to know."

Unless the cards had the name of Nicole's killer and Verity's whereabouts, I didn't expect them to reveal what I needed to learn. But I kept quiet. Sutton's calm manners and soothing voice were such a contrast to his earlier demeanor that I was interested in seeing where this reading was going. When he turned over the cards, I was confused by the first one, a little worried by the second, and surprised by the third. From left to right they were: The Fool, Death, and The Magician.

"Let's start from the beginning with The Fool."

"Sure. So, I was a fool in my past?" I put my finger on The Fool card. I found tarot cards to be fascinating with their unusual imagery and this card intrigued me. The person, The Fool, carried a stick with a bag hanging off of it. He stood at the edge of a cliff, holding a white rose with a dog jumping behind him. While I had done foolish things in my past, I had never placed myself in that situation.

"The cards and I are here to guide you, but you must decide what in your past The Fool reflects." Sutton smiled. "Let me ask you this, by the lack of a Southern accent, you are not from New Orleans. Did you decide to move here on your own?"

"Yes."

"See how The Fool is setting out on a dangerous journey? He is taking a leap of faith to go where he needs to go. Perhaps that's how you found your way to our enchanted city."

I couldn't deny it was a leap of faith that brought me to New Orleans. And it turned out to be a dangerous journey to find my past and establish a new life here. But the beauty of tarot card readings is that the cards can be interpreted in many ways including being forced to fit some situation in the person's life.

"So I survived my foolish journey and now I'm facing death?" I smiled, hoping to keep the mood light. My guess was that Sutton not only read the cards but the person he was reading for.

"I'm glad to see you're not frightened by the Death card." Sutton inhaled. "Many clients tremble when it appears, but it has a plethora of interpretations."

"A card with the grim reaper wearing a suit of armor while riding a white steed surrounded by dead and dying people doesn't seem encouraging," I said. "But I'll go out on a limb and guess it can be the end of something, not just your life."

"You are correct. The death card can symbolize the end of a life, but also of a relationship or a phase. Is something like that happening to you now?"

I was tempted to say no to prove him wrong, but everyone has some kind of change in their life. "Not recently, but over the past few months, I moved here, switched careers, made new friends, and started dating my boyfriend."

Sutton shook his head and pressed his hands on the table. "Yes, yes, those are all changes, but the card is emanating a distinct energy. There will be an upheaval in your life. It will shock you to your core."

Bad news — if I believed Sutton. "So I should expect to move, lose my job, my friends, and my boyfriend?"

"Oh, no, nothing like that! I'm sorry I shouldn't have scared you." Sutton grabbed my hands. "The energy around you and the cards show a change to someone, perhaps more than one person, in your life."

I tried pulling my hands away, but Sutton squeezed them harder. "Sutton, you can let go."

"Sorry, the spirits took over for a moment." Sutton released my hands. "Be careful over the next week. There will be a cataclysmic event in your life. Prepare yourself physically, mentally, and, of course, spiritually."

"I'll take that under advisement," I said this to placate Sutton, but I couldn't deny my brother came to mind. Were his messages to me and Jasper a sign that he was part of a major event to come? I didn't need a tarot card reading to tell me to be wary of my brother — Joey did that on his own.

"Good, now let's go to the future. While your present will be full of heartache and despair, there is light or, I should say, magic at the end of the tunnel." Sutton laughed as he pointed to The Magician tarot card. "And no, you won't be pulling a rabbit out of your hat."

I chuckled along with Sutton as I assumed he expected me to. He must use that line every time the card appeared. "What does The Magician stand for?"

"You'll be happy to know it's a good sign. Your future is full of endless possibilities if you focus on your strengths. Your career, your love life, whatever you want, is yours for the taking!"

"I'd say that's a good ending to this reading." I looked back toward the bar and signaled Rose for the check.

"Yes, it is a perfect card to have for your future, but Sammy, you can't wait for things to happen." Sutton traced The Magician card with his finger. "Nothing will fall into your lap, no matter how lucky you are. You can have the life you want, but you must stay on the right spiritual path."

Here was the part I was waiting for — the sales pitch.

Sutton took the cards up and put them back in the deck. "A spiritual cleanse will remove all the negativity from the past and present. Then you will be prepared to work toward your destiny."

I had to ask, "And how much is this spiritual cleanse?"

"Normally, it would be $1500 to start, but seeing as you're

now a friend..." Sutton leaned over the table and whispered. "I can offer it to you for $750. And for any additional sessions you might need, I'll give you a discount on them, too. But I'm sure you won't need too many."

"Why is that?" I tried to keep my face as blank as I could as not to show how utterly ridiculous his offer sounded.

"You seem in tune with your spiritual side, so I am confident you'll take to my guidance very well."

My skin crawled as Sutton leered at me. Just as he leaned over the table farther, Rose dropped a bowl of peanuts in front of his face. He jumped in his chair at the sound and scowled at Rose.

"Sorry, I should have brought these over earlier." Rose put the check down by Sutton. "Come again."

I winked at Rose before she walked away. Terry gave her a thumbs up as she passed his table. I didn't care which one of them came up with the interruption, but I was grateful for it. I'd had enough of Sutton for the evening.

"That was the rudest delivery of rancid peanuts I have ever endured." Sutton pushed the peanut bowl aside. Apparently, he forgot that the complimentary peanuts were always stale. So far, no one could tell me why they were still placed on the tables. My guess it was to separate the bar regulars from the first timers or the only timers if they actually ate the nuts.

He took out a pack of cigarettes from his vest, but quickly put them away. "Forgot I can't smoke here. Or anywhere it seems. I'm waiting for my new landlord to outlaw smoking in the courtyard."

"Were you outside smoking the night Nicole and Verity left?"

"I don't think so." Sutton tapped his fingers on the table.

"Really? I heard you saw them leave the Delmar court-yard at ten that night."

"Did I? I could have. I mean that was almost thirty years ago! I don't dwell on my past, just my destiny." He stood up from the table. "I see a cigarette in my future, however. You said you were buying tonight, so I'll head outside."

If I hadn't just asked Sutton about the night Nicole and Verity left, I would have just assumed he didn't want to pay for our drinks. The way he avoided looking at me as I asked him about that evening gave me pause. If he really didn't remember why not just say that? Sutton had more up his sleeve than a magician.

Sutton avoided Terry's table by taking the long way around the room. Terry and his table mates watched him as he scurried out the door, but not before Terry yelled, "Go find yourself an office, Sutton O'Berry!"

"You really don't like him, do you?" I walked over to Terry and put my hand on the back of his chair. "What did he do to you?"

"I've never let him read my cards, but plenty of others gave him a chance when he waltzed into town. And everyone agreed he just spewed nonsense," Terry said.

The other men at the table nodded as Terry spoke, but they never took their eyes off their cards. Terry and his friends played poker from time to time, using the peanuts from the bowl as betting chips.

Jimmy, who had the most peanuts in front of him, said, "Sutton used to pester people to let him read their cards. He'd say it was free, but then try to charge them afterward."

"He used The Gas Light to do his work?" I asked. "Ruby has her own shop and I've watched the tarot card readers set up at Jackson Square, but I've never seen anyone use a bar to do a reading."

"Maybe it would work in a tourist trap bar, but not here," Terry said.

"He tried to read my daughter's tarot cards here one night. Laura laughed in his face when he told her she was in danger from evil spirits, but he could rid her of them for the bargain price of $1000," Jimmy said.

"$1000? He wanted to charge me double," said Bob, a bar regular. "For that kind of money, I told him I'd keep the ghosts and charge them rent."

"I must be special, since he said it would only cost me $750." I grinned and put my hands up. "No, no. I didn't take him up on this exclusive offer."

"You're smarter than that, Sammy," Terry said.

"Sammy, don't you believe a word Sutton tells you," Jimmy said. "You follow your heart and you'll be all right."

They all agreed, so I had no doubt that Sutton had rubbed almost everyone in the bar, if not the French Quarter, the wrong way. Not that I planned to take what he said to heart, anyway.

"Thanks, I will." I smiled. "I should let y'all get back to your game. Although it looks like Jimmy is winning each hand."

"He must be using some of Sutton's magic to win." Terry winked at me. "Now, cher, you watch yourself around him and everyone else at Delmar Apartments. I know how you like to play detective. The past has a funny way of coming back and not always in a good way."

"Don't worry, I'll be careful." I wanted to ask Terry what he knew about the building and its tenants, but I didn't want to miss grilling Sutton for more information. Terry was here so often that it wouldn't be hard to find him later.

"I thought you had forgotten about me," Sutton groused when I met him outside The Gas Light. "Terry must have been giving you an earful about me. He is such a curmudgeon."

"I got the feeling you and he have a bit of history," I said.

"Not really. I think he just hates successful business people like me." Sutton took a drag off his cigarette.

I doubted Terry felt that way, especially about Sutton, but I let it go. "Did anyone else from the apartments hang out here?"

"I don't believe so. My interaction with my neighbors has mostly been in our courtyard." Sutton grinned. "Would you like to have a drink in the courtyard? Or my apartment?"

"That's kind of you to offer, but here's my boyfriend." I pointed over Sutton's shoulder at Connor, who walked up to us. "Connor, this is Sutton O'Berry from the Delmar Apartments."

"Now, now, introduce me as the renowned psychic that I am." Sutton tossed his scarf around his neck. "You both should let me do a reading for you. I have a special rate for couples."

"I have your card, Sutton. Thanks for tonight's reading," I said.

"You're welcome, but consider having the spiritual cleanse done." Sutton shook Connor's hand and hugged me. "And I'm a hit at weddings, so keep me in mind as entertainment at your reception."

"What in the world did he tell you about your future?" Connor put his arm around me after Sutton walked out of sight. "Did he predict when we were getting married? You haven't even told me what kind of ring you like. I need to play more gigs if you want one like Sissy's."

I dug my elbow into his side and laughed. "Simmer down. I'm not relying on a psychic, and I use that term loosely, to dictate the terms of our relationship. Don't worry."

"Oh, I'm not worried. I'm happy the way we are."

"Me, too." I got up on my tiptoes and kissed him. "But I do like Sissy's ring, so keep that in mind — in a couple of years."

"Yes, ma'am." He grinned, and we walked back to Thibodeaux Mansion. Marriage was the last thing on my mind right now, and I was relieved Connor felt the same way. This relationship was easy and fun. No matter what Sutton predicted, I would live my life on my own terms. But I wondered what a reading from Ruby would reveal.

But tarot card readings weren't a priority for me or for Ruby. We needed to find out what happened to Verity. And I wouldn't get answers from a tarot card deck.

15

———

The day after Sutton's card reading was uneventful until the evening. After a busy day at Lagniappe Books, Andrew and I entered our courtyard with plans to share a bottle of wine. Our resident psychic foiled our plans. Instead of her usual layers of scarves, Ruby wore a simple white shift dress and her feet were bare. Clutching a stick of incense in each hand, she rocked side to side in front of her front door.

"Well, that explains the smell of pine trees." Andrew wrinkled his nose.

"I had no idea pine tree incense existed." I coughed. "The courtyard smells like a hundred of those tree shaped car air fresheners."

"Shush!" Ruby's eyes opened wide, and she hissed at us. "Something is happening here."

"What is going on, Ruby?" I waved my hand in front of me to clear the woodsy scent. "Have you heard about Verity?"

"The spirits are restless. I need to listen to them."

Andrew walked over next to me, a handkerchief up to

his mouth. The bang of the gate being flung open startled all three of us. We turned our heads to stare at the striking forty-ish woman walking into the courtyard. I didn't recognize her; there was something about her that seemed familiar, but I couldn't place what it was.

Dressed in dark jeans and a black t-shirt, the woman carried a large gray duffel bag and a matching backpack. Her hair was pulled back in a high ponytail and she wore no jewelry. The practicality of her clothing and accessories matched her quick movements. She marched toward Ruby but stopped ten feet from her and dropped her bags in between them.

The stranger's green eyes settled on Ruby with the same disapproving stare that Ruby gave me regularly. Even before she spoke, I knew who she was.

"Still talking to the spirits, mother?"

16

―――――

"Verity?" Ruby's voice cracked. "Is that really you?"

"Surprised to see me? I assumed your spirits would tell you I was coming," the woman said.

Ruby dropped the two sticks of incense. Andrew rushed over and picked them up in one hand and used the other to steady Ruby's elbow. She shook, making the stack of bracelets on her wrist bang together in an off-key harmony. He guided her out of her doorway toward her daughter, but she stopped after a few steps.

"I'm fine, Andrew. Thank you." Ruby pulled away from Andrew's grasp and wrapped her arms around her body. "No, Verity, the spirits have said nothing about you for twenty-six years."

"So you remember when I left?" Verity mimicked her mother's stance by wrapping her thin arms around her body and staring at her with the same burning green eyes.

"Of course I do! I've searched for you all these years. Where were you?" Ruby snapped.

Andrew moved next to me and we both stared at them. While I didn't expect Ruby to be overly emotional, I assumed she would rush to her daughter. And Verity would do the same. Even if they weren't an affectionate family, a twenty-six-year separation called for a happier response than these two women showed. There was obviously more to their relationship and their story.

"What do you mean, where was I? Nicole gave you the letter that explained everything! You've never listened to me." Verity's high-pitched voice and the stomp of her foot reminded me of an angry teenager. It was as if she had reverted to her younger years with her mother. And Ruby felt the same way.

"Verity, stop acting like a spoiled child." Ruby sighed. "I have no idea what you're talking about. What letter? Do you know Nicole is dead?"

For the first time since entering the courtyard, Verity's armor came down. Her body slumped and her eyes watered. "Yes. I came back for Nicole. Why would I come back to see you?"

"Because I am your mother!"

"Really? You didn't respond to my letter. You cut me off."

"I cut you off? You did that to me."

"Hold on," I interrupted "You said letter, Verity. You sent your mother a message?"

"I wrote a letter and gave it to Nicole."

"I never got it." Ruby shuffled over to the table outside my apartment and lowered herself into a chair.

"Oh." Verity took the seat across from Ruby. "Nicole promised she would give you the letter before she left. And she always kept her promises. Always."

I had a lump in my throat as I watched Ruby and Verity realize what had really happened. My heart broke for them, thinking of all the years they lost. But I couldn't understand why Verity wouldn't have called or written to her mother. Andrew thought the same.

"Verity, I recognize this isn't my place, but why didn't you contact your mother after you left?" Andrew asked.

"It's a long story." Verity stared at Andrew and me. "Who are you two? Are you my mother's clients?"

"We're her friends and neighbors," I answered. "I went with Ruby to see what turned out to be Nicole's body."

"So it is Nicole." Verity wiped a tear from her face. "I hoped it wasn't true."

"She still wore your charm bracelet." Ruby's hand reached toward Verity's but she pulled back before she touched her. "Did you give her your bracelet?"

"Of course I did. Nicole wouldn't have taken anything from me without asking," Verity said. "So you thought it was me buried at Delmar Apartments?"

"Yes. You always wore that bracelet, but when I realized it wasn't you, I knew it had to be Nicole," Ruby said.

"Nicole went missing when I did, then?" Verity said. "That makes sense now."

"What do you mean?" Andrew had joined us after making a whispered phone call.

"We were leaving New Orleans on the same night. We planned to meet in a month in Seattle. She didn't show up." Verity looked down at the table. "Now I know she was already dead."

The meowing entrance of Cleopatra, Nefertiti, and Nubi broke the silence that followed Verity's realization. They jumped from the back wall of the courtyard and trotted to the table. Nubi rubbed up against my legs while Cleopatra and Nefertiti beelined to Verity.

"These can't be Horus and Ra." Verity reached down to let the cats sniff her hands. "Cats can live a long time, but thirty years?"

"No, these are Cleopatra and Nefertiti." Ruby picked them up. "Horus and Ra ascended to the great beyond three hundred and forty-nine days after you left."

"Oh." Verity dropped the hand that had been reaching out to pet the animals. "You still have a thing for black cats, don't you?"

"As a witch, it's a requirement." Ruby smiled as Verity laughed. "See, some things don't change."

"I'll give you that, mother." Verity turned to me. "So are you a witch, too?"

"I've been called many things, but a witch is not one of them." I grinned as Nubi climbed up my leg so I could pick him up. "This fur-ball picked me to be his human."

"You met him in a graveyard, so perhaps he thought you were a witch." Andrew winked at me. "Anubis has been a lovely addition to the community, along with his human."

"Your cat has an Egyptian name, too?" Verity drummed her fingers on the table.

"Yes, your mother named him when she took care of him for me." I glanced at Ruby. "It was very kind of her."

"So my mother is getting soft in her old age?" Verity grinned briefly, but she quickly returned to her stoic composure. "She always loved her cats, though."

I expected Ruby to say she loved Verity, too, but she didn't. Instead, she said, "Cats have been agreeable companions to me."

"You've always treated them better than humans," Verity said. "Are they still helping you with your work?"

"You know they never have. Those in the great beyond are my only helpers." Ruby glared at Verity. "You could have been my earthly helper. You are psychic, like me. Don't deny it."

Verity pushed her chair backwards. I cringed at the sound of the metal legs scraping the slate tiles. But the anger on Verity's and Ruby's faces made me flinch more.

"If I was a psychic, Mother, I would have known Nicole was dead."

"No one knew! Don't use that as an excuse to deny your birthright." Ruby placed her hands on the table and pushed herself out of her chair. "I will be inside if you want to come in. Otherwise we should talk after we both have had time to reflect and speak with the Goddess of Good."

"She's your Goddess of Good, not mine," Verity said to Ruby's closed door. "Nothing has changed in all these years."

"Verity, wait." I said. "You can't leave."

"Why do you care?" Verity marched over to her bags and grabbed them. "My mother will be fine."

"But how about you?" I asked.

Verity dropped her bags. By her intense stare, she must have been sizing me up. As a complete stranger, my concern must have confused her. Or she didn't believe my sincerity.

"Please stay for a moment, Miss Virtue." Andrew said. "An old friend of yours is on the way."

"Who?" Verity said. "Nicole was my only real friend."

The courtyard gate squeaked open, followed by the rapid clinks from a cane hitting the slate tiles. The familiar scent of lavender wafted in the air ahead of Papa Gede. Verity's eyes grew wide as he rushed over to her and dropped his tarnished brass python topped cane on the ground.

"Verity! I am so happy to see you, child." Papa placed his hands on Verity's cheeks. "You have been missed."

"Thanks." Verity grasped his hands and took them from her face, but she squeezed them gently before she let go. "It's good to see you."

"Your momma was right that you're still on this earth. I looked for you in the spirit world and didn't find you either." Papa tilted his head toward Ruby's front door. "We're happy you're home."

"Where's your hat, Papa Gede? You always wore it," Verity asked.

"Oh, I have no need for it, although I get cold in the winter." Papa ran his hands over his bald head. "And it's Papa these days. I'm just a regular man."

"You've never experienced the cold until you've lived in Canada." Verity laughed. "And you're anything but ordinary."

"We can attest that Papa is an extraordinary man." Andrew put his arm around me. "He is an excellent friend to me and Samantha."

"And they're good friends to Ruby, too." Papa's face crinkled as he smiled.

"It's quite the love-fest at Thibodeaux Mansion." Verity reached down and unzipped her backpack and took out a pack of cigarettes. "I never thought I'd see the day where my mother had friends."

"Now, now, don't be so hard on your momma." Papa shook his head. "And you shouldn't be smoking. Didn't you listen to me all those years ago? I gave you that gris-gris bag, so you'd stop that bad habit."

Verity put the cigarettes back in her backpack and pulled out a small bag. I recognized it as one from Papa's shop. I had my own, but it was for protection.

"You need to make me a new one. Are you still in the same place? I didn't know if you moved after Katrina," Verity said.

"I'm still there, but it's just me now." Papa's eyes watered. "I lost Virginia and Dotty in the storm."

Andrew's arm stiffened around my shoulders. He had also lost someone, his partner, in Hurricane Katrina. Papa had lost his wife and daughter. Besides Andrew's academic interest and Papa's spiritual interest in Voodoo, their loss was something they had in common.

"I'm sorry to hear that," Verity said.

"I know you are." Papa took out a handkerchief and wiped his furrowed brow. "Now, you said, Canada. You been hiding yourself up there? What in the world were you doing there?"

"Just living, Papa." Verity twirled the end of her ponytail as she looked around the courtyard.

"OK, I'll stop asking for now. I recognize that look. You'd always twist your hair when I went on too long about Marie Laveau."

"So Papa told you all about Marie Laveau, too?" I said.

"For a while, I thought I'd get into Voodoo. Once I met Papa and he talked about Voodoo, the real religion, I realized I wasn't ready to commit to it." Verity looked toward Ruby's apartment, where Cleopatra and Nefertiti stood like statues on the doormat. "I was already dealing with my mother's version of spirituality."

"Voodoo wasn't the way to rebel like you wanted it to be." Papa laughed, the lines deepening in his face. "I wasn't offended, but I had hoped you'd go back to your mother for spiritual guidance."

Verity jumped at the sound of Ruby's cats' meows. "I

swear, those two are clones of the cats we had when I lived here. They meowed constantly at me."

"They're welcoming you home, like we all are." Papa grasped Verity's hand. "You and your momma have a lot to deal with, but give her a chance, Verity. She searched long and hard for you. I don't just mean in the spiritual world. She hired a private investigator to find you. You sure hid yourself well."

"We'll catch up soon, but now I need to find a place to stay." Verity squeezed Papa's hand before dropping it to pick up her bags. "I want to rest before I speak with the police."

"You can stay with your mother."

"That's not a good idea, Papa."

"I know a place, Verity," I said. "Our friend, Beau, owns Hotel Jeanne. I'm sure he'll have a room for you."

"I vaguely recall the hotel," Verity said. "Isn't it haunted?"

"Depends on who you ask." I didn't want to tell Verity that Beau had hired her mother to speak with the ghosts there. I had a feeling she wouldn't stay anywhere that had a connection to Ruby.

"It's a lovely hotel and Beau will take good care of you," Andrew said. "Samantha, will you walk Verity there? I'll call Beau and tell him you're on your way."

Verity blew out her cheeks and tightened her grip on her bags. "Well, thanks. I'm sure I can find it on my own."

"I don't mind taking you there." I reached out my hand toward her duffel bag. "Here, let me help you with your bags."

"I should have guessed you wouldn't take no for an answer." Verity frowned and handed her bag to me. "I'm tired enough that I'll let you. I forgot all about Southern hospitality."

"Sammy will take care of you, but come see your momma after you've rested." Papa pointed his cane at Verity before walking to Ruby's door. "And come see me, too. I'll make you a new gris-gris bag and my momma's frog legs."

"That's a deal on the gris-gris bag." Verity gave the first genuine smile I'd seen from her to Papa. "But let's make it beignets instead of frog legs."

Papa laughed and opened Ruby's door. Verity's face dropped, and I followed her gaze to the collection of BB dolls. She shook her head. Whether from surprise or annoyance, I wasn't sure. Verity must be overwhelmed with emotions from being back home and finding out that her mother never received her letter.

Before I left with Verity, Andrew whispered in my ear, "Be gentle with her, but do find out what happened all those years ago. She might tell you more than she would Ruby."

That was my plan. Ruby needed answers, but I didn't know how much Verity would reveal, especially to a stranger, even if I used my best manners.

17

"So are you the neighborhood busybody or just trying to drum up business for your friend's hotel?" Verity blew a smoke ring as I met her on the sidewalk.

"Well, you don't hold back, do you?" So much for me using Southern hospitality. "I can understand your apprehension. You didn't trust too many people here in New Orleans, did you?"

"I'm going with busybody." Verity dropped her cigarette on the ground and stomped it out. "My mother wasn't friendly with the neighbors when I lived here. She always kept to herself."

"She is a private person." That was putting it politely, but I didn't need to tell Verity about her mother's psychic commentary on her neighbors.

"That's true. I'm her daughter, but I don't know everything about her." Verity sighed. "I definitely don't understand her, either."

"Everyone says that about their parents." I was speaking from experience. While I loved my adopted parents, the things I found out about them after they died in a car crash still haunted me.

"You're probably right. So tell me, did my mother ever mention me?"

I had hoped Verity wouldn't ask me that. I wanted to lie, but Verity struck me as someone who would see through my lies. "No, she didn't. But to be fair, we don't talk a lot. She mostly tells me I'm stirring up the spirits."

The laughter that erupted from Verity caught the attention of the tourists passing by on a mule-drawn carriage. They stared at her while the driver tipped his hat and continued with the tour. I was just as surprised as the tourists.

"My mother hasn't changed one bit. Thank you for being honest, Samantha."

"You're welcome. If we're being honest, will you tell me why you left?" By asking her I risked losing the little trust I hoped I had earned, but I couldn't help myself. "I'll admit that I am the neighborhood busybody if that helps."

Verity studied my face, but I wasn't sure what she was looking for. But apparently she found it. "You're kind of young to be playing Murder She Wrote, but I'll give you credit for not lying to me."

"I prefer to think of myself as a grown-up Nancy Drew. Thank you very much." I smiled and then hefted her duffle bag over my shoulder. "You can tell me about leaving New Orleans as we walk to Hotel Jeanne."

"Let's go up to Bourbon and back down to the hotel. "

"Are you sure? It's almost seven, so the crowds are growing. Unless you'd like a drink."

"I don't want a drink. I'm just curious to see it after all these years."

Verity's shoulders relaxed as we headed to Bourbon

Street. By going this way, we would steer clear of Delmar Apartments. Whether she wanted to avoid passing by Nicole's grave or running into the people she knew there, I wasn't sure. It was probably a bit of both. She had mentioned no one living there, but according to Sutton, she and Nicole hung out there all the time.

Bourbon Street was blocked off to cars in the evening so tourists could walk in the middle of the road and the sidewalks. People carried plastic to-go cups filled with drinks from the bars lining the street. We weaved in and out of them. I ducked as a handful of bead necklaces came flying from the balcony of a bar to my right. Verity caught a gold strand and the others fell to the ground and a group of women grabbed them.

"Are you going to wear it?" I asked.

"I forgot they throw beads even when it's not Mardi Gras." Verity handed her necklace to woman who didn't get one off the ground. "I don't think I've seen these beads since I've left."

"Is the French Quarter the same?" I asked.

"Yes and no. There are some different bars, but it feels the same," Verity said. "Bourbon Street is as sticky and tacky as I remembered it."

"Did you and Nicole spend much time here?"

"No, we avoided the tourist areas. We didn't need to come up here for liquor." She waved off a guy trying to shoo us into a bar, offering daiquiris of all flavors.

"I assume Myles and Sutton were the go-to guys for alcohol."

She twisted her head and stared at me. "You know them?"

"I met them when I went with your mom to view the

grave. I didn't talk with Myles, but I did with Sutton. He read my cards the other night at The Gas Light."

"Sutton and Myles both live there still?"

"Yes and Tabitha does, too. Although she and Myles are divorced now."

"I'm not surprised they got married or divorced. But I am surprised that Tabby and Myles didn't move if they're not together."

I explained Myles lived in his father's apartment while Tabitha had kept their place. Delores Riggins rented her same apartment, but Sandra Lewis and Myles Senior both had passed away. She listened to all the information without comment, but the tension in her body returned as I spoke.

"Verity, why did you go? Everyone says you and Nicole were best friends, like sisters," I said.

"We were like sisters." Verity took out her cigarettes but put them back immediately. "We wanted to leave town, so she was going to New York to get some money she'd left there and I headed out to Seattle to wait for her."

"How long did you wait?"

"Two months." Verity stopped at a Lucky Dog street vendor and ordered a hot dog with everything. We stepped a few feet away from the vendor and Verity took a few bites of her food.

"Did you try calling Momo or Nicole's father?" I asked.

"I disguised my voice and called both of them. They said she wasn't there, and I got off the phone before they could ask me any questions. I assumed she'd changed her mind and moved somewhere else."

"That must have been difficult," I said.

"It was, but I moved on without her."

"So you didn't go together? That seems strange..."

"We had to," Verity interrupted me, but quickly bit her lip.

"You had to?" I stared at Verity. "Were you two in a dangerous situation? It's odd y'all would leave separately when you were so close."

"It's just the way it had to be." Verity dropped her half-eaten hot dog in a trash can and we started walking again. Her face was expressionless, but she gripped her bag tighter. There had to be more to the story, but I didn't think I'd get anything else out of her.

"So you didn't come back or reach out to anyone in town?" I said.

"No, I cut my losses, put it all out of my mind."

"But you never really did, did you?"

"No, I guess not," Verity replied, but by the faraway look in her eyes, I suspected she was talking to herself rather than to me.

"I forgot the hotel was by Momo's place." Verity's whole body tensed as we got closer to Hotel Jeanne. Momo's house was next to the hotel's parking lot.

"Would you like to stop in and see her?" I asked.

Verity shook her head. "She might not want to see me."

"Momo told me she missed you," I said.

"You know Momo? Do you know everyone around here?"

"No, but Momo is a friend and she really has missed you. She asked me to find out what happened to you and Nicole."

"She did?" Verity stopped and stared at me. "Are you an actual detective?"

"No, but I have looked into situations for my friends."

"Situations?" Verity raised her eyebrows.

"Let's just say a lot of strange things happen in the French Quarter." I was relieved when Verity laughed. If she thought I was crazy, she might have left me on the sidewalk.

"That's how I remember this place." Her smile reminded me of the few times I'd seen her mother smile. "OK, so Momo asked for your help. Did my mother?"

"Actually, she did." I answered as Verity shook her head. "She and Momo want to know what happened to Nicole and to you. Trust me, Momo will be relieved to see you."

"I will go visit her, but not tonight." Verity rushed past Momo's front door. I looked up at her balcony, but she wasn't sitting at her table. The way Momo spoke about her, Verity had nothing to worry about. Unless, of course, she had something to do with Nicole's death.

Verity opened the door to the hotel, and I followed her in.

"Welcome to Hotel Jeanne," said Ambrose Fortner, the hotel's general manager, as we walked into the reception room. While his slicked black hair and posture were stiff, his smile was relaxed. It was a wonderful change from when I first met him. He was unhappy when Beau bought the hotel, but they had worked through their differences. Now their only disagreements were whether the random noises around the building were ghosts or old pipes.

"Hi, Ambrose. It's good to see you. I'm so glad you have a room available tonight," I said.

"I'm happy we could be of service." Ambrose turned to Verity. "Good evening Miss..."

"It's Verity Virtue." She opened her wallet and handed him two cards. "Thanks for fitting me in at the last minute."

"We're happy to have you. I see you live in Seattle now,

Miss Virtue." Ambrose looked down at the driver's license and credit card. "It must be good to be home."

"Not really."

Ambrose took the hint and quietly continued to complete the check-in paperwork. "Excuse me for a moment. I need to get some supplies from the office."

Once Ambrose was gone, I said, "Hold it, you told Papa you lived in Canada. What's going on?"

"I didn't lie, Miss Detective." Verity laughed, apparently not offended by the accusation. "I've lived all over but mostly Canada. But about three months ago, I made Seattle my permanent home."

"Why? Tired of the weather?" I tried to soften my accusatory tone.

"Ha! Seattle is freezing, too. But no, when I got divorced, I decided it was time to leave Vancouver. I took back my maiden name then."

"You just went back to Verity Virtue recently?" That must have been why no one found her under her legal name.

"Yes, I married a friend to make it easier to stay in Canada. But he finally wanted to marry someone else, so we divorced. I hadn't seen him in years, so it wasn't a problem." Verity tapped her fingers on the reception counter.

"Sounds like you were ready to return to your name."

Verity shrugged, so it wasn't really an answer. But I kept going.

"So Virtue is your last name? I assumed Ruby made it up for her business."

"Yes, legal and everything. I'm sure it's not her original surname, but my mother refuses to say what it was before. Maybe you can solve that mystery."

"I don't want to add another thing to the list of things Ruby hates about me."

"I doubt she hates you. I bet you remind her of me."

"Oh." Why Verity thought she and I were alike, I couldn't imagine. She pegged me as a busybody, so perhaps she was one?

"And your aura is crazy, too."

"You can see my aura?"

"I am my mother's daughter." Verity walked away and looked out the window. With her back toward me, I couldn't tell if she was joking or serious. Although Ruby claimed Verity had psychic abilities, just like her.

"I apologize for the delay." Ambrose returned to the reception desk with a stack of plastic key cards. "Now, Miss Virtue, we have rooms here in the main building and around the courtyard."

"I'd love a room by the pool. Where I live, I don't swim much."

"I have one available near the pool. It's been recently updated, so I am sure you will enjoy it."

Ambrose gave me the same questioning look he always did when he mentioned the pool. My cousin, Scarlett, was murdered in it, and I had been a suspect. I smiled at him to let him know I was fine. My cousin's death was tragic, but it didn't keep me away from the hotel. Ruby advised me that Scarlett's spirit wasn't at the pool. Not that I believed in spirits necessarily, but I couldn't deny a bit of unexplainable relief when Ruby told me that.

"And how long will you be staying with us?" Ambrose handed Verity's identification and credit card back to her.

"Let's start with three nights if you have availability," Verity responded.

"Of course. Anything for a friend of Samantha's."

Ambrose handed a plastic key card to her. The electronic key card system was one of the upgrades Beau made as the new owner. Adding more staff, including bellmen, was in the works. "I will help you with your bags in just a moment."

"No need. I can handle them." Verity turned around. "Never mind. Samantha is taking care of me."

"She is helpful in many ways. But I'm sure your mother has told you that," Ambrose said.

"You know my mother?" Verity looked Ambrose up and down. "You don't seem like the Ouija board and seance type to me."

Ambrose gave one of his rare laughs. "I am not, but I have watched your mother use her gift here at the hotel."

"Did she tell you that your mother said to behave?"

Ambrose paled. "Yes."

"Let me guess, you questioned my mother's abilities, so she pulled the 'your mother says to be quiet' shtick?" Verity headed out of the reception room.

"But she said the exact phrase my mother used," Ambrose insisted to the back of Verity's head. "Samantha, you heard Ruby. I am not crazy."

"You're not, I promise." I smiled at him before I followed Verity into the hallway. She was already heading toward the door to the courtyard, but she stopped in front of the library entrance.

"Isn't this room wonderful?" I said. "I helped sort through the books and we discovered a hidden letter from a previous resident."

Verity nodded and then shivered. So I wasn't the only one who felt the icy presence that swept through the room. She looked up, and I guessed she was looking for an air vent, as most people did when they experienced the chill.

According to Ruby, it was the Lovelorn Ghost roaming through the library.

Before I could explain the ghost story, Verity pushed open the door and entered the courtyard. She headed straight to her room. "The pool looks nice. What's wrong with it, though?"

"Why do you ask?"

"The manager gave you a funny look. Something obviously happened there." Verity raised her eyebrows. "And if my mother was here professionally, I assumed someone died near it or in it."

"My cousin, Scarlett, was killed here. I found her body."

"I'm sorry. You've seen more than your share of murdered women." Verity turned her head away from the pool and studied me. "Including Nicole?"

"Just from a distance."

Verity blinked as if she was trying to hold back tears. One slipped down her face and she let it drip onto her shirt. "I shouldn't have left her alone that night."

"Were you worried something was going to happen?" I put down her duffel bag and grabbed a tissue from my backpack. "I get the feeling y'all left town for a serious reason."

"Thanks." Verity took the tissue and wiped her face. "I need to think through that day. I must have missed something."

"Would it help to talk to someone?"

"Like you? I will say you are persistent, but in a kind way." Verity gave a half-hearted smile. "I'll go over things on my own tonight before I meet with the police tomorrow. But thank you for bringing me here."

"Here's my card. If you need anything, call me." I handed her my business card for Lagniappe Books.

"Thanks." Verity reached into her backpack and pulled a

business card holder. "Here's mine, because I'm pretty sure you were going to ask for my number."

I nodded as I accepted it and read out loud, "Verity Virtue, Editor and Ghost Writer. Really? Ghost writer?"

She laughed. "Trust me, I enjoy the irony of being a ghost writer. But I don't work on books about ghosts. I had to draw the line somewhere."

"We'll have to talk about what you write. It's possible we sell them at my shop."

"Can't, I'm afraid. I sign a confidentiality agreement with my clients." Her lips curled up in a smile. "And I'm good at keeping secrets."

"I am too, but I understand," I said. "Call me anytime if you need anything."

"Thanks. A bit of advice, Samantha, don't hang around Delmar Apartments. The tenants are not what they seem." She picked up her duffel bag and opened her hotel room door. "One of them is a murderer."

18

Verity warned me not to go to the Delmar Apartments, but I couldn't help myself. I woke the next morning feeling like I needed to clear my head. Verity's arrival must have stirred up the spirits in the building. I found Ruby humming as her cats swirled around her legs. Her face was pale and the circles under her red-rimmed eyes gave no doubt to her fragile emotional state. I wanted to ask her if she had spoken to Verity again, but her chanting grew louder. Not wanting to interrupt what I assumed to be a spell, I let her be.

Neal came down the steps and mouthed to me, "What's she doing?" I shrugged my shoulders and headed out the courtyard gate with him.

"I heard Ruby's daughter showed up yesterday." Neal stopped to tie his tennis shoes. "Is she like Ruby?"

"She and Ruby are more alike than they care to admit. She's direct and mysterious, like her mother."

"Two Virtue women in town are going to stir up the spirits." Neal laughed as he stood back up. "Did she say what happened when she left?"

"She's cagey about why she disappeared."

"But you'll find out, right?" Neal said. "Rumor has it you took Verity to Hotel Jeanne. You're a nice woman and all, but don't deny you wanted to grill her about her past."

"Verity asked if I was the neighborhood busybody, so you just confirmed it." I grinned. "She's meeting with the police today, so maybe we'll find out more after that."

"I bet she'll tell you more." Neal gave me a hug. "You have that way about you. Bye, Sammy!"

I waved goodbye to Neal as we left in opposite directions. Most likely, he was heading to meet Rose for breakfast at Libby's cafe. I would have preferred to go there for coffee and a chocolate chip scone, but I needed to run. A regular exercising schedule let me eat beignets — or at least that's what I told myself. But I'd eat them even if I didn't run.

I wanted to head directly to Delmar Apartments, but I made it the end of my route. Growing up, I'd never liked any sports, but my freshman college roommate begged me to join the running club with her. She promised it would keep me from gaining the infamous "freshman fifteen" and we'd meet cute boys. We met attractive guys, but the running only kept me from gaining five pounds instead of fifteen. But twelve years later, I still liked to run, especially here in New Orleans, where it was flat instead of hilly like San Francisco.

I started toward the river, but I changed my mind after I spotted a man a block ahead who looked like Joey. He was the same build and had the same hair color as my brother. But he wasn't facing me, so I wasn't sure it was him. Before I started running toward the man, he turned around. All the tension in my body released when I saw it wasn't my brother.

While there most likely would be a few other runners

along the path by the Mississippi River, I stuck to the streets in the neighborhood. I hated to admit I was concerned about running into my brother unexpectedly. If I did, I wanted to be in a well-populated area. Even though it was early in the morning, the French Quarter was quietly bustling with people heading to work, late-night partiers heading home, and tourists enjoying the cooler temperature. I pushed myself to run faster than normal, as if I could run away from my worries about Joey.

My run helped me put my brother out of my mind, but then I started thinking about Nicole's murder. On my way back home, I couldn't help myself. I just had to see if anything was going on at the Delmar Apartments. It was about 8:30 a.m., so I expected it to be quiet. I was wrong.

Myles and Tabby were fighting right in front of the door to the building. Although he was wearing the same Ward Construction baseball hat, I was positive the red on his face continued over his entire head. He shoved his hands in his pockets and turned them out. "There's nothing left, Tabby! Everything is gone!"

"I don't believe you." Tabby's eyes were blazing. "You're hiding some money somewhere. I will find out where it is."

"Come on, I'm being honest." Myles grasped her hand, but she bristled at his touch. "Don't be this way, sweetheart. We may be divorced, but we're still friends, right?"

Tabby jabbed her finger in his chest. "Get me the money or I call my lawyer."

"Tabby!" Myles shouted as she stormed away, but she didn't turn around. "Oh, hey, don't I know you?" Myles smiled at me as if he hadn't just been arguing with his ex-wife.

"We met the other day. When Nicole was uncovered." I had been pretending to tie my shoelaces a few feet away from them. I stood up, expecting Myles to scowl when he remembered I had been there with Ruby. He either didn't remember or didn't care.

"Of course. You were with that lady detective. She sure is a tall drink of water."

Christine would not have been impressed to be described that way, but I'd let her handle him if he said that to her face. "I came by with her and Ruby. I'm her neighbor."

The lecherous grin slid off his face. "Watch yourself with that witch. She is not a good person. But I gather she got her daughter back."

"You heard about Verity?" News traveled fast through the French Quarter. "Have you seen her?"

"No. A friend told me Verity's staying at that haunted hotel. I guess Ruby didn't invite her to stay with her. Not that anyone wants to be around that lady any more than they have to."

"You really don't like Ruby," I said. "How do you feel about Verity?"

I caught the brief flash of anger in his eyes. He coughed as if to hide his feelings. "Oh, she was a good kid. Annoying at times. Verity always acted like she was better than the rest of us. Except Nicole, of course. They were joined at the hip."

"Sutton said you and Tabby were good friends with them, too."

Myles chuckled, and for a moment, I saw why the teenagers liked him back then. His whole body relaxed into his laughter. "You know a lot about us for just being Ruby's neighbor. Are you sure you aren't a reporter?"

"No, no. I'm only a curious neighbor." I smiled as widely as he did and he let out another laugh.

"You sure you're not a writer? I could use some free PR for my business."

"Sorry, I'm not, I promise. You sell antiques, right?"

"Come to the shop. You'll have to walk, though. I can't run. Tabby is, I mean was, the athlete of the family." A touch of sadness crept into Myles' eyes, but he shook it off. "But I'm not so bad for an old guy, eh?"

I smiled politely and walked next to Myles, but I found him repulsive no matter his age. I still hadn't gotten over his cruel remarks to Ruby about Verity being missing when we thought it was her body in the grave. But I needed information. "I'm sure you could keep up with Tabby. What kind of athlete is she? A runner?"

"No, Tabby's a swimmer. Been one since she was a little girl."

That explained her broad shoulders and muscular arms. Swimming was a solitary sport which seemed to suit Tabby's temperament. At least what I'd seen so far, but I wanted to chat with her to confirm that suspicion.

"Now, remind me of your name. Suzy, right?" Myles said.

"It's Samantha. You're named after your father, I understand. Are you a junior or Myles the third?"

"I was junior, but Daddy died a few years back, so now I'm just Myles."

"Was your shop your father's?"

"Yes, it's been in the family for generations. Antiques are in our blood," Myles said. "Do you know where Verity has been all these years? Did she tell anyone why she left?"

We stopped at the corner to let traffic go by. The delivery trucks were coming in and out of the Quarter. I needed to pick up the pace with Myles so I could get back home and shower before we got our deliveries at Lagniappe Books.

"I think she lived in Canada. But I don't know why she left." Which was true, Verity hadn't explained the reason she and Nicole wanted to leave town.

"Canada? Wow, that's like another country."

It was another country, but I decided it wasn't worth pointing that out to Myles. Unless he was trying to make a joke, but he didn't strike me as the comedic type. And I realized he wasn't the best business man either when we got to his shop near the end of Royal Street.

It had good bones with its elegant wood facade and large framed windows. A faded sign hanging by the peeling front door said, "Delmar & Sons, Antiques for Fine Living." Myles unlocked the door to a pile of mail spread out on a faded Oriental rug. He flipped the light switch and four chandeliers flickered on and off and then on again. "These are the original fixtures my grandfather put in. Not the most reliable, but they're sentimental."

From the cobwebs coating the crystals and the brass holders, it looked like the chandeliers hadn't been cleaned since Myles' grandfather installed them. The same went for the antique tables, chairs, desks, and a lone wardrobe that lined the walls. In the center of the room stood a wrought-iron table with four matching chairs. Garden figurines shaped as angels and cherubs were on top of the table and in the seats.

"The outdoor section is lovely," I said.

"What? Oh, you mean this stuff." Myles picked up a statue of a boy cherub holding a bow and arrow. "These are popular."

"There's a rumor a statue was buried with Nicole." I picked up an angel sculpture. "Did you see one?"

"What? You shouldn't believe all the gossip around here." Myles put down the cherub. "Poor sweet Nicole is dead and we should let her rest in peace."

"That's a good point," I agreed, hoping Myles' lackluster response didn't mean he wouldn't keep talking. "I think her family will be relieved to bury her in the family mausoleum. Actually, this angel reminds me of the ones I've seen around my family's tomb."

"These are reproductions, I assure you." Myles grabbed the angel out of my hand and placed it down on the table. He stepped over to a desk near the back of the shop, took off his baseball cap and shoved it in a drawer, and pulled out a blue tie. He threw it around his neck without tying it and then put on a sports coat that hung on a hook on the wall.

"I'm a serious business owner. Everything that is a reproduction is noted."

"I can see you are passionate about your shop." I smiled, hoping it would lighten the mood. Why did he take offense when I said the statues looked like ones in the graveyards? And things went downhill from there.

"I am, but it's difficult these days. People don't buy antiques like they used to. The new generations think build-it-yourself furniture is good enough. And they like mass market decorations. Who needs a sign that says, 'live laugh love?' How ridiculous."

After staring at the dusty candelabras and ceramic figurines, I preferred that sign. Not that I had anything against antiques, but Myles' shop didn't have a great selection of them. By the large number of sales tags that said reproduction, the business was more of a reproduction store than an antique shop. But at least he was honest about his merchandise.

"Do you work alone? It must keep you busy."

Myles walked over to a table and straightened the assortment of china animal figurines scattered on the top. "It does. Tabby used to help me from time to time. I'd hoped I'd have a son or even a daughter to take over the business, but we weren't blessed with children."

For the first time, I had a little sympathy for Myles. His downcast eyes and his slumped shoulders made him appear a bit more human.

"I'm sure you'll find the right person to carry on with your family business. Close friends can be like family."

Myles shook his head and quickly switched into salesman mode. "Now tell me what antiques you like. I'll have something perfect for your home."

"I live in a furnished apartment, so I'm all set with furniture and accessories, thanks."

"Well, you come see me when you move somewhere new."

"Are there going to be apartments available in your building?"

"Would you like to be neighbors?" Myles winked at me. "I'll probably be moving soon, so I should check if there is an opening in your place."

"I'm sure you and Ruby would love being neighbors."

"That's right, you live in Thibodeaux Mansion, so I'll guess we'll just have to be friends."

Not on his life, but I smiled sweetly instead of using Sissy's favorite phrase for when someone annoyed her. Bless your heart isn't what it really sounds like. "I guess so. I need to run, but it was nice to chat and visit your shop, Myles."

"We should have drinks sometime." He walked me to the door and held it open for me. "And if you see Verity around, tell her to come find me. Let her know there are no hard feelings."

He closed the door, and I heard the click of the lock behind me. What did he mean by no hard feelings? Apparently Verity didn't leave on good terms with at least one person in Delmar Apartments.

19

———

There was one person who was definitely happy to see Verity: Momo.

After leaving Myles' shop, I returned home and took a hot shower to wash away the ickiness of my chat with Myles. When I left my apartment, I found Neal and Sissy relaxing at the back table, drinking coffee.

"Hey, Sammy! Come sit with us." Neal waved me over. "I got scones from Libby's cafe."

"You better get one before I eat them all," Sissy said. "They're your favorites."

"I thought I smelled sweet potato scones." I picked up Nubi from the chair next to Neal. "Has my cat been begging for food?"

"He's been an angel." Neal patted Nubi, who purred in response. "Sissy brought him and the other cats some cream."

"Of course she did." I laughed. Sissy claimed not to like cats, but she also frequently had treats for them. Neal and I had a bet about when Sissy and Rob would adopt a cat or two. The loser had to take the winner out to Acme Oyster

House for unlimited oysters. I hoped I would win because I'd been with Neal when he had oysters and losing would cost me an arm and a leg.

"They were thirsty." Sissy insisted as she poured more cream into three separate paper plates. "I think Cleopatra and Nefertiti have been outside for a while waiting for their human to open her door."

"Is Verity with Ruby?" I asked.

"She arrived about twenty minutes ago," Neal said in-between bites of his scone. "We introduced ourselves before Ruby whisked her inside."

"Verity was pleasant, but guarded. Coming back home must be difficult for her," Sissy said.

Sissy's words were confirmed when Ruby's door flung open and Verity stomped out. She pivoted on her heels to face her mother, who leaned up against her doorframe.

"I will not talk about my supposed psychic powers with you this morning." Verity crossed her arms. "Let it go."

"How can I? It's your birthright! It's your destiny!" Ruby reached for her daughter, but Verity took a step back out of her mother's reach. Ruby sighed. "Fine. We won't speak of it for now."

"Or ever." Verity snapped.

"Verity..." Ruby said. "Oh, here are Cleopatra and Nefertiti."

The cats meowed at Ruby, but continued lapping up their cream. Nubi finished his and trotted over to Verity, rubbing up against her legs.

"Which one is this?" Verity asked.

"That's Nubi," I said. "How are you? Was the hotel all right last night?"

"It was pleasant. No ghosts," Verity answered. "I met

your friend Beau this morning before I left. He's quite the charmer."

"That he is." I laughed. "He enjoys owning the hotel and chatting with the guests."

"I got that impression. He walked me here. He insisted, just like you did yesterday. More Southern hospitality, I assume." Verity narrowed her eyes at me.

"Of course." I smiled. "Have you spoken to the police yet?"

"I talked briefly to Detective Gammon. I'm meeting her and her partner this afternoon," Verity said. "Being the neighborhood busybody, you must know them."

Neal and Sissy both laughed, causing the cats to rush to the back of the courtyard and jump on the brick wall.

"What's so funny?" Verity looked at Neal and Sissy, who were using the napkins to wipe their eyes.

"Sorry, we didn't mean to sound rude," Sissy said. "Sammy is our own detective, but we all know the official detectives. One actually lives here."

"Oh, right, you mentioned your fiancé was a cop." Verity sat down next to me. "What's his name?"

"Rob Armstrong. He's a good guy." Sissy said. "And his partner is great, too. They'll figure out who killed your friend."

"Unless you already have, Samantha." Verity smiled, but her eyes were serious.

"Oh, she will." Neal pushed the box of scones over to Verity. "We're just hoping no one tries to kill her this time."

"What?" Verity dropped the scone back into the box. "You're joking, right?"

"Yes, they are." I glared at Sissy and Neal. Not that they were lying, but Verity didn't need to hear about the trouble I'd run into looking into a few mysteries. I didn't want that bit of gossip to keep her from talking to me. "You know how it is in New Orleans — people like to exaggerate."

Verity's skeptical gaze told me I hadn't convinced her, but she didn't have a chance to ask me more questions.

"Verity, someone is here to see you." From her doorstep, Ruby pointed at the entrance to the courtyard. Momo's eyes were still puffy, but her hair was back in its usual style, and she stood tall and steady.

"Verity! You are alive!" Momo gaped at Verity. "Oh, thank goodness!"

"Yes, Momo, it's me." Verity rose from the table and took a few steps toward her.

"Well, come give me a hug! Thank the Lord for some good news!"

Verity shyly walked up to Momo and put her arms around Momo gingerly.

"Give me a proper hug, young lady! I may be old, but I'm not fragile," Momo insisted.

Verity hugged her tighter. Momo wasn't a delicate woman, but for a moment, she looked broken. As she held Verity, but I couldn't help but wonder if she wasn't hugging her grandniece.

"Now, Verity, the police explained everything to me and, of course, we'll talk. But let me make this clear," Momo said. "I don't blame you at all. You wouldn't have hurt a hair on Nicole's head."

A tear trickled down Verity's face, and Momo wiped it away with a tissue. "Now, now, it's all right. We have some answers and we'll have more soon." Momo looked over at me. "Our friends will help us through this."

I nodded and then shot Neal and Sissy a look so they wouldn't chime in about my detecting skills.

"Let's go get beignets like we used to. You still like them, don't you?" Momo put her arm through Verity's and guided her toward the courtyard gate.

"I do," Verity said. "Mother, do you want to come?"

Ruby shook her head.

"You're welcome to join us." Momo was polite but I noted an undercurrent of friction in her voice.

"No, thank you. I am sure you two have much to catch up on." Ruby turned quickly, her chiffon layers whipping around her as she rushed inside.

Verity stared at her mother's door, but didn't say a word. She let Momo lead her out of the courtyard. I heard Momo's animated voice until the gate closed. I wished I could have gone with them and not just for the beignets. But I expected Momo would fill me in on their conversation even if Verity didn't.

"You'd think Momo was Verity's mom, not Ruby," Neal said.

"Come on, didn't you like your friends' parents better than yours?" Sissy said. "Everyone else's parents seemed cooler, especially compared to mine."

Neal laughed. "I guess so, but then again, I had a crush on my best friend's mom. She was really fun. And she always took us for ice cream."

"You'd like anyone who bought you food." Sissy pulled the box of scones away from Neal. "Sammy, you're quiet. What are you thinking?"

"Oh, just wondering what Verity is going to tell Momo," I answered.

Hopefully, it would be the truth for Momo's sake. Unless Verity had something to do with Nicole's death. I doubted Momo could handle any more bad news.

20

Just before noon, Andrew and I had a visitor at Lagniappe Books.

"Momo asked me to bring these to you."

The warm scent of powdered sugar permeated the shop as Verity opened the door. She held a paper bag from Cafe du Monde and a carrier with three coffee cups.

"Thanks, we can definitely use them," I said. "Andrew and I need a break."

"It is good to see you again, Miss Virtue." Andrew smiled at Verity as we sat down in the seating area at the back of the shop.

"Please call me Verity. Miss Virtue sounds like my mother." Verity took a gulp of her coffee. "Momo filled me in on you and Samantha. She likes you both very much."

"We like her too," Andrew said. "It must have been good to reconnect with her."

"It was, but I wish I hadn't waited so long. Or that it was under these circumstances," Verity said.

"How is Momo, really?" I asked.

"She's tough as usual, but there is despair in her eyes,"

Verity said. "But she perked up when she talked about you, Samantha."

"She did?" I put my beignet down before I took a bite.

"She said you're the neighborhood detective. And she's sure you'll get to the bottom of Nicole's death." Verity's eyes bore into me. "Momo has a lot of faith in you."

"We all do." Andrew placed his hand on mine. "Samantha has a knack for seeing what others do not."

"Hmm. Momo said you were one of the smartest girls she knows and insisted I take you with me to Delmar Apartments."

"She did?" I said.

"She demanded actually." Verity sighed deeply. "Normally I would have argued, but Momo didn't want me to go there alone."

"She is concerned something will happen to you, I imagine." Andrew brushed off a spot of powdered sugar from his shirt. "Would you like me to go as well?"

Verity studied Andrew. I covered my mouth so I wouldn't giggle. Andrew's salt and pepper hair and slight wrinkles around his blue eyes offered a hint of his "seasoned age," as he liked to call it. But I assumed it was his college professor uniform of khakis, a blue button-down shirt, and a pink bowtie that made Verity doubt his physical prowess in protecting her.

"While you seem in shape, I think Samantha and I can handle ourselves," Verity said.

"Well, thank you for not calling me elderly." Andrew smiled. "But you both will be careful, won't you?"

"Yes, we will. Verity, we can go around five when we close the shop," I said.

Andrew was already standing up and gesturing toward the front door. "Go now. Verity is eager to leave."

Verity definitely seemed anxious as she had already popped up from her seat and strode over to the front door. But the slight shake in her hand against the doorknob made me believe she was also scared of what or who she would see at the Delmar Apartments.

For the first block, Verity and I didn't speak. While her body was relaxed, I could see the apprehension in her eyes.

"Are we going to the apartment building to pay our respects to Nicole or to confront the people who live there?" I asked.

"Both." Verity stopped in front of an art gallery. A painting in the window showed a scene from Lafayette Cemetery. The rusted gates were locked and an overcast sky surrounded the plaster and brick tombs. The piece reflected Verity's mood — gray, dark, and closed off.

"Verity, what do you hope to gain by going back?"

"I have no desire to see anyone from the building, but one of them knows what happened to Nicole that night." Verity touched the window with a finger.

"I heard you and Nicole left the courtyard around ten that night."

"We did. But then Nicole went back to drop off some stuff before we left town."

"What stuff?"

"Just some things for Myles." Verity took her finger off the window and squeezed her hands by her side. "We needed to leave or they might have..."

"They might have what?" I rushed to catch up to Verity, who was taking big strides. "Why did you and Nicole need to go in secret?"

"Because they would have told my mother and Momo we were going," Verity answered, but she turned her head away as she spoke. "No other reason."

"Verity..." I pleaded.

"That's all, Sammy." It was obvious she was lying, but I dropped the subject until later. I tried another tactic.

"Did you ever talk about New Orleans with your new friends? Your ex-husband?" I asked.

"No. I never spoke about my life in New Orleans to anyone. Actually, I never talked about my childhood or teenage years," Verity said. "After a while, people stop asking you about your past if you don't answer."

"So you just forgot your whole life?" As someone who had moved to New Orleans to find out what happened to me before I was two years old, I couldn't comprehend forgetting seventeen years of my life.

She gripped her shoulder bag. "I tried putting my past in an airtight box. But something always leaked out. Memories of my mom cooking chicken fried steak, watching the artists paint in Jackson Square, listening to the street musicians play, and roaming the French Quarter with Nicole."

"So, your past was always with you?"

"I buried it deep." Verity stopped in front of Delmar Apartments. "But not as deep as I thought."

21

T he crime scene tape was gone and no one stood outside the Delmar Apartments trying to catch a glimpse of "the courtyard of death" as the media had dubbed Nicole's burial place. But all wasn't quiet at the building. "Shut up!" screamed a woman over the jarring symphony of male voices.

I turned to Verity to ask if she still wanted to go inside, but I didn't need to. She pulled at the locked gate and yelled, "Open up! It's Verity and we need to talk!"

Footsteps echoed off the hallway walls. "Verity, it is you!" Tabitha opened the gate and pulled her in for a hug. "I heard you were back. I'm glad you finally came to see me."

Verity pulled away from Tabitha's embrace, but gave her a slight smile. "Hi, Tabby. I returned when I found out about Nicole. I don't understand how she died here." Verity started toward the courtyard.

"It's been awful, Verity." Tabby followed her so I did, too.

Myles, Sutton, and Luke stood by the back wall of the courtyard. Luke had his arms crossed and looked like he was trying to keep Sutton and Myles away from the fountain, which was still in pieces. Sutton nodded as Myles pointed a finger at Luke and spoke in a hushed, angry tone.

"Myles, stop badgering Luke. Guess who's here!" Tabby walked around Verity, who had stopped in the center of the courtyard where Nicole had been buried. The hole had been refilled, but the slate tiles hadn't been replaced.

"Verity, look at you, all grown up!" Myles stepped over with his arms out as if he was going to embrace Verity. She stepped backward and crossed her arms. "Well, now, it's been too long. We searched for you when you left. You should have told us you were leaving town."

"We needed a change of scenery, but you know why," Verity said.

"No, I don't." Myles shifted his feet. "Are you here to tell me why twenty-six years later?"

"You're such a liar. Are you a killer, too?" Verity uncrossed her arms and shoved her hands in her pockets. "Why else was she in your courtyard?"

"It's a mystery, darling." Sutton stepped in front of Verity. "I searched the spirit world for both of you, but didn't find either of you. It appears both you and Nicole were hiding, but in different places. Is it true you live in Canada?"

"I did." Verity looked startled by Sutton's interruption, but her body and voice relaxed a little. "The great psychic Sutton O'Berry didn't know Nicole was here?"

"It's my biggest regret that I couldn't find her in the other realm. Her spirit must have left instantly." Sutton dropped his chin to his chest but quickly raised it up to look at Verity. "Why did you leave? I'm shocked you would go without Nicole. You were two peas in a pod."

"We planned to meet later, but she didn't show up." Verity looked down at the ground and then held her head high. "She never left since one of you killed her."

The courtyard erupted again as Sutton, Myles, and Tabby argued with Verity. Luke slid over to me and whispered. "This is nuts. Should I call the police?"

Before I could answer him, the door of the apartment on the second floor opened up. A tall woman with rollers in her silver hair and a brown tabby cat in her arms came out and leaned over the railing "Children, stop this now. This is our home, not a place for shouting."

"Sorry Mrs. Riggins. I didn't think you could hear us." Myles smiled at her, but she didn't return it.

"Myles, Junior, I'm wearing my hearing aids. I was watching my soap opera, but y'all are doing one of your own out here."

"We apologize, Mrs. Riggins. We're all just shocked by Verity's appearance." Tabby put her arm around Verity, who glared at her but didn't shake it off.

"Verity, I'm happy to see you're alive." Delores Riggins walked down the stairs and dropped her wiggling cat onto the ground. "I'm so sorry about your friend. God rest her soul."

"Thanks, Mrs. Riggins." Verity picked up the cat who had trotted over to her. "This can't be Mr. Roux."

"That's Mr. Roux the Third. I've had a lot of cats over the years. I can't believe you remembered him." Mrs. Riggins accepted her cat from Verity. "But then again, my cats always enjoyed hanging out with y'all in the courtyard."

Mrs. Riggins motioned for the group to come over to her, and she told a story about the cats hiding in the courtyard. While they politely listened to her, I walked over to the fountain. Luke joined me.

"We've met before, right?" Luke asked.

"I was here after the body was discovered. I'm Samantha,

Ruby's neighbor, and I came with her when we assumed it was her daughter buried here."

"Oh, I felt like I've met you before that." He shook his head and pointed at Verity. "So that's the woman who went missing when the dead girl disappeared."

"Yes, that's Verity Virtue. She was Nicole McBride's best friend. The entire group used to hang out in this courtyard."

"And Verity thinks one of them murdered her friend? That explains a lot." Luke took off his baseball hat and wiped his brow with the back of his hand.

"What do you mean?" I asked.

Luke proceeded to tell me how disruptive Myles, Tabby, and Sutton had been ever since he bought the apartment building. He had expected Myles to be combative since he hadn't wanted to sell it, but financially, Myles had no choice. Mrs. Riggins was the only tenant who welcomed the changes he planned to make.

"So she didn't care if you refurbished the fountain?" I asked.

"Not at all. She just warned me her cat would use it as a drinking fountain," Luke said. "If everyone was as easygoing as Mrs. Riggins, I would have finished this project by now."

"I heard the man who found the body with you disappeared afterward," I said.

"Yes, Ray did a runner." Luke shook his head. "He was a hard worker, but he didn't talk much about his personal life."

"Why do you think he left?"

"Probably had a bad run-in with the police or something like that. Ray leaving is just another setback in this renovation from hell." Luke put his hat back on. "Let me give you some advice. Don't buy a building with tenants in it."

Or a building with a dead body buried in the courtyard, but that went without saying.

"Mr. Ward, can I speak with you? I keep coming home and finding my shower leaking. My cat is not turning it on, so something else is going on," Mrs. Riggins called out as she left the group standing around her.

"Did you check with your cat sitter? Perhaps she turns it on to entertain your cat?" Luke smiled, but his shoulders tensed as he spoke.

"I asked her and she said she hasn't. And she's as honest as the sun rises. You come look at it right now." Mrs. Riggins turned swiftly and climbed the stairs with the meowing Mr. Roux. Luke sighed, but he trotted over to the staircase to follow Mrs. Riggins.

"Her cat sitter is here all the time. I bet she uses it as a love nest." Sutton slid next to me and winked.

"Was the pet sitter or Mrs. Riggins here the morning Nicole was found?" I said.

"Thank goodness, no. There was enough drama without them," Sutton said.

Mrs. Riggins didn't strike me as the dramatic type, but Sutton fit the bill.

"Verity, let's stop this arguing. Come sit with us and let's drink a toast to our dearly departed Nicole." Sutton gestured toward the table in the corner. "You must fill us in on where you've been all these years."

"And you can tell us why you left." Myles put his hand on Verity's shoulder, which caused her to wince. She pulled away from him and raised her hand. My stomach churned, anticipating she was going to hit him, but Verity dropped her hand as quickly as she'd raised it.

"Myles, you know why Nicole and I were leaving," Verity snapped. "Do I need to bring it up in front of outsiders?"

Suddenly, Myles, Tabby, and Sutton stared at me, the outsider. If Verity hadn't pointed out I was still there, they might have talked freely. By the tense faces of those three, as well as Verity, I was out of luck.

"Samantha, darling, it was kind of you to bring Verity here, but we need to talk about old times." Myles flashed a smile at me. "You understand, don't you?"

"I need to leave to meet with the detectives working on Nicole's case." Verity grabbed my hand and pulled me toward the exit. "We'll just have to catch up later."

"But Verity, wait..." Tabby called out as Verity pushed me through the gate. Verity rushed to the next corner and pulled a pack of cigarettes out of her bag.

"What's going on Verity?" I coughed as the cloud of smoke from Verity's cigarette swirled around her.

"Sorry to rush you out of there, but I actually need to see the cops." Verity took a drag and then crushed her cigarette on the sidewalk. "They all looked guilty, so I don't know if they all were in on it or they just feel guilty that Nicole was buried under their noses."

I had to agree Myles, Sutton, and Tabby had acted suspiciously, but then again, so did Verity.

"If one of them didn't kill and bury Nicole, then who did?" I asked.

"Are you accusing me?" Verity looked like I had slapped her. "Not that I need to defend myself, but I didn't kill my best friend."

"I didn't mean to imply you did." Well, perhaps I was questioning her innocence. She wasn't telling me the whole truth about the night she and Nicole were supposed to leave, but did that make her a murderer?

"Listen, I did some bad stuff as a teenager, but I would

never, ever hurt Nicole." Verity stared me straight in the eye. "I've got to go meet the detectives, but let's talk later."

"Sure. You know where to find me."

"I do. And Sammy." Verity stopped walking and turned back toward me. "I loved Nicole like a sister. If I'd known she had been murdered, I wouldn't have left. I would have killed whoever took Nicole away from me."

And with that, Verity rushed down the street. I wanted to believe she had nothing to do with Nicole's death, but until she told me the whole truth, I had to keep her on my list of suspects.

22

Following Verity to her appointment with the detectives wasn't an option so I returned to Lagniappe Books. Between waiting on customers, restocking shelves, and researching upcoming book releases, I had no time to think about anything but work. Around 6 p.m. I went back home and waited for Verity to call me. After catching up on my laundry, paying bills, and dusting the cobwebs in my apartment, I finally admitted she wasn't going to call. When my head hit my pillow, I fell asleep with a new plan of action for my investigation. As soon as I woke up at 8 a.m. the next morning I called one of my favorite partners in crime.

"You want to play detective on your day off? And my day off?" Sissy said.

"It will include shopping and lunch, I promise."

"Where?"

"The Garden District."

"I was going to say yes anyway, but I'm even more intrigued now that you've said the Garden District. Who or what are we investigating there?"

"Tabby Calloway Delmar."

"Who?"

"She is Myles Delmar's ex-wife, but when Nicole was killed, she was living with Myles as his girlfriend. And she was friends with Verity and Nicole."

"OK, I'm in. And on the way, I can tell you what I learned from Rob last night."

"Hurry up then! I'll even spring for coffee." I hung up and raced to get dressed. Sissy could have as much coffee as she wanted if she shared the latest news about the investigation.

"Verity said she and Nicole had a falling out with Myles? Over what?" I handed Sissy her cafe au lait and a bag of beignets. She insisted we stop at Cafe Beignet before walking to the Central Business District to catch the streetcar to the Garden District.

"That's all Rob would say, but I got the feeling that's all Verity told him." Sissy opened the bag and inhaled the sweet scent of powdered sugar that coated the beignets.

"I can believe that. She's been very vague about why she and Nicole were leaving." I sipped my iced cafe au lait. Even though it was only 9:00 a.m., it was already hot. "I get the impression she and Nicole were in some kind of trouble with Myles."

"Do you think they were doing something illegal, like selling drugs?"

"Sutton claims he would have known if they did that in the courtyard."

"This from the man who claims he didn't hear them

unearthing the body that morning?" Sissy laughed. "Or did he use his psychic powers to figure that out?"

"Considering he said his spiritual cleanse would give me the life I want, I wouldn't rely on his psychic powers." I rolled my eyes. "He knows more than he's saying. Whatever happened twenty-six years ago, no one wants to talk about it."

"Well, let's hope we'll have more luck with Tabby."

The dark green streetcar pulled up to our stop, and we climbed aboard. When I rode the streetcar for the first time with Neal, he corrected me when I referred to it as a cable car. "You're not in San Francisco anymore!" Neal had said and then explained the difference. Cable cars used cables in the streets to run while overhead cables powered streetcars. I found both modes of transportation charming.

Wooden benches lined the sides of the street car's interior, with dual rows of single light bulbs above them illuminating the interior. Not that extra light was needed as the sun shone through the windows that weren't covered with green shades. It was still stuffy inside even with all the windows open. When the streetcar moved, I put my hand out the window to feel the breeze, but Sissy pulled it back in.

"When we pass the trees, your hand will get scratched," she said.

"Thanks, mom," I said.

Sissy gave me her "don't fool with me" look that she used on her patients at the hospital. "We'll be out of the Warehouse District soon and onto St. Charles, and the trees will slap your hand silly."

She was right, of course. Trees and bushes lined the route in the residential area of the Garden District. I sat back and took in the views. This neighborhood differed completely from the French Quarter. Originally, the neighborhood was a plantation but in the 1820s it was subdivided and large homes were built with lush gardens and decorative fences surrounding them.

"So, are you and Rob going to move out here when you have kids? That one should have enough room." I pointed to a gorgeous two-story, sage green home with white trim. A wrought-iron fence enclosed the massive oak tree and ferns that made up the garden.

Sissy sighed. "My momma emails me listings of these houses. Although she keeps trying to get us to move back to Metairie, too."

"I can handle you moving here, but not out of town."

"I couldn't get Rob to leave the French Quarter even if I tried." Sissy squeezed my hand. "Don't you worry, we're not leaving. Eventually, we'll find a bigger place to live, but for now, we can make do in my apartment."

I squeezed her hand back. "So you won't desert me at Thibodeaux Mansion until you get married?"

"You're going to be stuck with me for a while, much to my mother's chagrin." Sissy put her hand up to her forehead dramatically. "Momma is beside herself that we haven't set a wedding date. Honestly, Rob and I are fine with the way life is right now, so no need to rush into some big elaborate shindig that my momma wants to plan."

"You could elope and throw a big party later."

"Trust me, we've considered it." Sissy laughed. "But for now, we're just going to enjoy being engaged."

"Sounds like a good plan." I pulled the cord to request the next stop. "And now it's time to continue with today's plan — talking to our suspect."

We walked past the iconic blue and white striped building that housed Commander's Palace to go to the cemetery across the street from the famous restaurant.

"When you pulled the cord on the streetcar, I thought you were taking me to Commander's Palace, not Lafayette Cemetery."

"It's too early for Commander's Palace and we have work to do so we can't indulge in those twenty-five cent martinis."

"You're right on both counts." Sissy sighed. "Promise we'll come back after you solve this mystery."

"We better get going, then. First, let's stop at the cemetery."

"Why? You've been before, right?"

"Yes, Neal took me and Jasper on a tour a month ago. I forgot to take a picture of the Collins tomb for Madeline."

My best friend from San Francisco, Madeline Collins, asked me to snap a photo of the tomb so she could research if she was related to the family buried here. I tried to persuade her to come visit and check it out in person. "Samantha, if I visit I may never leave and my husband and child might not like that." Maddie had laughed.

As Sissy and I walked through the cemetery, I noticed the statues and vases surrounding some mausoleums. They reminded me of the ones I saw in Myles' shop and of his reaction when I commented on them. Could you sell items from your mausoleum? It was legal to sell your tomb if everyone in the family agreed, but did that also apply to unattached items? Sissy didn't know, so I'd have to look into that later. It would explain why Myles sold those items, but not why he was defensive.

After our quick stop at Lafayette Cemetery, we walked up to Magazine Street. The Graceful Girl Boutique was a small clothing and accessories shop. The front window showcased sundresses featuring bright floral patterns with matching sandals. My Aunt Charlene would love this store as she favored bright clothing — the brighter the better.

"Good morning! Are you looking for anything in particular today?" Tabby greeted us after we entered the shop. Fortunately, she appeared to be the only person inside. I could chat with her without being interrupted. Clothes hung on every inch of the walls and three round tables piled with clothing and accessories filled the floor space. A sales counter was in the back of the shop and had more accessories showcased behind it.

"Actually, we met the other day, and you said to come see you if I wanted this belt in other colors." I pointed to the green belt around my black linen shorts.

"Of course! I remember you," she said. "You wanted to talk to my husband, I mean my ex-husband. Are you friends with him?"

"No, I met him when I came with Ruby Virtue when Nicole McBride was discovered in the courtyard," I said. "And I came with Verity yesterday."

"You did? I was so distracted when Verity arrived." She looked at the sales counter and began folding a pile of scarves. "Are you related to Ruby and Verity?"

"No, I'm Ruby's neighbor. And so is Sissy." I pointed to Sissy, who was going through a rack of sundresses. By the speed with which she pushed the dresses aside, it appeared Sissy didn't like any of them.

"How lovely to meet you. That dress would suit you well. Red must be your color." Tabby came out from behind the sales counter. She wore the dress Sissy was looking at but in buttercup yellow.

"I can't say I wear red often, but I'll try it." Sissy walked toward the left side of the sales counter where two small dressing rooms stood. "Sammy, check for a belt in red like yours."

Sissy never wore red, so I knew she was giving me time to chat with Tabby. Not that Tabby needed any encouragement. She was already back behind the sales counter, taking down belts before Sissy had closed the dressing room's curtain.

"I have the belt in red, which is perfect for your friend. You can't wear red being a redhead," Tabby said.

It sounded like a statement, not a question. But she was right, I didn't wear it. I wore black most of the time. I was trying to venture out of my comfort zone and pick other colors. But the yellow belt with black polka dots Tabby handed me was definitely not one I wanted.

"How about this one?" she said. "It's the last one and I don't think I'll get anymore in."

Having worked retail in my teenage years and now as a bookseller, I recognized this ploy to get rid of the last of an item that wasn't selling. "I'm not much for patterns. But this cobalt blue belt is pretty. Do you have any scarves in this color? Or earrings?"

"I sure do!" Tabby began pulling items down off the shelves.

"Great. So how are things at your apartment building? It must have been so stressful after they found Nicole."

Tabby kept her back to me, but answered, "It was dreadful. I can't believe Nicole was there all this time."

"I heard you and Myles searched for her and Verity after they disappeared."

"We did, of course. They were our friends." Tabby turned around with a smile plastered on her face, but I could see she was flushed.

"Verity said she and Nicole spent a lot of time in the

courtyard with you and Myles." I picked up a pair of garish rhinestone earrings and pretended to inspect them. "Y'all must have had a lot in common to hang out so much."

"No, not really." Tabby shook her head. "They were sweet girls who seemed lost. Since Myles and I were a few years older, we took them under our wing, so to speak."

"They were both new to New Orleans, so I imagine they were out of sorts. How kind of you and Myles to befriend them." I looked up from the earrings to see Tabby staring at me. "I bet the girls had crushes on Myles, though. How did you handle that?"

Tabby laughed so loudly that Sissy peeked her head out from the dressing room and stared at her. Sissy gave me the "what in the world was that about" look before closing the curtain again.

"Myles was a catch back then, but he was mine." Tabby tapped her elegantly manicured fingers on the counter. "He still acts like we're together, but we are most definitely not."

"I'm sorry to hear that." Sissy came out of the dressing room wearing the red dress. "I got engaged a few months back and I'm always looking for marriage advice."

Tabby looked down at Sissy's left hand. "Well, you might be all right by the look of that ring. Just make sure he keeps his money for your whole marriage."

"My friends say money can be a difficult part of marriage." Sissy twirled around, making the dress float up in the air. "How long were y'all married?"

"Twenty-five years. We just divorced." Tabby walked over to Sissy and put the red belt around her waist. "Here, try the belt with this. It'll give you another way to wear the dress."

Although math wasn't my strong suit, I could do subtraction quick enough to realize she and Myles married right after Verity and Nicole disappeared. Coincidence?

"So you must have married around the time Nicole and Verity left," I said. "Or did you marry before they disappeared?"

"Oh, it was a few months later, I guess. Who can remember?" Tabby picked up a pair of red stilettos and handed them to Sissy. "Try these with the dress, too. Unless your fiancé is short. Men can be so defensive of their height."

Rob towered over Sissy, but that wouldn't have kept her from wearing heels. Sissy was the most confident woman I knew, and Rob wouldn't have cared if she was taller. Myles seemed to be in Tabby's shadow when I saw them together, but I thought more from Tabby being confident, not her physical presence.

"Oh, my fiancé is as tall as can be. Is your ex-husband short?" Sissy put her hand on Tabby's arm. "You have a wonderful figure, so I hope he didn't want you to hide it."

Tabby straightened up and flicked her auburn hair over her shoulders. "Well, thank you for the sweet compliment. I've been a swimmer all my life, so it keeps me fit. Even at my old age."

"Oh, you're not old!" Sissy put the heels on. "Wow, you got my size right without asking."

"I'm good at sizing people up." Tabby laughed. "So, how about it? Is this the outfit to make your fiancé swoon?"

"It might be. Let me get changed and I'll think about it." Sissy went back to the dressing room.

Tabby turned to me. "How about you? Need a new dress for a night on the town? I don't see a ring, so maybe you're looking for a dress to impress someone?" She pulled a sequin dress with a plunging neckline from a display rack. "This will turn any man's head."

"Oh, that's a bit too much for me. But my boyfriend might like it." I smiled, but then frowned. "But Sutton warned me danger was headed my way and that might get me into trouble."

"Sutton read your cards? Don't believe what he says. That man will do anything to keep a woman talking to him." Tabby shoved the dress back on the rack. "You've met him and Myles and now me. You're just like Verity and Nicole, aren't you?"

"How's that?" I smiled, trying to lighten the mood as Tabby's demeanor changed from pushy saleswoman to suspicious woman.

"Oh, I mean, you've met all of us." Tabby returned to the sales counter and held up the blue belt. "Did you want anything else to go with this adorable belt?"

I guess I was buying a belt. At least I could use the belt more than I could use Sutton's psychic reading. The things I had to do to get information. But I wish I got more out of Tabby. Sissy must have thought the same.

"Tabby, how long have you had this shop?" Sissy asked.

"I started working here when I was in college, but I bought it when I graduated."

"Is this where you met Verity and Nicole? Verity didn't strike me as having been a swimmer." Sissy pulled out her credit card and handed it to Tabby.

"You got that right." Tabby said. "She and Nicole were so uncoordinated. And no, I didn't meet them here. Their idea of fashion back then was ripped jeans and faded t-shirts."

"So they were friends of Myles, then?" I asked. Tabby frowned at me. I guess I was bad cop to Sissy's good cop. And thankfully Sissy played the role well.

"I bet you and Myles felt sorry for the girls." Sissy lowered her voice. "Two unsophisticated newcomers must have been thrilled to meet you and Myles. Y'all were so kind to take them under your wings."

Tabby handed Sissy back her credit card and nodded. "Yes, Myles met them at Café du Monde and felt sorry for them." Tabby cackled. "Oh, that sounds horrible. But really, the girls were out of their element, and we tried as hard as we could to help them fit in."

Tabby was putting on her best Southern charm, but her eyes betrayed her feelings — disdain, annoyance, perhaps even anger at Verity and Nicole. What in the world went on with that group at Delmar Apartments?

"Beau said she left a while ago." I shoved my phone in my pocket. I'd tried the hotel after Verity didn't answer her cell phone.

After we left Tabby's shop, we walked back toward the streetcar to return to the French Quarter. Sissy agreed that we'd save Commander's Palace for a day when we could enjoy a leisurely lunch. Also, she understood how badly I wanted to find Verity. While I only learned a little about Nicole's and Verity's relationship from Tabby, it just confirmed my theory that there was more to their desire to leave New Orleans.

"Maybe she's visiting her mother. Should we go to Ruby's shop?" Sissy asked after we settled into our seats. "It's somewhere on Decatur. Have you been?"

"No, I don't know if Ruby would even let me inside." I laughed. "But let's go by and see if Verity is there."

"But first, food. I'm starving. If we're not having a fancy lunch, let's have some down-home cooking."

We got off the streetcar and walked down Decatur Street to Coop's. I had written it off as just a bar with gambling machines. Sissy enjoyed introducing me to new restaurants, and when I took my first bite of fried chicken, I realized she might have saved the best for last.

"You've been holding out on me, Sissy. This is incredible." I put down the chicken breast and wiped my lips with a napkin from a stack on the table.

"Everyone has a favorite fried chicken place. Rob actually likes the chicken from a corner store in the Marigny." Sissy picked up her fork. "But you need jambalaya with your chicken, and I love this one."

"Can't say I've had rabbit and sausage jambalaya before." I took a bite of the delicious rice dish. "Connor keeps telling me he'll teach me how to cook, but I rather like having him cook for me."

"You're a smart woman." Sissy laughed. "He's a keeper. How's his music career going these days?"

Recently, Connor quit his job as a restaurant manager to devote himself full-time to his music. I told her about Connor's latest gigs as a substitute trumpeter for a few bands playing at the bars on Frenchman Street. He'd also joined a few groups along Royal Street for some impromptu sessions. Fortunately, he'd saved most of his management salary since budding musicians made little money. And it didn't hurt that his parents owned the building he lived in, either.

After lunch, Sissy and I went to see if Ruby was in her shop. Neither of us had been there before. I would have known it was Ruby's place even without the weather-worn wood sign hand-painted with the business name Virtuous Spiritual Services. Statues of Egyptian gods and goddesses of varying shapes and sizes filled the window along with displays of crystal necklaces.

"Those must be Cleopatra and Nefertiti." Sissy pointed

to a pair of cat statues. "Cats have always been important to her, it appears."

"And so has Verity." There was a faded sign in the right corner of the window. It was barely legible but I could read the words "Verity" "Nicole" "Missing" and "Reward."

Sissy shook her head. "I'm such a horrible neighbor. I've lived in the same building as Ruby for almost three years and if I'd come by here, I would have known she had a daughter."

"No one in the building knew." I put my arm around her shoulders. While Ruby wasn't friendly to any of us in Thibodeaux Mansion, I felt terrible that I hadn't visited her shop. I'd been to everyone's business, even William's accounting firm.

Sissy tried the doorknob. It was locked, so she knocked. "It's about time we made an effort to get to know Ruby."

"Doesn't look like it will be today, though." Ruby didn't answer the door after Sissy and I both knocked loudly. "Let's go home, Sissy. She could be there with Verity."

It turned out Ruby wasn't home, or if she was, she wasn't answering her door.

"You'll just have to put your detective hat away now," Sissy said. "My feet are done for the day, so I'm going to curl up on my sofa with a glass of wine and binge watch the latest season of Midsomer Murder. Want to join me?"

"Normally, I would say yes to a wine and mystery marathon, but Connor and I are going out tonight." I hugged Sissy. "But thanks for the offer and coming with me today. I hope you had fun."

"Oh, I did. Have a good time tonight and try to forget about real-life mysteries for a bit."

"Wait!" I called to Sissy, who was halfway up the steps to the second floor. "I need you to ask Rob a question."

"I haven't even gotten to my apartment and you're already back to being a detective." She laughed, but she came back down the steps.

"I can't help it." I grinned. "He might not tell you, but do you mind asking him if there was anything else buried with Nicole?"

"What? It's the end of our day together and now you're bringing this up?" She put her hands on her hips. "Woman, you'll be the death of me."

"Oh, please, you enjoy seeing if Rob will tell you about a case." I grinned. "Ask him if they found anything else in Nicole's grave. Frankie heard there was an angel statue buried with her, but Sutton said he didn't see it. There's nothing about it in any of the media reports and no one connected to the case has mentioned it..."

"But Frankie's gossip usually is true," Sissy interrupted me. "That's a strange thing to find with a body, but nothing about Nicole's murder is normal. I'll see what I can do."

"You're the best." I hugged her. "Now go enjoy your fictional mystery while I enjoy a night without one, I promise."

I planned to follow Sissy's advice and have a good time that didn't include murders or mysteries. But then again, this was New Orleans, and an evening that didn't include ghosts wasn't guaranteed.

"You want me to meet you at a seance room? You're not taking me to Ruby's shop, are you?" I asked Connor. His laughter came through my cell phone loud and clear. "By your response, I'm going to assume that's a no."

"Sammy, I assure you Ruby is not involved in this

evening's outing. I said *the* seance room not *a*. You haven't been to Muriel's Restaurant yet, have you?"

No, I hadn't. Connor explained that there was a lounge in Muriels's Restaurant named the Seance Room. A former owner of the restaurant, Pierre Antoine Lepardi Jourdan, supposedly haunted the building, particularly the second floor.

"OK, I'll meet you there in twenty-five minutes. Order a Pimm's Cup for me and don't let the ghost drink it." I hung up the phone and threw on lightweight jeans, my new belt, and a sleeveless top. Although it was seven o'clock, it was muggy out. A pair of wedge sandals would dress up my outfit a bit, but I'd still be able to walk on the bumpy sidewalks.

It wouldn't take twenty-five minutes to reach Muriel's, but I liked to take my time walking and stopping to listen to a musician or two. Fortunately, Connor understood my love, perhaps obsession, with street musicians. I'd never lived where performers set up on the sidewalks and played for crowds big and small. It was more common than not that I would get lost in the soulful music or tap my toes to a peppy number.

As I always did, I paused at the corner of Royal and St. Peter to listen to a four-piece band featuring a clarinetist and singer whose musical gifts consistently drew a large crowd. I danced along with the tourists and locals alike to one of my favorite numbers, *Lulu's Back In Town*. As the song neared the end, the hairs on the back of my neck stood up. While music always affected me, the sense of dread wasn't from the song. I looked around, expecting to see someone I knew, but I didn't.

After the music ended, I clapped along with the crowd and reached into my pocket for the cash I always kept to tip the street musicians. As I dropped the money into the tip bucket and gave a quick hello to the band, once again the hairs rose on the back of my neck. I quickly stepped away and spun around. No one I knew was there, but as I walked toward Toulouse Street, a man caught my eye.

He was twenty feet away and I only saw his profile, but he seemed familiar. Wearing jeans, a white t-shirt, and a yellow baseball cap, he looked like any other man walking down the street. But where had I seen that hat before?

Then the man glanced at me, gripped the strap of the red backpack on his shoulder, and smiled before running off. The people around him yelled and gave him dirty looks as he pushed through them. One man shouted, "Where's the fire, dude?"

He wasn't heading to a fire. He was running away from his sister.

24

My brother ran down Royal Street.

I reached for my cell phone inside my pocket as my head said to call Rob and Christine. But my gut said to chase after him. Joey would be miles away by the time they showed up. I would call them but I had to catch up to him.

I set off, annoying the same crowds that he had. I kept my eye on the yellow baseball hat like the one Luke Ward and Myles each wore. Joey had to be the missing construction worker from Delmar Apartments. When I reached him, I would confirm it. Hopefully my pepper spray was powerful enough to stop him before he could get away again.

My regular runs around the neighborhood made it easier to run, but the high-heeled sandals didn't help. With my heart racing and my feet pounding, I weaved in and out of the crowds. Most people got out of my way, but a few yelled at me as I rushed by them. Normally I would have apologized, but politeness had to go by the wayside to grab him.

Joey never looked back. He kept running, so I did too. I would catch him. I had to.

But then he made a right on Conti Street and turned left onto Bourbon Street. The crowds on Royal Street paled in comparison to the ones on Bourbon Street. With bars lined up on each side of the road, there was no shortage of places to drink, dance, and listen to music. Not only did visitors bar-hop, they hung out on the sidewalks and the street, which was cordoned off from cars. From the loud music seeping out of open doors to the insistent shouting of people selling drinks, it was an overwhelming scene.

Joey pushed through the crowds faster than I could keep up, so I focused on his yellow hat. I lost him at the corner of Bourbon and Bienville and was about to give up when I saw the yellow hat pop up again ahead on the right. I rushed in that direction and yelled, "Stop, Joey! Stop!"

The crowds parted as my high-pitched screams rose above the noise. They must have thought I was crazy and they wouldn't have been wrong. All I cared about was catching my brother. The gap narrowed as I picked up speed. My eyes focused on the yellow hat. My heart pounded, but I was sure I could catch up to him.

That was until a bachelorette party exited a bar. A woman wearing a wedding veil and a sash that said,"Bride to Be" led a group of a dozen young women carrying cups brimming with beer. They towered over me as they sauntered in front of me.

"Excuse me! Excuse me!" I pushed gently through the crowd, as I didn't want the wrath of tall, tipsy women keeping me from finding Joey. After managing to extricate myself from the group, I started running again. I saw the yellow hat now a full block away.

The hat bobbed up and down in the sea of the dancing

drinkers in the street. Then Joey stopped. With all my might, I raced toward him and grabbed his arm. "Joey, stop!"

The man turned around. It wasn't Joey.

"Oh, I'm so sorry." I stammered.

"Well, hello there, darling. I'm not Joey I'm afraid." The man grinned.

I nodded as I tried to catch my breath. All the adrenaline of the chase spilled out of me like someone stomping on a tube of toothpaste. The man was the same height as Joey and he wore a yellow hat, but other than that, he looked nothing like my brother.

"I'm sorry. I was trying to catch up with a friend wearing a hat just like yours." I turned away, blinking back tears of frustration and disappointment. Joey wasn't here. I must be seeing things.

But I wasn't.

"Did you want the hat?" the man raced around me and stopped in front of me. "A guy shoved it on my head as he rushed past. Could he have been Joey?"

The man handed me the cap, and it said, "Ward Construction." I gulped, trying to keep down the bile that crept up my throat. "Did you get a look at him?"

"Sorry. He ran off so quickly. Did he do something?" he asked.

The answer was a resounding yes, but I didn't want to explain myself to this stranger.

"It's nothing. He must have just thought it was funny. I'll catch up with him later." I plastered a smile on my face. "Thanks for the hat. Sorry to bother you."

"No problem. Hope you find him," the man shouted as I raced away.

Me, too. I had to find Joey somehow, someway.

I tried to pull myself together before I met Connor at Muriel's, but I didn't do a good job.

"Sammy, you look like you've seen a ghost." Connor jumped up from his chair in the Seance Lounge when I walked into the room. "Did you meet the ghost when you came in?"

"No. I saw my brother on Bourbon Street on my way here."

Connor said a few expletives under his breath as he embraced me tightly. He led me to the couch and handed me his drink. I wasn't normally a fan of Sazeracs, but at that point I didn't care. I finished it and shuddered. It could have been from the strong whiskey or my nerves. Connor waited next to me, holding my hand. After I calmed down, I explained what had happened.

"So that's why you're carrying the hat," Connor said when I wrapped up my story. "We should call Rob and Christine. I bet they can get DNA off the hat."

I smiled at Connor. While I appreciated his concern and his ideas, I was sure Rob and Christine had enough to do with Nicole's murder. And I doubted they had the budget to run a DNA test on the hat. "I'm sure they're too busy. And it might not have even been Joey."

"I know you're positive it was your brother. If you don't want to call, will you at least text Rob?"

I nodded and texted Rob. *I saw Joey on Bourbon Street. He was wearing a Ward Construction Hat. I lost him, though.*

"Done. How about a drink of my own?" I said. "And tell me all about this room. It's unusual, to say the least."

"I thought you'd like it." Connor waved over a server standing in the lounge's doorway. After ordering another

Sazerac for himself and a Pimm's Cup for me, he explained that the ghost of the former owner supposedly haunted this area of the building. With its red decor from floor to ceiling, antique furniture and Egyptian artifacts, including a sarcophagus, the room looked like the perfect place for a seance.

"The ghost stays in this part of the building since he hung himself here," Connor said.

"That's awful." I shuddered. Suddenly, the room lost its charm and quirkiness for me. I'd been in plenty of places in New Orleans that were said to be haunted, but tonight I wasn't in the mood for stories from the past.

My phone rang. "It's Rob. I should take it."

"Why don't you go out on the balcony? It's just down the hall. I'll bring our drinks."

"Hi, Rob. Can you hold on a minute?" I stepped out to the balcony that overlooked Jackson Square. "I can talk now. Sorry to bother you."

"You should always call me if you see your brother. Now tell me what happened. But first, I'm putting you on speakerphone so Christine can listen, too."

I heard someone typing on a keyboard as I spoke. I assumed one detective was taking notes as I told them about chasing Joey. When I finished my story, Rob sighed and Christine said, "That confirms it, I guess."

"Confirms what?" I asked. "You knew my brother was in town?"

"We thought he might be the missing worker from the Delmar Apartments."

"What?" I screeched loud enough for the people walking the underneath the balcony to look up. I lowered my voice and asked, "Why didn't you tell me?"

"Sammy, it was just a working theory. We had no proof,"

Christine said. "Mr. Ward's description of Ray West was similar to Joey, but it was Ray's familiarity with the neighborhood, especially places that you frequent that made us suspicious."

"And now that you saw Joey wearing a Ward Construction hat, there's a very good chance that he is the missing worker," Rob said.

"Can you think of why he would work there?" Christine asked. "You don't have any connections to the building or the people there besides Ruby, correct?"

"I assume it was a convenient place to keep an eye on me and Jasper." I grasped the drink Connor brought out to me and took a gulp. "Joey was only twelve when Verity and Nicole disappeared, so he couldn't have had anything to do with that."

"We agree. It's just troubling that he's so close to your home. Are you alone right now?" Rob said.

"No, I'm with Connor. But I'm not worried about Joey hurting me. He could have easily snuck up on me on the street, or anywhere else and killed me." I mouthed "I'm fine, really," to Connor who looked horrified.

"Perhaps, but you shouldn't be alone," Christine said. "I'm sending officers to go by your apartment right now, and they will patrol your block during the night."

"Thanks. I appreciate y'all calling. You must be busy with Nicole's murder," I said.

"You should always call. Your brother's case is an open investigation and if he is Luke Ward's missing worker, it's just another reason to find him," Rob said. "Is Connor there with you now? Can I speak with him?"

I handed the phone to Connor and stared out at the street below. A few tarot card and palm readers sat on folding chairs with their tools of the trade displayed on cloth-covered tables. The tuba player from a brass band passed a hat around the crowd for listeners to put in their tips. A solitary singer wailed a sorrowful tune that reflected my mood. While I wanted Joey to be caught, it meant confronting him and coming to terms with what he did to me. I wasn't confident I was ready to face him.

Connor handed my phone back to me and I listened to Rob as he insisted I stay at Connor's apartment tonight and that I avoid going anywhere alone. While I promised I would, I had no plans to hide away until they found my brother. But I planned to look over my shoulder until then.

"I think you should stay with me tonight," Connor said after I ended the call.

"I am perfectly capable of taking care of myself."

"Of course you are." Connor took my hand in his. "But there's nothing wrong with erring on the side of caution. Especially when it comes to your brother."

"I just don't like Rob asking you to take care of me." While I had to admit I was thankful for friends who cared about me, I didn't appreciate being treated like I was helpless.

"Sammy, they actually asked me to let my parents know that a patrol would check the building tonight." Connor reached over and kissed me on the cheek. "They're just worried about you. Honestly, if any of us could take care of ourselves against a killer, we all know it's you."

I smiled, but he was not entirely correct. I had fought off murderers before, but not my brother. Was I ready to fight him again?

"Do you want to eat here or go back home?" Connor asked. "I can get a table inside."

My aching feet didn't feel like walking, but I did like the idea of kicking off my shoes and curling up on the couch with Connor. "Let's go. Are we staying at your place or mine?"

"How about mine? I'll cook dinner."

"We have to bring Nubi in with us." I followed Connor from the balcony and down the stairs to the front door of the restaurant. "I don't want him by himself."

"Do you think Joey would hurt him?" Connor asked.

"Probably not, but I don't want him anywhere near Nubi. Or anyone else, for that matter." I squeezed my eyes to keep back the tears. "I need to let everyone in the building know. Oh, no, I need to call Jasper."

"Already done." Connor showed me his phone when I opened my eyes. "See, I sent a message to our group chat."

"But Jasper..."

"I sent a separate text to Neal first so he could tell Jasper. They're on a tour now, so Jasper is safe. Don't worry about him. You know Neal will take care of him." Connor's voice reflected the confidence on his face. "He'll be safe, I promise."

"What about Ruby?"

"My mom called her and left a message on her voicemail. Everyone is taken care of, so it's time for me to take care of you."

"What did you have in mind?" I grinned.

"Many things, but let's start with dinner." Connor put his arm around me and steered me toward home. "I'm going to teach you how to make shrimp and grits."

"I've made grits before," I insisted.

"They were instant grits, weren't they?"

"Maybe..."

"Those don't count. And I bet you haven't cooked shrimp. Poor Nubi doesn't even know what shrimp is."

"Of course he does. He's a cat."

"Since you never cook, I assumed Nubi might be unaware of what real food smells like." Connor laughed as I playfully swatted his arm.

"I should be offended, but you're right on all counts."

"Let's grab Nubi and head to my apartment. We'll try Muriel's another time and then we'll see the ghost."

I wanted to dine at Muriel's, but I wasn't eager to meet the ghost. I had enough of my own ghosts to last a lifetime.

25

"I'll get you a new frying pan today, I promise." I kissed Connor goodbye and followed Nubi down the steps of the main building of Thibodeaux Mansion. The three of us enjoyed a quiet evening, except for the fire alarm going off when I burned the shrimp. I blamed Connor as he distracted me by playing my favorite song, *What a Wonderful World,* on his trumpet. Fortunately, with another pan and no distractions, I cooked the shrimp to Connor's and Nubi's liking.

"You don't need to," Connor called after me. "You won't know which one to get. And I mean that in the kindest way."

That was true, so I didn't argue with him before I left the foyer and entered the courtyard. Nubi beelined to my front door, where Rob waited. He stretched out his arm and Nubi gobbled up a handful of treats before I got to my door.

"You're spoiling Nubi like Sissy," I said. "He's going to move in with you if I don't step up my game."

"Oh, no, he's your baby. I'm just the uncle who spoils him." Rob scratched Nubi on the head before standing up.

"You look no worse for the wear after yesterday's encounter with Joey. How are you feeling?"

"I'm OK, but since you're here, I assume I won't feel that way for long." Rob followed me inside after I unlocked my door. I immediately went to my kitchen and started making coffee. Rob and I shared a love of coffee and, by his serious look, I would need multiple cups. Or maybe even something stronger.

Rob and I didn't speak as I prepared our drinks. Once we sat down at the kitchen counter with our mugs, he said, "I spoke with Luke Ward last night and showed him a photo of Joey."

"Did he recognize him?" I blew on my coffee before taking a sip.

"He wasn't 100% positive, but he thought it could be your brother. He said his hair was longer, and he always had stubble on his face."

"Did he say what Joey was like? Did he mention any family or friends?" I asked.

"Luke said Ray told him he was from Mississippi originally but was looking to settle back into New Orleans." Rob put his mug down on the counter. "Other than that, he kept to himself. Luke paid him weekly in cash, so he didn't have any paperwork or personal information on him."

"I just can't believe he's been in town." I ran a finger around the rim of my mug as if touching it would keep me tethered to reality. Even though I had seen my brother with my own eyes, it was still hard to believe he was back in New Orleans.

"Well, the postcards he's sent lately seem to indicate he's been in town."

"But it's too much of a coincidence that Joey is the missing construction worker," I said. "It sounds absurd."

"Sammy, I'm supposed to be some hardened detective who sees everything in black or white, but I don't." Rob laughed softly. "I believe in coincidences, but I also believe in facts. Is that the hat you got last night?" He pointed to the grocery bag I had carried with me into the apartment.

"Yes. When we got to Connor's place last night, I put it in there, so no one else has touched it."

Nubi jumped onto the counter and meowed as if to agree. Rob stroked his back, making Nubi's tail stick straight up. "Nubi is looking out for you, too, isn't he? Well, Mr. Nubi, we're all looking out for your human."

I picked up my cat and placed him on the floor. "I'm fortunate to have everyone looking out for me. Did the police officers patrolling last night see anything?"

"No, it was all quiet. But that doesn't mean you shouldn't be on guard. Promise me you'll be careful." Rob put his hand on mine. "Sissy will kill me if your brother touches one hair on your head."

"I won't let my brother hurt me, I promise. I wouldn't want Sissy killing her fiancé."

Rob stood up and laughed. "Thanks. But really, Sammy, take care and if you see Joey, call 911 and me and Christine."

"Thanks. But I imagine you're pretty busy with Nicole's murder. Any updates you can share? Perhaps something else was in the grave besides the charm bracelet?"

"You mean an angel statue?" Rob sighed. "If it wasn't against the law, I would kill Officer Edwards. He's got the biggest mouth on the force."

"Sorry, I didn't mean to get him in trouble."

"Oh, you didn't. Frankie asked me about the statue when I stopped to get coffee later that day," Rob said. "I nipped that rumor in the bud."

"So no one else knows about the statue rumor?" I made the air quotes gesture when I said statue rumor.

"Frankie promised on her grandmother's manicotti recipe that she only told you, so I believe her," Rob said.

"If Frankie swore on a family recipe I would believe her, too." I grinned. "But you found something, didn't you? There's no smoke without fire, right?"

"When are you applying to the police academy?" Rob laughed.

"Come on, you know I won't gossip about it." I put on my most angelic face. "And I was there at the scene, so I'm bound to silence."

"That's not how that works, but yes, we found something. That's all I'll say. We need to hold a few things back. I'm sure you've read about that in your books." Rob pointed to my bookshelves filled with mystery books and the New Orleans themed books the apartment came with.

"OK, I won't ask about any additional evidence," I said. "But how is the case going otherwise?"

"It's early days, but we're making some progress." Rob smiled, but his tense voice made me think he was lying. "Has Verity confided in you about the real reason she left town? I don't mean to put you on the spot, but I have to say she's not as forthcoming as I had hoped."

"No, she keeps saying they just wanted to leave, but I agree. There's more to her story than she's sharing." I opened my door for Rob. "Has Ruby given you any insights?"

"You have met Ruby, right?" Rob's laugh made Nubi jump down from the chair he was napping on and rush over to Rob. "She's as close-mouthed as ever. I hope we'll have better luck with Verity. It would be good to get someone off our suspect list."

Rob's phone rang, and he excused himself. I watched as he headed toward the courtyard gate. Verity, as a suspect, made sense, but I couldn't picture her hurting her best friend. But then again, I knew little about her and Nicole, really.

I needed to talk to Verity and convince her to open up to me. Or at least to the police. She spoke with such affection about Nicole that I couldn't imagine her killing her. But then again, I never imagined Joey trying to kill me, and he did just that. People weren't always what they seemed. I just hoped that wouldn't be the case with Verity.

26

———

I had to put my plan to question Verity on the back burner when Momo called. She said little, just asked if I would come by this morning. I told her I'd be there in forty-five minutes. After a quick shower, I made it to her house in a half an hour. Momo's breaking voice was all I needed to get to her as fast as I could.

I used the ornate lion's head knocker, but Momo must have been waiting in the hallway. She immediately swung the door open. "Sammy, thank you for coming so quickly."

"Momo, what's wrong? You're shaking." I grasped her hands. "What happened?"

"It's just too much, honey." Momo squeezed my hands and took in a deep breath. "I searched Nicole's room again. It was a ridiculous thing to do since Nicole's father and I did it when she disappeared."

"It's not ridiculous. I would do the same thing."

Momo dropped my hands and stood back for me to come inside. "Yes, you would do that, wouldn't you? Let me show you what I found."

I followed her up the stairs to a bedroom. Lady Clementine sat in the doorway, looking like the cat that ate the canary. "Oh, my sweet kitty, the mess you made this time was a good thing," Momo said.

"Did Lady Clementine find something?" I bent down to scratch the cat on her head. She purred in response.

"Let me show you."

I followed Momo into the plain bedroom. An antique canopy bed with faded pink linens, a nightstand, and a matching dresser filled the room. Unlike the rest of the house, no artwork or mirrors hung on the wall.

"You probably expected it to look like Nicole still lived here," Momo said. "It did for a year, but then I put everything away. I realized when she returned, the bands and movie posters would be out of date. Now I realize it would have been a shrine to the dead."

Lady Clementine's plaintive wail summed up what I felt — utter sadness. I picked the cat up and carried her to the bed where Momo sat. She jumped out of my arms and curled up next to Momo.

"What did you find in here?" I looked around the room, trying to imagine a hiding place Momo could have discovered twenty-six years after Nicole's disappearance. "And where?"

"Like I said, I came in here to look once more for anything I might have missed. I couldn't find anything and when I got up to leave, my bracelet fell off and dropped to the floor."

"Let me guess. Lady Clementine decided it was a toy for her and batted it around the room."

Momo dipped into the pocket of her pants and held up a thin gold bangle. "Bingo. Nicole gave me this, so I was irritated when my kitty knocked it under the bed."

Lady Clementine meowed, either in defense of her playing with the bracelet or just confirming Momo's story.

"When I reached for the bracelet, my sleeve caught on a nail from a floorboard." Momo pulled at the loose threads from the cuff of her jacket. "When I pulled my sleeve up, the board came with it and I discovered a hiding place."

"What was in there?"

"Open the drawer of that dresser. I put it in there and then called you."

I opened the drawer and took out a wooden cigar box. After I placed it on top of the dresser, I lifted the lid. "I understand why you were shocked when you found this."

Inside the box was a handful of yellowed papers, a bottle of vitamins, and a plastic pregnancy tester.

"There are no lines, so Nicole might not have been pregnant," Momo said.

"I doubt she would have kept a negative test," I said gently, and I didn't think the lines would still show after twenty-six years.

"You're right." Momo wiped a tear from her cheek. "The papers underneath seem to confirm it."

I opened the folded papers, and they were sheets from a phonebook. It was a list of obstetrician offices in New Orleans. "I'm sorry Momo. This must have been hard to find."

"It was." Momo sighed. "I wish she had told me. If she was running away because she was pregnant, that breaks my heart."

"Have you shown this to Verity?" I put the papers and pregnancy test back in the box.

"I left her a message to come and see me after I called you." Momo stood up from the bed. "Let's go outside. I need a cigarette and a drink."

I followed Momo through the hallway to the balcony. Apparently she had already been out here since there was a bottle of bourbon and a glass with her frosted pink lipstick on the rim. A pack of cigarettes sat next to a china teacup, which she always used as an ashtray. She gently lowered herself into one of the wrought-iron chairs. I suspected Momo was in her eighties, but today she looked to be a hundred. Finding Nicole's body and now this new information was draining the life out of Momo.

"I know it's early to be drinking even by New Orleans standards, but honey, I am spent." Momo poured a dollop of bourbon in her glass and sipped it. "Do you think Nicole's pregnancy got her killed?"

I shook off the bottle raised in my direction. "It's definitely a possibility. We need to talk to Verity."

"Let me call her again." Momo took out her cell phone. "If she doesn't answer, I'll try the hotel. If she's there, Beau or Ambrose will track her down for me."

Momo put her phone on the table and set it to speakerphone. As we listened to the phone ringing, a voice shouted up from the street. "Momo, are you calling me?"

I leaned over the balcony railing to see Verity holding a cell phone up to her ear. Even from two stories up, it was clear how exhausted she was. Her shoulders were slumped, and she ran a hand through her loose hair. The news about Nicole's pregnancy wouldn't help her mood. Then again, this might not be news to her.

27

Unless Verity was an incredible actress, she hadn't known about Nicole's pregnancy.

Momo asked me to let Verity in and grab Nicole's secret box before we joined her on the balcony. Verity raised her eyebrows and cocked her head toward Momo's glass of bourbon, but sat down across from her. I handed the box to Verity and sat with the two women who had loved Nicole.

Verity opened the box, and her mouth dropped. I explained how Momo had found Nicole's hiding place and discovered the hidden test and papers. When I stopped, Momo poured a drink for Verity and me. I ignored mine, but Verity finished hers in one gulp.

"Oh, god, I'm an idiot." Verity clutched the edge of the table, making it shake slightly. "She felt nauseous a lot, but I assumed it was nerves."

"Who do you think was the father?" I asked.

"Sutton or Myles." Verity looked nauseous herself. "She hung out with them more than I did, and she hinted she had slept with one of them, but I took it as a joke."

"Sutton would have been too old for Nicole, surely." Momo poured more bourbon into her and Verity's glass.

"He was, but he always came into the courtyard with beer and cigarettes," Verity said.

"How about Myles? And didn't his father live in the building, too?" I said.

"Myles Senior?" Momo's pinched face apparently worried Lady Clementine, who meowed loudly and jumped out of Momo's lap. "I can't even fathom the possibility."

"I wouldn't consider him. Mr. Delmar was rarely there." Verity clenched her fists. "His son or Sutton are most likely the father."

"Could it be anyone else?" I asked.

"I doubt it. We didn't have other friends. And Nicole admitted she had a crush on Myles when we first met him, but I assumed it was over," Verity said. "Sutton read Nicole's tarot cards a lot, but I figured he used it as an excuse to hang out with us. Maybe it was more than that."

"I don't know which one of them is worse — Myles or Sutton," Momo said.

Verity threw back the rest of her drink and stood up. "Let's find out."

28

"Oh, Verity, do you think that's wise?" Momo followed Verity down the stairs to the front door.

"Momo, please, you want the truth, too." Verity turned around to face Momo. "Are you coming with me?"

Momo left the hallway and shuffled into the living room. She lowered herself gingerly onto the couch. "I'm too old to storm off to Delmar Apartments and accuse one of them of getting Nicole pregnant. And even if I wanted to, Nicole's father will be here soon."

"Mr. McBride is coming here? He never came when Nicole was alive." Verity sat next to Momo and held her hand.

"He did when you two went missing. He and Nicole hadn't spoken much after she moved in with me. But he's showing up now." Momo slipped her hand out of Verity's and pushed herself up from the couch. "I've got to prepare myself. He's distraught and naturally, he blames me for Nicole's death."

"It's not your fault," Verity and I said in unison.

"You girls are sweet, but I was responsible for my grand-niece and I obviously mucked it up."

"No, you didn't. Nicole and I did. We were stupid kids just thinking about ourselves. We never considered how our actions would affect our families. I'm so sorry." Verity's face turned bright red. "I'll make it up to you and find out who killed Nicole."

Verity rushed out of the room and the front door slammed shut.

"Sammy, go after her, please." Momo grasped my arm hard enough that I winced. "I've seen how she is when she's angry and this is worse. I can't bear for her to get hurt or in trouble."

"I will, but promise me you'll call Rob Armstrong and tell him about the pregnancy test." I looked Momo in the eyes. "He needs this information right away."

"Be careful Sammy! And thank you!" Momo called out as I flung the front door open. I shut it behind me and braced myself to dash down the street after Verity. But I didn't have to.

"Are you ready?" Verity dropped her cigarette and crushed it onto the sidewalk. "I expected Momo would insist you come with me, so I figured I'd save you the trouble of chasing after me."

"You assumed correctly. Are you sure you want to confront Myles and Sutton?" I asked.

"Of course I am! Whoever got her pregnant must have killed her and I need to find out which one of them did it." Verity started down the street. "Come on, you want to know almost as much as I do, Nancy Drew."

She was right about me wanting to know who killed Nicole. But I wasn't as confident that the father was also the murderer. Was her pregnancy enough to kill her, or was there something else going on with that group at Delmar Apartments?

Verity wouldn't talk as we went to Delmar Apartments. After my fifth question about Nicole, she stopped and said, "If you say one more word, I'm going by myself."

I kept quiet as we walked. I preferred to have Verity consider me an ally instead of a babysitter. Not just for Momo's sake, but for Ruby's sake. Neither of them could bear to lose Verity again. But by her increasing anger with each step toward the apartment building, my concern grew that she would explode when we found Myles and Sutton.

Verity's actions when we arrived confirmed my fears. A deliveryman came out of the building as we walked up, so Verity grabbed the front gate before it closed behind him. "Myles Delmar and Sutton O'Berry, get out here now!" she screamed as she lumbered down the hall to the courtyard.

"They might not be here," I said.

I don't think Verity heard me or if she did; she didn't care. She stomped to the center of the patio and raised her arms in the air and shook her fists. "Come out or I'll tell the cops that one of you got Nicole pregnant and killed her!"

The click-clack of high heels rushing down the hall preceded Tabby entering the courtyard. "Verity! What are you screaming about? I heard you from the street."

"Did you know your boyfriend, wait, no, your ex-husband got Nicole pregnant?" Verity stepped up to Tabby and though she only came up to Tabby's shoulders, her presence appeared to scare her. She took two steps back and swung her large purse in front of her chest like a shield.

"Verity, what are you talking about? Nicole was pregnant? How do you know?" Tabby squeezed her purse. "And why would you accuse Myles?"

"Oh, come on, Tabby, you knew Myles liked Nicole."

"He also liked you, and he didn't knock you up." Tabby dropped her bag to the ground and wiped her hands on her jeans.

"Of course not! I wouldn't let that man touch me with a ten-foot pole!" Verity's face turned a shade bordering on purple. "But Nicole hung out here without me. I bet while you were at swim practice."

"Verity, you're just being ridiculous." Tabby picked her purse up and swung it over her shoulder. "Have you accused Sutton yet? He followed you and Nicole around like a puppy dog. No, more like an old hound dog."

Verity's heavy breathing slowed down as she closed her eyes. Her silence made me think she was considering Sutton as the father of Nicole's baby. When she flicked open her eyes and marched to Sutton's backdoor off the courtyard, she looked like she was ready to accuse him, too. She banged on his door and called his name repeatedly.

"Is Verity telling the truth? Was Nicole pregnant?" Tabby stepped next to me and we watched Verity.

"Would it surprise you if she was?" I raised my voice over Verity's.

"No, well, yes," Tabby stuttered. "Nicole had a crush on Sutton, for sure."

"What about Myles?" I asked, but Sutton whipped open his door.

"Why are you screaming at this godforsaken hour?" Sutton tied the belt of a faded blue kimono around his waist.

"Sutton, it's not that early." Tabby strode over to Sutton

and put her arm around him. "Verity claims Nicole was pregnant."

Sutton shook Tabby's arm off his shoulders and stepped over to his table. He dropped into a chair and took a pack of cigarettes out of a pocket in his robe. With a slightly trembling hand, he lit a cigarette and inhaled deeply.

Verity sat down across from him and grabbed the pack. She took one out but didn't light it. Instead, she tapped it on the table. Sutton pushed his lighter over to Verity. "My dear, can you explain your rantings and ravings? I was communing with the spirits when you interrupted me."

"You were more likely sleeping off a bender from drinking spirits, not communing with them," Tabby snorted.

"Tabby, will you shut up and let Verity speak?" Sutton snapped.

"Were you fooling around with Nicole?" Tabby asked.

"I didn't touch a hair on her pretty head," Sutton said.

"But you did like her, right?" Tabby said.

"Would you shut up, Tabby?" Verity finally lit her cigarette and took a drag. "I'm doing the talking here."

"I think they're here to do the talking." I pointed to hallway. Their faces dropped when Myles walked into the courtyard with Rob and Christine close by.

"Mr. O'Berry, we'd like to talk with you at the station," Rob said.

"Me?" Sutton squeaked.

"Yes, by Miss Richardson's and Miss Virtue's presence, I assume you are all aware that it is possible that Nicole McBride was pregnant when she was killed." Christine gave me and Verity one of her trademark death stares. I was used to it, but Verity looked away.

"Nicole was pregnant?" Myles turned a shade of green

that I had only seen in a puddle on Bourbon Street in the early hours before the cleaners came by.

"How can you tell from her skeleton?" Tabby stood up from the table and moved over to Myles. She put her arm around him.

"We will discuss the details during our interviews," Christine said. "We would like to speak to you later, Ms. Calloway-Delmar and Ms. Virtue, so expect a call."

"Of course." Tabby smiled at Christine. "Myles and Sutton will be happy to speak with you first, I'm sure."

Sutton and Myles frowned at Tabby, so I doubted they were happy to talk with Christine and Rob. But Sutton returned to his apartment to change while Christine walked Myles out to the front of the building to wait. Tabby came back to the table and sat in Sutton's now empty seat and took her cell phone out of her purse.

"Please don't talk to anyone else about this recent development," Rob said. "It's best to keep this information to ourselves."

Verity nodded, but didn't look up. Tabby said, "Of course, Detective Armstrong. We will."

"Sammy, can I speak with you for a moment?" Rob walked to the back of the courtyard and leaned against the wall. I joined him and he lowered his voice. "I just wanted to let you know we alerted all officers to look out for your brother. Has he contacted you today?"

I shook my head. While I had hoped Joey would have been located, I really hadn't expected him to be. He had done a good job of hiding in the French Quarter for a few weeks with none of us noticing him.

Rob squeezed my shoulder. "Be careful until we find him. And if Verity should share any information..."

"I'll call you." I interrupted Rob. "We should go."

Verity and Tabby were walking out of the courtyard, and I didn't want Verity to get away. Rob led the way out of the courtyard and onto the street. Christine and Myles were standing outside Sutton's front door, both scrolling on their phones. Rob joined them, so I looked for Verity.

To my surprise, she and Tabby were hugging like long lost best friends. Were they closer than they led me to believe? And Tabby seemed awfully calm for someone whose ex-husband was suspected of impregnating a teenage girl and murdering her. Before I could catch up to them, Tabby waved down a taxi and she and Verity got in. If it had been a movie, I would have hailed the next cab and followed them. But finding a taxi in the Quarter wasn't easy and Tabby grabbed the only one in sight. And what would I do after I caught up with them? They obviously wanted to talk alone.

My finger was itching to dial Verity's cell phone number, but I called Momo. She picked up the phone in two rings. I reassured her that Verity was fine and that the detectives were already talking to Myles and Sutton.

Sutton, now dressed in jeans and a button-down shirt, and an agitated Myles, walked with Christine and Rob. I wanted to follow them, too, but Christine would have waved me off. While both Sutton and Myles seemed shocked by the news, if Verity was right, one of them had an affair with Nicole and got her pregnant. A confession would make life a little easier for Momo and Verity. They needed closure.

And so did I. When would my brother make his next appearance?

29

———————

It wasn't just Verity's past that was coming to light. Mine was too.

I returned home after leaving Delmar Apartments to find an envelope under my door. I didn't need to open it to know who sent it. No one else called me Sarah Jane. My Aunt Charlene still used my birth name occasionally, but she was in Huntley, Mississippi. And it wasn't her style to leave a note.

I tore open the envelope and unfolded the letter. Joey's scrawl covered the notepaper.

Dear Sarah Jane,

Sorry to run off yesterday, but I wasn't ready to talk to you yet. I hope that guy gave you my hat. Can you give it back?

Now that I'm out of a job, I've got a bit of time and I'm ready to talk to you today.

Can you find me? Let me give you a clue:

Let's get to the heart of the matter, or rather, the center of it all. The landscape has changed and even the name, but it's still the same place. The heart of the French Quarter.

*Come meet me and we can get to the heart of our matter —
our family.*

Love,

Your Brother

P.S. I'm coming alone, so I expect you to do the same. Otherwise, we'll have to meet another day. Or not.

I sank into my loveseat, trying to catch my breath. The sound of my heart beating filled my ears. My hands shook as I read the note over and over again. It was just like the one he gave me that lead me to the cemetery. And that meeting ended with me locked in the family tomb.

I didn't like that he said to come alone or he wouldn't come at all. I got the impression that there was no exception to his demand. My head told me not to go without someone, but my heart told me this was my only chance to see him.

It wasn't the first time and it wouldn't be the last time I decided to follow my heart. I didn't trust Joey, but at least he wanted to meet somewhere that didn't involve mausoleums. Our meeting would be in a very public place. His clues could only mean one location. The center of the French Quarter was Jackson Square, formerly known as the Place d'Armes.

And that's where I needed to go if I wanted to find my brother and put this part of my past behind me.

Jackson Square bustled with musicians, entertainers, and tourists even in the mid-day heat. People of all ages danced to the jazz music while others wandered the area listening to tour guides and taking photos of the famous New Orleans landmark. Tarot card and palm readers sat at tables shaded by umbrellas to predict the fortunes of those willing to pay for that information. I didn't need my cards read to know I was about to have a life-altering experience. Confronting my brother was foolish, but I needed answers from him and he would only talk on his terms.

Large black iron gates marked the entrance to the park area of the square on Decatur Street and Chartres Street. Standing in between the gates of the Charter Street entrance and St. Louis Cathedral, I stared up into the stained glass windows of the church. While I wasn't Catholic, the church was a calming place to me, even from the outside. So many people found peace inside this cathedral that I hoped it would offer me a bit, too.

What was I hoping for? I wanted my brother to tell me the truth. Did he mean to kill me all those months ago? Or had he changed his mind? I needed these answers so I could put this part of my history behind me.

My other hope was that I could convince Joey to turn himself in to the police. I had no idea what he planned to do here in New Orleans. Perhaps he was going to see Rob and Christine after he met me. I wasn't that naive though. He had been a fugitive, a successful one at that, for four months, so why would he turn himself in now?

No matter what happened today, Joey had to be brought to justice.

I took out my phone and called Rob. The call went to voicemail, so I left a message, "It's Sammy. Joey sent me a letter to meet him somewhere in Jackson Square. I'm here looking for him now." I texted the same information to him.

Contacting Rob was the right thing to do, but I hoped I had enough time to speak with Joey before Rob arrived. I turned back one last time to look at the cathedral. Calling the police could keep me safe physically, but a bit of spiritual protection might help my soul.

30

Stepping through the gates, I looked around, but Joey wasn't there. I didn't expect him to wait by the statue of Andrew Jackson with the line of people waiting to take their picture in front of it. If I couldn't find him, he would find me. I walked to the left of the statue and sat on a bench.

How long should I stay? I fiddled with the pepper spray key chain in my hand, wondering if I would need to use it. Just after I checked my watch for what seemed like the thousandth time, the hairs on the back of my neck stood up.

"I brought pralines."

I glanced up to see a box of Aunt Sally's pralines in the hands of my brother. He wore a black baseball cap, a Saints t-shirt, and dust-covered jeans. Joey looked like any other person in the French Quarter and by that I meant a normal person. But I knew better. He was a murderer.

"Are they poisoned?" I hoped the snarky tone would hide my fear. Although we were in the middle of Jackson Square, I didn't know what Joey planned for our meeting. His warm grin and kind eyes reminded me of the man I met when I first moved to New Orleans. Joey was fun and compassionate. Until I learned he was Samuel, my brother, and a killer.

"OK, I deserved that." Joey sat on the other end of the bench, putting the box of pralines in between us. "I guess candy won't get you to trust me. Or forgive me."

"Are you here for forgiveness?"

"Well, I'm not here to kill you."

I clutched my keyring tighter and scooted a few more inches away from him. I scanned the park to see if Rob, Christine, or any police officers were around, but I didn't see them. Tourists listening to their guides, couples sharing beignets and coffee on the other benches, and a variety of people walking through the area comforted me. If I needed help, one scream would get the attention of someone if not everyone around us.

"OK, that wasn't funny." He took off the baseball hat and placed it on the bench. After he ran his hand through his shaggy brown hair, he said, "Sorry."

"You've got five minutes." I stared down at my watch. "Go."

"For someone who doesn't have the upper hand, you're mighty sure of yourself." Joey laughed. "Oh, you are serious. Fine."

"You've got four minutes left."

"I wanted to ask you to meet me at the family tomb, but I didn't think you'd come."

"I wouldn't have."

"I promise I wouldn't have put you in it."

"That's not the most reassuring thing to say."

"It's all I've got." Joey opened the box of pralines and took one out. "Sure you don't want one?"

"Positive. We're here to talk, so talk."

"Fine, but first, I had nothing to do with that skeleton Luke and I dug up."

"The woman was buried twenty-six years ago, so you couldn't have been involved."

"Listen, I'm not all bad, really. I made sure Luke didn't rebury the body and that he called the cops. I'm not cold-hearted enough to cover up a skeleton."

"So you're a saint now?" Once I said it, I wished I hadn't been so snippy. He might leave at any moment and I'd never hear what he had to say.

"I guess I deserve that. But I'll tell you this. I didn't hide the bodies of the people I killed. Someone who lives there murdered and buried that girl."

"Why do you say that?" I was getting off topic, but my curiosity got the better of me.

"That smug guy who used to own the building and his snotty ex-wife were always butting their nose into wherever Luke and I worked. So did that old psychic. He's almost as crazy as Ruby."

I smiled involuntarily, but I quickly hid it. His observations piqued my interest, but I needed to talk about our issues no matter how much I wanted to find Nicole's killer.

"But you were coldhearted enough to hit me and leave me for dead in a tomb." My temperature rose along with my anger. "Did you forget the key when you locked me in? Or did you mean to leave it there?"

"To be honest, I planned to lock you in there and throw the key in the river before I left town." He sighed and leaned back against the bench. "I was so angry with you, but then you asked for your doll. That stupid doll."

Before I moved to New Orleans, my water-stained doll was the only connection I had to my life before my adoption. Once Joey revealed himself as my brother, the doll became a dark reminder of my past. I couldn't bear to throw the doll out, but now she sat in a box in my closet instead of displayed on a bookshelf.

"I vaguely remember calling out for it, but since you had hit me on the head, I wasn't quite conscious."

Joey looked away, but not before I glimpsed regret in his eyes. Whether it was regret for hitting me or for not killing me, I didn't know. He said, "I couldn't tell if you did that on purpose to distract me or if me knocking you upside the head unearthed your memories."

"No, I didn't do it on purpose and it didn't bring up any memories — at least no more than me calling for the doll." If any recollections of my toddler years had come to me, I would have been happy. But when I woke up inside the tomb, all I thought about was my immediate present, and that meant finding a way out.

"That's too bad." He sighed once again. "After you called out for your doll, I was confused. Killing you didn't seem right, no matter how angry I was at you."

So I had my answer: Joey had planned to kill me, but changed his mind. It didn't make up for what he did, but knowing he hadn't left me to die in the end was strangely comforting. But it wasn't enough to make me forget that he had murdered other people.

"Too bad you didn't feel that way about Kelly and Matt."

"It seemed necessary at the time. I did what I had to do." Joey sat straight up and looked at me. "Listen, I realize you'll never forgive me for what I've done, but baby girl, I've changed."

"Stop, just stop. First you can't call me baby girl. You have no right to use any terms of endearment with me."

"How do I get you to understand I'm not all bad? I just wanted to be your brother."

I would never tell him I still referred to him as my brother, but not as a term of affection. It was just a fact that we were related. My adopted parents and then the friends who I considered family here in New Orleans showed me that blood wasn't thicker than water.

But my relationship with Jasper and even Charlene proved that blood relations could be a good thing, too. That would never be the case between me and Joey.

"Do you have any photos of our parents? Any mementos of them?" I asked. "Aunt Charlene says you took everything of theirs when you left Mississippi."

"Aunt Charlene?" Joey narrowed his eyes. "You're calling her aunt?"

"Yes, she's been more family than you. And Jasper has been, too."

"Charlene was nicer than Scarlett, I'll give you that," Joey said. "Jasper tried his best to make me part of the family, but the rest of them never let me forget I was a burden."

"I am sorry about how life turned out for you, but it doesn't excuse what you did," I said.

Joey buried his face in his hands, and his shoulders shook as if he was sobbing. Was this an act? Maybe he finally felt guilty about his actions, but I would never truly believe him as much as I wanted to.

"Joey..."

"Will you call me Sam instead of Joey?" He sat up and wiped his wet eyes with his hands.

"No."

"But it is my name. And you know that."

"I've only known you as Joey. Whoever Sam was to me disappeared from my memory."

"I hoped you'd say my name at least once."

How could he think I would call him Sam as if we could go back to when we were children? I would never do it.

"Time is up." I looked down at my watch as if I had been keeping track of time. I should have though; Rob could rush through the park gates at any moment. "Do you have any photos or anything from our parents? I want them."

"I'll get them to you."

"When? Before or after you're in jail?"

"Baby girl, I'm not going to jail."

"You can't just keep running. The police are going to catch up with you." I clasped my hands together to keep myself from grabbing Joey by the shoulders and shaking some sense into him. "You need to turn yourself in. It's the right thing to do for the victims and for you."

Joey tapped both feet as his eyes bore into me. He appeared agitated but also confused. Was he actually taking what I was said to heart? Would he do the right thing? I looked over to St. Louis Cathedral, hoping for a miracle.

I didn't get one.

"I can't do that, Sarah Jane. Jail isn't for me." He shook his head. "I'll figure my way out of it. I always do."

"Not this time." I tried to stand up but my legs wobbled, so I sat back down.

"I promise I'll leave our family stuff for you in a quiet place that's locked up tight." He stood up. "I need to go now. You'll give me a minute or two before you call the cops, won't you?"

"I already called them."

He didn't say a word. He didn't have to. The sadness that passed over his face said it all. For a moment, I regretted calling the police. The betrayal he felt was palpable. But the reality of the situation returned to me. We were family, but he still was a murderer and I wouldn't let him get away with it.

Did he realize that, too? He shoved his hat on his head and took a step, but then he turned back around. "You had to call them, baby sis. But part of me hoped you wouldn't." He gave me that charming smile he used the first time I met him. "You can still have the pralines, though."

My brother ran out of the park, leaving me alone one more time.

31

———

Joey was gone. I wanted to stay on the park bench and cry for what I had lost, but I couldn't. I needed to find him again.

He had about a thirty-second head start so when I exited the park, he had already run to the other side of Decatur Street. I watched him go up the steps to the Washington Artillery Park. It was a popular viewing spot for tourists to take pictures of Jackson Square. And it also led to the Moonwalk, which bordered the Mississippi River. Cars whizzed by me, so I couldn't get across. I should have pepper sprayed him when I had the chance when we were talking, but it was too late now.

"Sammy! Are you OK? Is he here?" Rob grabbed my arm as I stared at the traffic light, willing it to turn red so I could run across the street. Joey was already out of my sight so even if I had made it across, I wouldn't have known which way to go once I got to the Moonwalk.

I nodded. "He's wearing a black baseball cap and a Saints t-shirt. He ran that way." I pointed to the steps for the Washington Artillery Park.

Rob got on his radio and gave Joey's description to the officers. Groups of them rushed up the stairs and headed in both directions of the river. I didn't hold out much hope. My brother would blend in easily with everyone else in the French Quarter. No matter which direction he ran, he had several places to hide in, like shops, hotels, and bars. He could have left the area on the Riverfront Streetcar.

"Let's go over here and talk." Rob led me back into Jackson Square. The sudden influx of officers disrupted the usual flow of tourists lining up to pay for a carriage ride. While the tour guides were used to keeping their mules calm while drumming up business, Rob and I standing there were another distraction for them to deal with.

"Sammy, you should have called 911." Rob gestured to a park bench under an oak tree. "You shouldn't have come here on your own."

"I needed to talk to him." I flopped on the bench and crossed my arms and legs. My body grew warm, and it wasn't just from the heat. Rob had every right to reprimand me, but I didn't want to hear it.

"Your brother could have killed you." Rob sat next to me, his radio clenched in his hands.

"He didn't."

"Sammy..." Rob put the radio on the bench. "But he could have. The point is, Joey is a killer."

"But he's also my brother." I gulped down a sob and turned my head away from Rob.

Rob put his arm around me. "Sammy, just because he's family doesn't excuse him from what he's done. You know that, don't you?"

"Of course I do!" I stared down at the ground. "I had to talk to him. But I called you."

"Yes, you called." Rob sighed. "What was so important that you had to risk your life?"

"I needed to know if he really meant to kill me or if he changed his mind." As soon as the words came out of my mouth, the tears dripped down my face. Looking back, it sounded crazy that I put myself in danger to find out if Joey left the key in the tomb on purpose. Did it matter? It didn't change what happened. And it wouldn't change his future — jail.

"By your tears, you got your answer." Rob handed me a pack of tissues. "He decided not to leave you for dead in there, didn't he?"

"No." I accepted the package and took a tissue out, but held it in my shaking hand. "And I also wanted to try and get him to turn himself in. I knew it would be better if he did that instead of being caught, but he said no and then he left me once again…" I stopped talking as the tears started again.

"Sammy, look at me."

I wiped my tears and turned to Rob, expecting his face to be full of disappointment and anger. Instead, there was compassion in his eyes. "I've met many people who have to deal with the aftermath of having a killer in their family. Some deny it no matter what the evidence shows, some just pretend that person never existed. But the ones who make it through the least scathed are the ones who accept it for what it is and move on. Can you be that person?"

"Yes." I shoved the pack of tissues in my pocket and stood up. "You're right. I can't change what happened, but I can try to help you find him now."

"Good." Rob got up and hugged me. "Brace yourself. Christine is walking up, and she looks madder than a wet hen."

I'd never seen a wet hen, but I'd take Rob's word for it

that Christine looked like one. She headed straight to Rob. Standing in front of him with her back to me, she didn't even acknowledge I was there. "Rob, no luck on finding him yet. Any ideas on where he fled from the witness?"

"Christine, you can ask Sammy yourself." Rob stared over Christine's shoulder at me and I swore his eyes were telling me to prepare myself for the worst.

She turned around and put her hands on her hips. My short statue felt more evident as she towered over me, her nostrils flaring and her eyes narrowed. "Sammy, I'm going to assume Rob has already explained you should have called 911 instead of leaving him a text."

"I left a voicemail too," I said weakly.

"You shouldn't have come alone. We would have protected you," Christine said. "And now he's escaped. He might kill again."

My chest hurt and I realized I had stopped breathing. As I took in a few deep breaths to calm myself. I hadn't considered Joey could be on the way to murder someone. But in my heart, I didn't believe he was.

"I doubt he will." I raised my hands up in the air in response to Christine's shaking head. "I'm sure it sounds crazy, but I believe he met me to close this chapter, so to speak."

"Do you think he'll kill himself?" Rob asked.

"No, I believe he's just moving on," I whispered. "It felt like he was saying goodbye."

"Where was he was heading, then?" Christine took out her notebook and pen. She clicked the pen with such force that I thought she might have broken it. The pen wasn't damaged as she scribbled notes as I began to speak.

"He said he had to wrap things up." I turned my head

away from the detectives toward St. Louis Cathedral. "So he might go to our family tomb to say goodbye to our parents."

"OK, where else?" Christine asked. Rob was already on his phone calling for officers to check out St. Louis Cemetery No. 1.

"He could visit our old house on Governor Nicholls Street. Or Cafe du Monde. Or Aunt Sally's for more pralines," I said. "He wasn't carrying a backpack with him, so he might need to go back to wherever he was living."

"That is helpful information." Christine gave me a cold, hard stare. "Sammy, you can't run off on your own when it comes to Joey. You've hindered our investigation, you realize, don't you?"

"I do and I'm sorry." I was sorry for making things hard on the detectives, but I wasn't sorry for meeting my brother.

"Let us handle it from here on out." Christine went to leave but turned back around. I waited for her to reprimand me again, but she placed her hand on my shoulder. She didn't say a word and exited the park through the Decatur Street gate.

"What she said." Rob put his phone away and sighed. "No sign of your brother anywhere so far, but that doesn't mean he left town. I'll have an officer walk you home now."

"It's OK. I can go by myself. Or I can call someone." I only offered to phone someone after Rob frowned.

"No offense, Sammy, but I need to make sure you actually go home." His frown changed to a slight smile. "I know you all too well and you want to find your brother. But you need to leave it to us. Please."

Rob hugged me and then steered me toward an officer standing by the exit on Decatur Street. "Officer Wilson, escort Miss Richardson home. Nowhere else, you understand?" By the look Rob gave me, that last part was for my benefit.

"Thanks, Rob. Please let me know as soon as you hear anything," I said.

"Same to you." Rob waved goodbye as he walked away.

As much as I wanted to stay, it was best that I go. My phone kept vibrating with text messages, so I had a lot of explaining to do to my friends. The walk with Officer Wilson would give me time to brace myself for the tongue-lashing I'd get when I returned home. They would be angry that I met Joey by myself. And once they found out he was missing once again, I would never have a moment to myself.

32

I was right. Everyone except Ruby was waiting for me in the courtyard. Rob had called Sissy, so they had time to gather before I arrived. They designated Andrew as the group's spokesperson. "Samantha, we all understand your need to meet Joey. But you cannot put yourself in danger. Your Thibodeaux Mansion family loves you too much."

I hugged everyone after Andrew spoke. Neal whispered in my ear, "Sammy, I know he's your brother, but he's also a killer. I won't let him hurt you or anyone else." Sissy embraced me the longest and hardest. "Girl, be careful. We can't lose you."

I was relieved Jasper was with Neal. While I didn't think Joey would come after Jasper, I didn't want him to be alone. Jasper pulled me aside. "You should have taken me with you. We're in this together now, cousin. But I get why you went. Don't do it again, you hear?" I nodded, so he agreed to go with Neal on his tours that evening.

Connor waited by my front door with a sour look on his face. But when I stepped toward him, he opened his arms and held me as I gulped down my sobs. "Sammy, you've got to remember you're not alone. I will support you no matter what."

We stayed in my apartment for the rest of the day and night, waiting for updates from Rob and Christine. Joey hadn't been found by the time we finally stumbled into bed after midnight. I woke up at 7 a.m. and started the coffeemaker immediately.

Physically and emotionally, I was exhausted, and I had too much work to do today at the shop. Andrew called last night to offer to handle the vendor meetings on his own, but I said no. Keeping to my normal schedule would keep me from thinking about Joey. I hoped.

As I poured a cup of coffee, Nubi trotted out of the bedroom and to the front door.

"Nubi, don't you want breakfast first?" I joined a meowing Nubi. "Do you have big plans with Cleopatra and Nefertiti today?"

I opened my door, and Nubi sat in the open doorway. "What's going on, Nubi?" My stomach dropped, and I called out to Connor. Was Joey here? Cats have a sixth sense, especially Nubi. But my cat wasn't warning me about my brother, but another relative.

"Jasper Elvis St. Martin, wake up! Your momma is here!"

She didn't need to yell she was Jasper's mother; her thick Southern accent was recognizable even to me before my first cup of coffee. Connor and I stepped out into the courtyard and I looked up to the second-floor balcony. Aunt Charlene wore one of her trademark bright floral dresses, but she'd changed her hairstyle and color. It wasn't as puffy and it was a more natural shade of blonde than before.

Had Jasper called his mother to tell her about my brother's return? And did she drive all the way from Mississippi to see him? I wouldn't have been surprised if she had, but she had not.

"Momma, what are you doing here? I phoned you all last night, and you didn't call back." Jasper pulled his rumpled t-shirt down over a pair of running shorts and shut his apartment door behind him.

"Aren't you going to invite me in? Or are you entertaining a young lady?" Charlene put her hands on her hips and tapped her foot.

"No, on both counts. Neal is still sleeping. Although I don't know how with all your banging." Jasper hugged his mother. "But it is good to see you."

"Now that's my boy." Charlene squeezed her son so hard that Jasper grimaced.

"Oh, hey, Sammy, Connor, look who's here." Jasper mouthed the word "help" to me after noticing me downstairs.

"Hi, Aunt Charlene," I said.

Charlene let Jasper go and trotted down the stairs. I braced myself for her hug. She stopped dead in her tracks when I said, "I take it you're here about my brother?"

"Your brother? What's going on? Did the police catch him?" Charlene's eyes grew wide under her thick eyelashes. "This is the first I've heard of it. Why didn't either of you call me?"

"I did, Momma." Jasper guided his mother over to my outside table. "I left you a ton of messages, but I didn't expect you to show up this morning."

"I drove in last night and I don't answer my phone in the car," Charlene said. "And by the time I got to my room, I was too tired to call you back. I wanted to surprise you both."

"You did, Momma. But why are you here?"

"Do I need a reason to visit my only child and my only

niece? And my niece's boyfriend?" Charlene huffed. "Aren't you happy to see me?"

"We're all happy to see you, Miss Charlene." Connor flashed that smile that made me melt. It worked on Charlene too, as she relaxed into the chair.

"Thank you, Connor." Charlene pointed a finger at Jasper. "Look, even Connor's happy I'm here."

Jasper rolled his eyes. "Yes, Momma."

"We're all glad you came to visit." I sat down across from my aunt and put my hand on hers. Connor stood behind me, his hand on my shoulder. "We're just surprised, especially after my brother showed up yesterday." I explained about that Joey had been working at Delmar Apartments and how I talked with him yesterday. She received the news unexpectedly well. No tears, no angry outbursts, nothing. Instead, she pulled her hand back and took out her compact out of her purse.

"Your brother will get his comeuppance, I'm sure." Charlene stared into her mirror and brushed away a stray eyelash.

"Momma, is that all you have to say?" Jasper took the compact from his mother's hand. "Do you understand that Sammy actually talked to him? That he could have hurt her again? Aren't you worried he's going to come after me or you?"

Charlene snatched the compact back and shoved it in her bag and zipped it shut. "No, I am not worried. It sounds like he knows you and Sammy are prepared to deal with him if he comes back. I know I am."

"What does that mean? You're not carrying daddy's pistol around, are you?" Jasper reached for his mother's purse, but she held it tight.

"Keep your hands to yourself, young man. No, I don't

have a gun, just this little thing of pepper spray." Charlene opened her bag and took out a tiny can of pepper spray in a pink glittery holder. "I showed it to Ambrose last night, and he said it would work fine if I needed it."

"Are you staying at Hotel Jeanne?" Unless she had developed a secret friendship with Ambrose, she had to have seen him at the hotel. And I doubt fine was the word he used when he saw the bedazzled pepper spray. More likely, he told her it was "interesting."

"I am. Beau had offered to let me stay there for free when I come to town, so I took him up on it." Charlene said. "I'm sure he would have extended his hospitality even if I didn't say I wouldn't sue him for Scarlett's death."

"Momma." Jasper sighed. "He had nothing to do with what happened to Scarlett."

"Well, you know how people like to sue everyone for everything. Several attorneys contacted me, but I said no." Charlene smiled. "It's just my nature to be kind."

"You're another Mother Teresa, Momma." Jasper rolled his eyes, but he patted her on her shoulder. "You drove yourself to town last night?"

"Yes, I got in late, so that's why I didn't call you." Charlene said.

"But I saw you go out last night." All four of us turned around as Verity walked up to us.

"And who are you? And why are you spying on me?" Charlene snapped.

"Sorry, I guess that was rude." Verity smiled, but Charlene didn't return it. "I'm staying at the same hotel. Ambrose told me you were Sammy's aunt. You left just before I did last night."

"Ambrose shouldn't be telling everybody who I am." Charlene said.

"Miss Charlene, this is Verity Virtue, Ruby's daughter," Connor said.

Ruby opened her door and frowned. "Now I understand what all the commotion is outside."

"Hi, Miss Ruby! I met your daughter." Charlene waved Ruby over, but she didn't move. "Isn't she the spitting image of you, Miss Ruby?"

Everyone stared at Charlene. Apparently, I wasn't the only one who thought that was far from the truth.

"Not physically, I mean, but surely spiritually you are like your momma." Charlene faced Verity. "Do you read tarot cards, too? I'd love a reading."

"No. I'm a rocket scientist," Verity deadpanned.

"Really? Well, ain't that something?" Charlene stood up. "Jasper, you go get dressed so you can take me to breakfast. I am famished. Sammy, you'll come too."

"I can go for coffee, but then I have to go to work." It was more of a demand than an invitation, but that was Charlene's way.

Jasper returned to his apartment with his mother trailing along. For his sake, I hope he and Neal had improved their housekeeping skills. When the door closed, Verity sat down at the table.

"I think I could have told your aunt I was anything but a spiritualist and she would have moved on from me."

"Don't take it personally. Charlene's attention span is short to put it politely," Connor said.

"I keep forgetting I'm back in the South where everything is met with a smile — but not always genuine."

"Oh, come on, not everyone's that way," I protested.

"You give people the benefit of the doubt more than I do." Verity frowned. "I didn't learn that until it was too late."

"You're referring to your friends at Delmar Apartments, I take it. All of them or just one?" I said.

"All of them. I don't trust any of them."

"Not even Mrs. Riggins and Mr. Roux the Third?"

"OK, I guess they're both off the list of suspects." Verity stood up. "At least for now."

Sissy rushed down the balcony stairs, and Rob and Christine walked into the courtyard.

"Here to see me?" Verity asked the detectives.

"No, we're here for Sammy," Rob's voice was gentle, not what I expected. When I looked at Christine and saw the sadness in her eyes, I knew why they were here.

"Joey's dead, isn't he?"

33

My brother was dead.

Christine confirmed it with just a nod of her head. I clutched the table as my vision blurred and heart raced. I squeezed my eyes shut, ignoring all the voices that overwhelmed my ears.

"Sammy, look at me." Sissy's voice cut through the noise. "Are you all right?"

I opened my eyes and looked at Sissy, who was bent down next to me. "Yes, I'm fine. The news just surprised me."

"Of course it did. Now, give me your wrist so I can check your pulse." Sissy held my wrist. Connor was talking to Rob and Christine a few feet away, so I couldn't hear their conversation. Verity left the table and went to speak with her mother. She then returned with a glass of water and placed it in front of me. Ruby stayed in her doorway with an unlit bundle of sage in her hand.

Sissy stood up and said, "Your pulse is back to normal. How are you feeling now?"

"I'm OK, thanks." I gave her a half-hearted smiled. She

put her hand on my cheek. Ruby beckoned her over, so Sissy and Verity headed over to her.

"Sammy, I'm so sorry." Connor took Sissy's place next to me. "Do you want to go inside?"

"No, I want to hear what happened." I pushed myself up from my chair. It was déjà vu of the morning Christine and Rob came to tell Ruby that Verity was possibly dead. The difference was Verity turned out to be alive. I didn't think the same would happen with Joey.

"What happened to him? Where is he?" I asked.

"I'm sorry, Sammy. Your brother, Samuel Joseph St. Martin, was found dead at Delmar Apartments this morning," Christine said.

"Delmar Apartments?" My stomach dropped, imagining him buried in the same spot as Nicole.

Connor, Sissy, and Verity joined me with the detectives. Ruby moved out of her doorway but didn't come over. But even with the quick glance I gave her, I saw the tension in her jaw and the slight shaking of her hand holding her sage bundle. Jasper and Charlene rushed down from the balcony after Sissy texted them to join us.

"Are you serious? Samuel is dead?" Charlene gasped, either from the shock of finding out her nephew was dead or from bounding down the stairs. "What happened? Where is he? Who killed him?"

"Momma, let the detectives explain." Jasper put his arm around his mother. He and I exchanged glances, knowing we would have a lot to discuss later.

"Joey was discovered inside Mrs. Riggins' apartment. Apparently, he was squatting there whenever she went out of town." Rob explained that the pet sitter entered the home this morning to find the cat, Mr. Roux the Third, sitting next to his body. Joey had been struck on the back of his head.

"Did he suffer?" Charlene asked.

"I doubt he even knew what happened," Christine said.

"That's a shame," Charlene whispered under her breath, but we all heard it. Everyone stared at her, but honestly, I couldn't blame her. Joey had killed her husband, so there was no love lost. But it was still callous and stupid to say in front of the detectives.

"Please excuse my mother. She's in shock," Jasper apologized.

"I am not. I just wish they had found him alive so he could have paid for his crimes," Charlene said. "But justice will reign when he tries to enter the pearly gates."

I ignored Charlene, and so did the detectives.

Rob asked, "Sammy, are you sure your brother didn't have a backpack when you met him in Jackson Square?"

"I'm positive. Didn't I say he had a red backpack with him when I saw him on Bourbon Street?" I said.

"You did. Are you sure it was red?" Rob said. "We found a black backpack next to him this morning."

"I'm sure," I said. "What was in the backpack?"

"Did you find any of my husband's things in the bag?" Charlene asked.

"Momma, that's enough. We're going upstairs." Jasper grabbed his mother's elbow and pulled her away. "We'll get more details later. For now, let's talk about why you're really here."

Charlene protested all the way up the stairs, but let her son take her to his apartment. After his mother stepped inside, Jasper leaned over the railing. "Sammy, I'm sorry about your brother. Call me, OK?"

I nodded and turned my attention back to the detectives. "Can you tell me what Joey had with him?"

"Just clothes, toiletries, and a book." Christine flipped

through her notebook. "It was *Murder at the Vicarage*. I assume that's where he picked the name Raymond West."

"I didn't know you were an Agatha Christie fan." I smiled slightly at Christine.

"We have more in common than you think." Christine closed her notebook and returned my smile.

"You didn't find a red backpack with him then?" I asked.

"No, but we're still looking." Christine said.

"Do you know who killed him? Or why?" Another dizzy spell was coming on, so I leaned on Connor, who stood behind me. He put his arms around my waist to support me.

"Not yet. We'll keep you posted. I promise." Rob's firm voice and Christine's vigorous nodding gave me hope they would make his murder a priority — even though Joey was a murderer himself.

"But we need to ask you..." Christine started, but I interrupted her.

"Where I was last night?" I wasn't offended. "Connor and I were home all evening."

"We stayed in all night," Connor said.

"Thank you both. We'll be in touch soon," Christine said.

They excused themselves and left the courtyard. Sissy hugged me and promised to call me later. She bounded up the stairs to Jasper's apartment to check on him and Charlene. I appreciated how Sissy always anticipated what I needed before I asked.

"Samantha, I will pray to the Goddess of Good for you." Ruby lit her sage and waved it in a figure eight in front of her. "There is still trouble to come."

Verity shook her head. Ruby ignored her daughter's disapproving manner and closed her door without another word. I was glad Ruby acted as her usual dramatic self. I needed something to seem normal in this overwhelming moment.

"Let's go inside, Sammy," Connor said.

"Hey, I'm sorry about my mother and your brother." Verity stepped in front of me before I got to my apartment. "Sissy and my mother told me a bit about your situation with your brother. I thought my life was full of drama, but I think you've won the award for the most dramatic life story."

"I guess so. It's an award neither one of us wanted," I said.

"That's true." Verity's shoulders sagged as she sighed. "I'll call Tabby and find out what she knows."

She left the courtyard. I appreciated her concern and that she was calling Tabby; I needed to know what the residents of Delmar Apartments had to say for themselves. One of them might be Joey's killer.

34

—————

Connor made another pot of coffee to replace the one I had made before I received the news about Joey. We sat on the couch and sipped our drinks. Connor's presence was comforting, and it was good to be with someone who didn't insist I talk about my feelings. My emotions were all over the place. Sadness was the prevailing sentiment not just for Joey's death but for what might have been.

Jasper felt the same way. He came to see me after walking his mother back to Hotel Jeanne.

"Momma said to call her later. She figured you needed some time to yourself." Jasper accepted a cup of coffee from Connor and sat across from us.

"I bet it was you telling her to give me some space." I smiled at my cousin.

"Maybe." He smiled back, but his face grew serious. "But no matter what Joey did, I am sorry he's dead."

"Me, too." I said. "He took a lot of risks coming back here. Staying in Mrs. Riggins' apartment with the cat sitter coming in and out was pretty crazy. The cat sitter or any of the tenants could have caught him."

Jasper laughed. "I'm not surprised, actually. He did crazy stuff when we were growing up."

"Really? Before we knew who Joey was, he seemed like a fun, carefree guy, not someone who'd break into apartments." Connor reached for my hand. "Or do any of the other things he did."

Jasper put his mug on the table and sat back in his chair. "Joey was an adrenaline junkie, and he loved a challenge. If he found an open door, he'd walk right in. It didn't matter if it was a store or a house. He'd get in and out with no one knowing he'd been there. He even snuck into the Huntley Police Station."

"You've got to be kidding!" Connor's eyes grew wide. "Didn't the police catch him?"

"Nope. He took two donuts from the break room and came right back out." Jasper grinned. "I've never had better stale donuts in my life."

"That's insane." I shook my head. "So sneaking into Mrs. Riggins' place must have been easy."

"Probably. He never got caught before." Jasper picked his drink back up. "I guess last night his luck ran out."

My brother went from being a boy who escaped a hurricane to a man who was a successful fugitive for four months. In one night, it ended in the least likely of situations — being murdered in Mrs. Riggins' home in Delmar Apartments.

After he finished his coffee, Jasper had to leave. I followed him to the door. We hugged, and he set off to do a repair job for Beau at the hotel. I decided to follow suit and go to work, too. Connor tried to talk me out of it, but he stopped when I said, "I need to feel normal for a bit."

While I got the impression Connor didn't quite understand, he didn't protest. I promised to check in with him later and sent him to his band practice. He walked me to Lagniappe Books.

"Call me anytime, Sammy. You don't have to go through this alone." Connor kissed me. "We're all here for you."

I stepped inside the shop to find Andrew sitting in the back seating area with two cups of coffee. "Connor texted you were on your way, so I made a fresh pot." He stood up and embraced me. "I am so sorry, my dear. I cancelled our vendor appointments. They can wait."

"You didn't need to do that." I sank into the loveseat.

"I hate to tell you the news about your brother's death is all over the neighborhood. That's all they would have asked you about. You don't need to talk about it to anyone." He handed me my cup. "You should only speak to whomever you wish to and whenever you are ready."

"I'm ready if you are."

Andrew sat down next to me. "I am. How are you? And don't say OK because that's not an honest answer. You're being brave, but I see the pain in your eyes."

"I can't fool you, can I?" I said.

"No. You can't fool anyone who loves you. Connor and Sissy are beside themselves, but don't want to force you to talk."

"They're good people." I took a sip of my coffee, smiling that it had the right balance of coffee to creamer. Andrew understood me so well. "I'm sad. I'm angry. I'm confused. In a horrible way, I'm relieved that the problem with Joey is over. But I didn't want it to end this way."

"How did you want it to end?"

"I didn't want him to die." I wiped a tear off my face with

a handkerchief Andrew handed me. "The only good solution was for Joey to turn himself into the police."

"He would have never done that."

"I guess not. But at least if he had I could have visited him in jail."

"Would you?" Andrew looked me straight in the eye, so I had to answer him.

"Yes. No. Maybe." I put my mug on the table. "Now that I don't have the chance, I'd say the answer is yes. But I don't know why. He never apologized to me yesterday."

"Would an apology make it right?"

I shook my head. "I'm mourning what could have been, not what was."

Andrew held my hand as I cried for the brother I wanted, not the one I had. I mourned for the life he could have had, not the one that he got after Hurricane Geoffrey took away his family.

"You don't need to resolve your emotions now." Andrew handed me another handkerchief when I finished crying. "Samantha, not everything in life can be resolved quickly, if ever. You're not a character in a made-for-TV movie. You're an actual human being with many emotions."

"I hate being confused. I either want to be angry or sad. Not both."

Andrew laughed softly. "Oh, my dear, if emotions were simple we wouldn't have most of the books we sell in this shop." He pointed to the mystery section. "Can you imagine any of your favorite mysteries without complicated feelings or difficult relationships? You'd be bored to tears."

"It's different in a book. It's not my life I'm reading about." I sat up straight. "But I understand your point. I just wish I had closure."

"But don't you? He came to you and explained himself," Andrew said.

"You're not going to tell me he'll get justice in the after-life, so I shouldn't worry?" I smiled slightly, trying to lighten my mood by joking.

"That sounds like something your Aunt Charlene would say." Andrew laughed. "Or even Ruby or Papa. But honestly, Samantha, you don't need to concern yourself with forgiveness for your brother now, or perhaps ever."

I rested my head on Andrew's shoulder, letting what he said sink in. I didn't have to reconcile my feelings about my brother yet. But I wanted to find his murderer whether I forgave him or not.

35

Andrew insisted I work in our private office for the day. At first, I assumed he was worried that my emotional state would be off-putting to our customers, but he really was trying to protect me from the media and curious people. It didn't take long for reporters to come to the shop after they didn't find me at Thibodeaux Mansion. Andrew politely but firmly told them and anyone there to gawk that I wasn't there and they needed to leave.

He welcomed our regular customers who offered condolences that I overheard from the office. Even our fellow shop owners stopped by to check on me, which warmed my heart. And then there were the visits from my friends. Neal dropped in first, which surprised me. My brother had killed his best friend, and I hadn't expected him to comfort me. But he came into the room and pulled me out of my chair for a bear hug. "I want you to know that I'm sorry you're hurting," he said before rushing out. After that, I put my head down on the desk and let my exhaustion and sadness out through tears and a brief nap.

"Samantha, time to eat." Andrew woke me up. "Don't say

you're not hungry. Verity and Beau are here and brought gumbo from Frankie's."

"Beau and Verity?" I wiped my face with a tissue and smoothed down my hair.

I walked out of the office to find Beau and Verity waiting in the seating area. Containers of gumbo, a loaf of warm French bread, and four cups of sweet tea covered the coffee table. Beau grasped my hands and kissed me on the cheek. "Sammy, my darling, you have had quite the shock. I'm so sorry."

Verity stayed in her chair as I sat down across from her. "Hey, Sammy. Beau suggested we bring food over for you and Andrew."

"Thank you both." I'd only drank coffee so far and with the savory scent of seafood gumbo filling the air, I decided to try to eat a little food. After devouring two pieces of buttered bread and a bowl of soup, I admitted I was hungry.

"I'm glad you're eating. Grief can play havoc on your health if you're not careful." Beau handed me a chocolate chip cookie. "No, eat this, too. Frankie made them just for you."

"I don't want to disappoint her." The cookie was slightly warm and gooey just the way I loved them.

"I have to say, I don't remember everyone being so friendly when I lived here," Verity said.

"You were a teenager. As I recall, teenagers don't trust adults," Beau said.

"Speak for yourself. I looked up to adults when I was young," Andrew said.

"You were never a teenager. You were born a serious old man." Beau laughed.

"You better take back the word old or he's not buying

you any more drinks at the Carousel Bar." I put my arm around Andrew.

"Well, fellow old man, let's clean up this food so Verity can talk to Samantha." Andrew thrust an empty bag at Beau. "Why don't you two take the rest of the cookies to the office? And please make a fresh pot of coffee."

"Thanks." I gave Andrew a hug before leaving. A productive chat with Verity was exactly what I wanted.

I started the coffee maker while Verity took a seat in the office. "Thanks again for bringing the food."

"You're welcome. Flowers didn't seem right." Verity picked at a piece of cat hair on her jeans. "I had no idea you'd been orphaned and that your adopted parents paid your uncle to keep quiet about your existence. That's quite the story."

"It is. And when you add the part about Joey to it, it's even crazier."

"Truth is stranger than fiction they say."

"Tru dat as they say here in New Orleans."

"If you ever want to do a book about your life story, I'd be happy to be your ghost writer," Verity said.

"Does that mean you're staying in New Orleans?" I asked.

"You've heard of this thing called email and the internet right?" Verity took the cup of coffee from me and waved off the cream and sugar. "I work with my clients remotely for the most part."

"Well, I'll think about it. You did say you didn't write ghost stories and at this point, most of the people in my biography are ghosts." I poured an extra tablespoon of flavored creamer in my coffee, hoping the sugar would perk me up.

"Speaking of ghosts, my mother suggested I try to contact your brother for you, but I nixed that idea quickly."

"Can you reach the spirits like her?" I sat in the chair behind the desk and propped my chin on my hands. I'd seen Ruby in action, so I wondered if Verity had those same skills.

"No." She pursed her lips. "I won't deny that my mother has said some strange things in her capacity as a medium, but I can't say with certainty that she isn't just skillful in reading people. And by people, I mean the living."

"How are you at reading people? Did you talk to Tabby?" I hoped she had some news. Rob called earlier, but he had no new information to give me. Or, at least, none he wanted to share.

"Yes, I met Tabby at Cafe Beignet. She claimed no one knew your brother was crashing in Mrs. Riggins' apartment. Her theory is that he was stealing from the apartments and his partner killed him to take everything for himself."

"That's an interesting theory." I sipped my coffee. "I don't think my brother ever had a partner in his endeavors." And by that I meant murder.

"Even though Tabby has been nice since I've been back, I can't say I trust her. There's just something off about her." Verity frowned. "But then again, she always had her nose stuck up in the air when it came to me and Nicole."

After my visit to Tabby's shop, I could confirm that for Verity, but I didn't see any reason to do that. She appeared to have a good handle on that. "Did you get anything else out of Tabby?"

"Not really. She seemed eager to separate your brother's murder from Nicole's."

"So you think they're related?" My gut told me that but I was surprised Verity believed that too.

"It seems odd that the man who discovered Nicole's body would be murdered days later." Verity said.

"I agree. Joey must have found something about Nicole's death. He warned me to stay away from the building."

"Really?" Verity raised her eyebrows. "Did he say why?"

"He said that Myles, Tabby, and Sutton butted their noses into his and Luke's work."

"Because one of them buried Nicole there," Verity said.

"I agree. Did Tabby say anything about Myles or Sutton?"

"No, she claims she didn't see either of them last night because she wasn't feeling well and went to bed early."

"Do you believe her?" I asked.

"Not really." Verity stood up. "Sorry to run, but I have to meet my mother. I'll call you if I hear anything else about your brother. I know how tough it is to lose someone, even if your relationship was complicated."

Verity rushed out the door before I could respond. Was she referring to her relationship with Nicole as much as mine with Joey? If so, that differed from what she'd been saying up to now. Perhaps I needed to put Verity back on the suspect list for Nicole's murder. Did I need to add her to my list for Joey's death, too?

36

After Verity left the shop, I was able to quickly take her off my suspect list for Joey's murder. Beau told me he saw her sitting on Momo's balcony around ten last night. He had joined her and Momo for a nightcap that lasted well after midnight. I was relieved; I hated thinking Verity was my brother's murderer.

Between Beau, Verity, Neal, Libby, and William coming to see me at the shop and then Sissy bringing dinner to my apartment after work, I hadn't a moment to myself. After eating dinner with Sissy, my nerves were finally settling. But then at 8 p.m. Jasper and Charlene knocked at the door. As much as I wanted to turn them away, I didn't. They were Joey's family, too, and we hadn't talked since the morning. They offered their condolences, but Aunt Charlene couldn't help but make a few offhand comments about justice being served. While I agreed Joey needed to pay for his crimes, being murdered wasn't a just punishment.

After sitting around my living room listening to Aunt Charlene drone on again about Joey's death, I decided it was time for her to leave. I stretched my arms over my head and yawned loudly, hoping Aunt Charlene would take the hint. She didn't, but Sissy did.

"Miss Charlene, let me walk you to your hotel." Sissy stood up from the loveseat and grabbed her bag on the kitchen counter. "Sammy looks tuckered out and Jasper should make sure her apartment is secure until Connor gets home."

Jasper looked at Sissy, then back and me, and smiled. "Oh, yes, Momma, Sammy needs me here."

"But I need you, too." Aunt Charlene pouted.

"I have to admit I have an ulterior motive," Sissy walked over to Charlene and kneeled by her chair. "My momma and I can't agree on flowers for my wedding. Jasper told me you are a walking encyclopedia when it comes to flowers. I hoped you would give me some advice."

Charlene's face lit up, and she jumped out of her seat, almost knocking Sissy to the ground. Charlene grabbed her purse and opened the door. "I would be delighted, Sissy! When is your wedding? What are your colors..."

She was out the door without a goodbye to me or Jasper.

"You both owe me big time." Sissy looked wide-eyed as Charlene yelled her name from the courtyard.

"Yes, we'll help with your flowers." I gave her a quick hug.

"No, make it liquor. I bet I'm going to need to it." Sissy grinned and ran after Charlene.

I closed the door to a confused-looking Jasper, still sitting in his chair.

"Did Rob and Sissy set a date already?" Jasper asked. "And I never said Momma was an encyclopedia of flowers."

"A walking encyclopedia of flowers, you mean." I grabbed two Abita beers out of the refrigerator. "I mentioned to Sissy that your mother liked to garden, so she gushed about it. She knows how to get people talking. But no, they haven't set a date yet."

"She is a good friend." Jasper took the beer I offered him. "I know she did that to help you out, but Momma will love chatting with her. She said today she couldn't believe she wouldn't get to plan Scarlett's wedding."

Losing a child meant missing out on so many milestones, and I could only imagine how much Charlene wanted to plan a wedding for Scarlett. "Sissy will handle your mom delicately, don't worry. And she'll have your wedding to arrange, right?"

Jasper laughed. "It'll be a strong woman who dates me and lets my mother have a hand in planning a wedding. She can do your wedding to Connor."

"We are nowhere near getting married. Thank you very much." I took a gulp of my beer. "But I do have a funeral to figure out."

Jasper put his beer down on the coffee table. "Are you going to bury him in the family tomb?"

"Is it even up to me? Legally, I assume your mother is the next of kin."

"Oh, I'm sure Momma is happy to leave it up to you, Sammy." Jasper picked his beer back up. "She's still in shock over his death."

"Really?" Charlene's flip remarks about justice being served didn't match with her being in shock. "She seems at peace with it."

"Hmm, I hadn't thought about it that way. Momma is always so dramatic about everything. I brush off a lot of what she says and does, I hate to admit."

"Speaking of drama, has she said why she really came here to visit?"

"She said she was thinking of moving to New Orleans."

I choked on my beer and put the bottle down. "Please tell me you're joking."

Jasper explained his mother originally was here to explore the idea of moving to the French Quarter. She figured Sissy would leave her apartment soon so she could rent it. Or maybe she and Jasper could be roommates? And for a job, she could work at Lagniappe Books.

Aunt Charlene was family, and I liked her, but I didn't want her that close. And for Jasper's sake, I definitely didn't want her to move here. For the first time in his life, Jasper was on his own and thriving. If she settled here, I expected her to micromanage his life.

"But Momma had drinks with Andrew and Beau tonight and now she has new plans," Jasper said.

"They convinced your mother not to move here?"

"I talked to Andrew afterward, and he said Momma was just feeling lonely. It's the first time she's lived on her own since she married my father."

"Oh, that makes sense." Now I felt guilty that I hadn't considered Aunt Charlene's feelings. She went from living with her parents to her husband's house to being all alone. But I still didn't want her to derail Jasper's new life in New Orleans. "What is she going to do?"

"She asked her friend Gigi to move into her house. They're like sisters." Jasper grinned. "And they're taking a cruise to the Caribbean next month. Momma has always wanted to, but my father never did."

"That's fantastic!" I picked up my beer again. "Andrew has a way of figuring out what book someone needs and he just did it for your mother's life instead."

"Funny how we listen to anyone but our family, huh?" Jasper laughed. "But if Momma's happy..."

"We're all happy." I finished his sentence, and we clinked our beer bottles.

While not all my family relationships had gone as planned, this one had. And for the first time since Ruby asked me to come with her to Delmar Apartments, I was reminded of the joy of family. Even with Aunt Charlene's quirks, I appreciated having her and Jasper in my life. I wished my brother had the same experience I had with them.

At least I would bury him with our parents, the people he loved the most. So I had a funeral to plan.

37

"Sorry, Nubi, it's another text." I scratched the white fur spot on my cranky cat's head. We woke up to my phone dinging with messages from my friends and Jasper. I answered them all with the same message: *I'm fine. Thanks. We'll talk soon.* I was too tired to type more than that this morning.

Leaving Nubi in my bed, I dragged myself to my bathroom. Jasper had stayed until about ten last night and then Connor called from his gig on Frenchman Street. He had offered to cut short his set, but I told him no. While I wouldn't have minded his company, I hoped I would get a good night's rest with just me and Nubi at home.

It took a dose of over-the-counter sleeping pills to help me rest, but nightmares woke me up through the night. Looking at my reflection in the mirror, it would take every make-up trick I'd learned to cover up the bags under my eyes. But there were no cosmetics to hide the sadness that covered my face.

After showering, I turned on the coffee maker and another text came through. I considered ignoring it, but I was glad I didn't. Libby texted that Luke Ward was working out of her cafe today, so if I had questions for him, I should come over.

I threw on my tennis shoes, grabbed my backpack and a Preservation Hall baseball hat. Nubi jumped on the coffee table, scattering the magazines and unearthing my keys.

"Thanks, little one." Nubi was more likely reminding me to feed him instead of helping me. I added extra kibble to his dish and rushed out. Artistic Coffee and Creations was only a few blocks away, so even in my exhausted state, I power-walked there quickly. Opening the door, the comforting smell of freshly ground coffee welcomed me at the same time as Libby.

"Darling, come here!" She wiped her hands on her flour-covered apron as she came out from behind the bakery counter. "I can finally hug you."

I hid my head in Libby's shoulder as she hugged me tightly. My eyes ached from crying, and I didn't want to start again. She whispered in my ear, "You're grieving, but you'll get to the bottom of your brother's death. Go talk to Luke and I'll bring your coffee and scone to you."

Libby might have been Connor's mother, but she treated me and everyone else at Thibodeaux Mansion as if we were her children, too. Sometimes she could be overbearing, but today her mothering was just what I needed.

Luke sat at a corner table under a painting titled, *Summer Rain*. It fit his apparent mood with its dark blue colors splashed haphazardly on the crooked canvas. He scowled at the laptop, banging the keys with two fingers. I didn't know if he would welcome me interrupting him, but I took a chance.

"Hi, Luke. May I join you?" I sat down. "I'm Samantha Richardson. We've met a few times at your building."

"You're the sister, aren't you?" He closed his laptop and stared at me. "I thought you looked familiar, and now I realize it's because you're Ray's sister. I mean Samuel. Or was it Joey? Honestly, I'm confused about who he was."

So was I, but I didn't want to discuss that issue with Luke. "His real name is, was, Samuel Joseph St. Martin. He gave you the name Raymond West, right?"

"Yep, Ray was quiet, but a hard worker and clever. He suggested working in the courtyard without telling the tenants." Luke took a sip of his coffee and sighed. "Part of me wishes I'd never touched that fountain, but then that poor girl would have been there forever. I wouldn't want that for my kin."

"Nicole's family is relieved she's been found, so you did a good thing. Although I'm sure it hasn't been easy for you or your renters."

"You can say that again. I was behind schedule already. Since losing Ray, I've had to find workers from out of town. The locals I've talked to say the place is cursed. No one wants to be another dead construction worker." Luke turned red. "I'm sorry. That sounded crass. You must be upset about your brother. But you didn't know he was working for me, did you?"

"No, our relationship was complicated." That was putting it mildly. "Can I ask you a few questions about him?"

"I don't know how much I can help you, but I'll try."

"Do you know where he was staying or keeping his stuff? The police assume he squatted in Mrs. Riggins' apartment, but they didn't find any of his things except a black backpack."

"I hope he didn't or Mrs. Riggins will have my hide." Luke rubbed his temples. "Ray carried either a black backpack or a red one. The police guess he stole from the apartments, but so far all I've heard is some food is missing."

"I wonder what he did with his stuff, then? And where is the other backpack?"

"If you find it, let me know. I'm missing some tools and I'm guessing Ray had them in the other backpack."

"Like what?"

"A small shovel, a hammer, a screwdriver, and a tension wrench are the ones I remember. I told the cops he could have used the wrench and screwdriver to pick the lock on Mrs. Riggins' door. But they said they found a key on him. He made a copy of the master key." Luke picked up his coffee mug and put it right back down. "I don't even know how it got a hold of it."

"He was always resourceful. But no one else said they had things go missing?"

Luke shook his head. "Seems like he was careful to steal from the tenant who was rarely there. But he must have made an enemy of someone."

"Did he know someone was buried under the fountain?" Joey had nothing to do with Nicole's murder, but did he overhear someone or find something in the courtyard?

"I don't know." Luke lowered his voice. "By his reaction, I doubt it. He seemed as shocked as me when we found the skeleton. And when we found the bracelet, he insisted we call the police right away."

At least Joey was truthful when he told me that part yesterday.

"But I'm pretty sure he wanted me to make the call so he could take something from the grave," Luke said.

I saw Libby coming our way, but I shook my head. She got the hint and returned to the counter. While I needed caffeine and sugar, I didn't want Luke to stop talking. But Luke assumed my shaking was directed at him.

"Now, I don't mean to speak ill of the dead. I really did like Ray, but I swore there was something next to the skeleton, like a figurine or sculpture. I didn't get a good look. But when I came back from calling the cops, there was nothing there."

"Did you tell anyone about that?"

"Just the police. They asked me not to say anything to my tenants. I guess I shouldn't have told you, but..."

"I appreciate you trusting me. Did you ask my brother about it?"

"I didn't get the chance. Ray went out front, supposedly to wait for the cops while I kept everyone away from the grave."

"And then he disappeared." I closed my eyes as the tears welled up. As much as I was trying to treat this as another mystery, the reality that I was discussing my dead brother hit me hard.

"Hey, I'm sorry. This must be tough." Luke handed me a napkin when I opened my eyes. "No matter what he did and whatever his name was, he was your family."

Libby appeared with two cups of coffee and a plate of pastries. "I thought you might want a refill, Luke. And Sammy needs her favorite scones."

"Thanks, Libby. I appreciate the service. You tell me when to free up the table." Luke reached into his pocket and pulled out his wallet.

"No, no, this round is on me. Neighbors help neighbors around here." Libby smiled and took up Luke's empty cup. "Now you just holler if you need anything else. You, too, Sammy."

I nodded since I couldn't speak. I had taken a big bite of

the warm sweet potato scone. But Libby didn't need me to answer. She had a knack of anticipating my coffee and scone needs even more than I did.

"She's so kind." Luke tilted his head toward Libby. "I wish I'd met her before I bought Delmar Apartments. She's been giving me all kinds of helpful hints about owning a place in the French Quarter."

William and Libby took over Thibodeaux Mansion, tenants and all, so I bet they had a lot of advice for Luke. Fortunately, they hadn't run into the same issues as Luke.

"I need to get back to my spreadsheets before my accountant calls, so please excuse me." Luke lifted the lid of his laptop. "But if I think of anything else, I'll let you know."

I gave him one of my business cards and stood up. "Thanks. I'm sorry you had all these problems. The French Quarter is a great place. I hope you'll stay."

"I haven't decided yet, but thanks."

Luke grasped my arm when I stepped away with my mug. "I've heard about your brother's troubles, but I'd still like to come to his funeral. He was good to me and I should pay my respects."

I nodded and then retreated to the bakery counter. One person thought enough of my brother to want to attend his funeral. I didn't expect many people to come to the cemetery. But I had to figure out how to go about organizing the service. I did know I needed to give the tomb key to the undertaker...

I dropped my mug on the counter. Now I knew where Joey hid his belongings.

38

Libby rushed over to me when I dropped the coffee cup on the counter. "Sammy, are you OK?"

"Sorry. My mind was somewhere else." I checked the mug and it wasn't chipped. Not that Libby cared. She had already come out from around the counter with a glass of water.

"Come sit down with me for a minute." Libby guided me to an empty table near the front door.

"Thanks. I need a moment to collect my thoughts before I head out." I sipped the ice-cold water and my body relaxed.

"Did you learn anything from Luke? He really did like Joey. Then again, we all did before he..." Libby didn't finish her sentence. She looked down. "I'm sorry, darling. My heart still aches over Matt's death. Joey caused so much pain, but for you the most."

I nodded. There was nothing to say. Joey scarred everyone he touched when he came to New Orleans, especially my friends at Thibodeaux Mansion. It would have been easy for everybody to lump me in with my brother.

Not that I condoned what he did, but my arrival started a chain of events that led to Matt's death. But instead they took me in as one of their own. And today was no different.

"Now, now, I can tell how troubled you are." Libby tucked a loose piece of my hair back in my hat. "Wearing that cap isn't hiding your pain. But I can also see you're determined to figure out what happened to your brother."

"I am." I reached out and squeezed her hand. "I think I know where Joey's hiding place is."

"Where? What do you think you'll find?" Libby leaned across the table. "Should we call Connor to go with you?"

I let go of Libby's hand and stood up. "Connor would offer to help, but there's another man who is better suited for this job."

Libby followed me to the cafe door and stood in front of it, so I had to stop. She was protective of her son, but that wasn't the reason she was stopping me from getting someone else to help me. "Sammy, where are you going? You've got to tell me!"

I moved her away from the door and pulled it open. "I need to go to the cemetery."

"Cemetery? What in the world are you talking about, Sammy?" Libby followed me out of the cafe.

I stopped in front of a horse hitching post and leaned against it. "When I saw Joey he said our family belongings were locked in a quiet place. I can only think of one spot."

"Your family tomb." Libby wrung her hands on her flour-covered apron. "Are you OK to go back there? You could send someone to check for you. No, of course not, you must go."

I didn't need to explain myself; Libby had figured it all out on her own. I kissed her on the cheek. "Thanks for understanding. I'll call Mr. Hugo on my way there. I promise I won't unlock the tomb on my own."

"Just be careful!" Libby called out as I left her waving in front of the cafe. "And you better tell me what you find!"

Would I find anything? If Joey had a hiding place, the mausoleum would be perfect. No one would open it until there was a death in the family.

After finding a quiet spot on Royal Street, I called Mr. Hugo. Fortunately, he was working today. I asked if he would let me into the cemetery. As a tomb owner, I had the right to go inside. Anyone else needed to visit with a licensed tour guide.

"I'm sorry to bother you. I just wanted to get in quickly without a fuss," I said.

"And you don't want to do it alone, do you? I can hear the worry in your voice, child."

I couldn't hide anything from Mr. Hugo. "If you don't mind, I'd appreciate the company."

"I'll meet you at the gates. You can always count on me. Remember that."

He didn't question why I was asking him to escort me to my tomb. Mr. Hugo had been involved in a few of my escapades at the cemetery, so he was used to my calls.

I didn't have to explain myself when I stopped by my apartment, either. No one was home when I ran inside to grab the mausoleum key I hid in my copy of the Nancy Drew book, *The Black Keys*. I kept my head down as I rushed through the Quarter to the cemetery. Wiping his brow with a handkerchief, Mr. Hugo stood outside the gates to St. Louis Cemetery No. 1. Even wearing a short-sleeve shirt and lightweight pants, he must have been boiling in his dark brown uniform. Before I went up to Mr. Hugo, I bought two bottles of water from the vendor by the gates.

"I think you need this. I know I do."

"Thanks, Sammy." Mr. Hugo took the bottle I handed him. "It's hot enough to fry an egg on the sidewalk and it's only June."

"I feel like I'm back in Florida." I took a swig of my water. "Without the pool in my backyard, though."

"Talk Miss Libby into putting one in." Mr. Hugo laughed and pulled up his belt, which held his flashlight and a set of keys. "I'll come visit you every day if you get a pool."

"You're welcome even if we don't have a pool."

He smiled, but then he furrowed his brow. "Now, let's talk about why you called. First, I didn't say how sorry I am about your brother."

"Thanks. He's the reason I'm here. I need to open the tomb."

"Open it?" He coughed and capped his water bottle. "Honey, why do you want to do that?"

"I think he used it to hide his stuff, including family mementos," I explained. "If there's anything in there, I promise I'll call the police."

"I know you will." Mr. Hugo took his key ring off his belt. "Let's visit your ancestors."

I inhaled deeply and followed Mr. Hugo into the cemetery. Time to find out if my brother left behind something more than terrible memories in our family tomb.

39

———

We weaved in and out of the tombs and tourists to get to my family's mausoleum. Even in the blistering sun, tour groups filled the aisles, taking pictures and listening to history told by guides. When the cemetery was established in 1789, did anyone imagine it would be a tourist destination?

"Breathe, dear child," Mr. Hugo said as we stood in front of the St. Martin mausoleum. I didn't visit the tomb often, but when I did, I would close my eyes and breathe deeply. Mr. Hugo would wait until I opened my eyes, and then sing *Amazing Grace*. This time when I opened my eyes, he was singing but still standing next to me.

When he finished, I wiped the tears from my face. "Thank you for being here with me."

"I am honored to be here for you. Now, what do you plan to do first? Did you brother have a key, too?"

"I don't think he did. Apparently, he took some tools from his construction job, so I wonder if he picked the lock or forced it open."

My family tomb differed from most in that a door

protected the interior. Most had a name plaque bolted over the front that was removed for a burial. The St. Martin mausoleum opened with a key. Caskets were positioned on one of three shelves, like a loaf of bread going in an oven. With the heat and humidity of New Orleans, the tombs actually acted like an oven, helping the bodies to decompose. The old remains were brushed down a shaft to make room for a new coffin. The system was efficient and allowed for unlimited generations to use the mausoleum.

To the right of the door was our name plaque, which included my birth name, Sarah Jane St. Martin. Jasper suggested having it covered, but I said no. That part of my life was in the past, buried so to speak, and I would keep it that way. If I was buried in the tomb, I wanted the name I used for most of my life etched upon the marble.

I inspected the lock and found scrapes around it. I took the key off the chain around my neck and unlocked the tomb. The humid air mixing with the musty smell from the interior made me cough. No one had been added to the mausoleum for twenty-eight years, so there were no human remains to confront. The middle shelf now held three shoeboxes.

Mr. Hugo leaned around me to look inside. "Unless your brother was burying his pets, those boxes must hold your family heirlooms."

"Do people bury their pets in tombs?" I pulled one box out, hoping I wouldn't find a hamster skeleton. My brother wouldn't pull a mean joke like that on me, would he?

"I've seen all kinds of things, honey. But I doubt your brother buried his pet hamster. Do you want me to hold it while you open it?"

I put the box in Mr. Hugo's hands and lifted the lid. I gasped, and I dropped the lid on the ground. In the box was a picture of the bride and groom in the faded picture. Aunt Charlene had sent me photos of my parents with Jasper when he moved to New Orleans, but none of their wedding. Seeing their smiling faces, just starting their life together, brought me joy but broke my heart. The next pictures did the same: Joey's baby photo, Joey holding me as a newborn, and the whole family posing with Santa Claus.

"You sure were a cute baby." Mr. Hugo handed the box to me and picked up the lid. "Your brother did one good thing. He left you these pictures. Are you ready to see what else is in there?"

My brother included a note in the next box. I read it out loud, "Sarah Jane, here are a few pieces of Mama's jewelry and Daddy's wedding ring. I found these in Uncle Preston's stuff after he died. My guess is he kept these as a last resort for money since he didn't have one sentimental bone in that evil body of his. Love, Samuel."

Inside were two plain gold bands, a small diamond engagement ring, a simple cross on a chain, and a pair of pearl earrings. I held each piece in my hand for a moment, but when I picked up my mother's ring, I dropped it back in the box. These must have been taken from my parents' bodies after they were found after Hurricane Geoffrey.

"Sammy, it's all right if you're feeling strange holding this stuff. It's normal not to bury people with their personal effects."

"Oh, I know." I looked into Mr. Hugo's concerned eyes. "I'm happy I have their things, but I wish I remembered my parents."

"You still can't remember anything about your folks?" Mr. Hugo closed the box and placed it on the ground next to the other box.

"No. Every time I see a picture of them, or Aunt Charlene tells a story, I keep hoping a memory of my own will appear," I said. "My memories are buried too deep or just gone."

Mr. Hugo put his arm around me, and I rested against him. I wanted to run home and crawl into bed and forget about my past and the present for a little while. But I couldn't. I needed to finish what I started.

"One more to go," I said.

"I'll get it." Mr. Hugo grabbed the box, and we heard it rattle. "I hope I didn't break anything inside."

I lifted the lid. "No, you didn't." I dipped my hand in the box and let casino chips drip through my fingers.

Mr. Hugo whistled. "Your brother must have been a good gambler. Those are from casinos in Biloxi."

"He was spotted in a casino in Biloxi a few months back, so I guess he won a lot."

"And he left it for you."

"I don't care about the money." I slapped the lid on the box. "No amount of money could make up for what he did. He probably didn't leave it for me. I bet this was his escape fund."

"Maybe. Maybe not." Mr. Hugo shrugged his shoulders. "You should just sit on that for a while. Is there anything else?"

I gathered my nerves and ducked my head inside the shelf. I was afraid of missing something, but I didn't want to be inside the tomb any longer than I had to. Mr. Hugo would have checked for me, but after Aunt Charlene got stuck looking for her husband's stash, he probably was wary. I couldn't blame him. Although I had room to move around, I felt claustrophobic in there.

The shelf appeared empty, but just as I was about to remove my hands I glimpsed a shape in the back. I stretched my arms and my fingertips and touched a hard object. Stepping on my tippy toes, I grasped the item and pulled it out.

"Your brother left you an angel?" Mr. Hugo took a fresh handkerchief from his pocket and handed it to me. I wiped the dust and sweat off my face and inspected the statue. It reminded me of the one I saw in Myles' shop.

"This looks like a tomb decoration. It's not from ours, though." I turned it in my hands, noting the chips and worn wings. While it was less than a foot tall, it must have weighed almost fifteen pounds. Dirt and dark splotches dotted the base, perhaps blood stains.

"I've seen ones like that before. It looks mighty old." Mr. Hugo took it from me and looked it over. "Do you know people used to steal these and sell them? The reason I got this job years ago was to protect this place against grave robbers."

"Grave robbers? Did they steal bodies, too?" My stomach lurched at the thought of people taking bodies out of the tombs.

"I'm sure some of them took bones, but they mostly stole stuff like vases and statues." Mr. Hugo pointed over to a tomb across the aisle. "That mausoleum used to have a beautiful marble statue of a vase with cascading flowers. The family even offered a reward for its return, but it's never been found."

"That's horrible." I looked up at the cross with intertwined roses on top of my family's tomb. Although I had only known of the mausoleum for a few months, I was attached to it, and I would be angry to have it damaged or stolen.

"It is. Bad enough people desecrate tombs like they do to Marie Laveau's tomb, putting those x's on it as if she would help someone just by doing that." Mr. Hugo shook his head.

"But taking things that families chose and used their hard-earned money to honor their families is evil. No God-fearing person would steal from a cemetery or buy stuff plundered from one."

"Does it still happen? The stealing I mean?"

"Probably, but not like it did in the nineties. There was a big scandal with some antique stores supposedly selling stolen tomb ornaments."

"Really? Any stores in particular?"

"Now, that was a while ago, but the shop owners arrested were from outside the city," Mr. Hugo said. "There were rumors about some stores on Royal Street, but no one was arrested as far as I remember."

Ruby would have mentioned if Myles or his father had been arrested. But that didn't mean he or his family's shop wasn't involved.

"But you're sure it was in the nineties?" While the hurricane that took my parents happened then, something else came to mind.

"Yes. Why do you ask?" Mr. Hugo said.

Verity and Nicole disappeared in the nineties, and apparently a statue was buried with Nicole. And Myles had knowledge of the value of antiques. This all couldn't be a coincidence. I needed to talk to Verity, but first I would do the right thing.

"Mr. Hugo, I need to call Rob and Christine. I think this angel is from the grave at Delmar Apartments."

40

Mr. Hugo left me at the tomb to let Christine and Rob through the cemetery gate. I had assured him I was fine on my own. Truth be told, I needed time to myself before the detectives arrived. Joey's personal items wouldn't be too interesting to them, but they meant the world to me. It was a bit of my history, which is one reason I had moved to New Orleans. Learning about my life before I was adopted came with so much heartache that at times I wasn't sure it was worth it.

But now, looking at the photos of my parents, of us as a family, I didn't regret discovering the truth. I just wish it hadn't included my brother turning out to be a murderer. But I couldn't change the past.

Identifying his killer might give me some sense of closure. Finding the angel statue gave me hope I was on track to solve more than one mystery. Joey must have taken the angel from Nicole's grave, and the murderer wanted it.

Was he or she still anxious about the missing statue? I believed they were, and I wondered if it was connected to the 1990s cemetery thefts Mr. Hugo mentioned. The time matched Nicole and Verity's disappearance. The way Verity alluded they had to leave made me suspect they were involved in something illegal. And with Myles' family owning an antique store, it would be the perfect place to sell items, especially to private clients.

I was dying to call Verity, but Christine and Rob arrived. I stood up, bracing myself for a reprimand from both of them. So I did a preemptive apology. "I'm sorry. I should have called you first, but I didn't know if I would find anything."

"I doubt that. You're pretty sure of your hunches," Christine said. "But let's see what you found."

The detectives walked over to the boxes I had stacked against the tomb, along with the angel sculpture. Christine pulled out a pair of latex gloves and picked up the statue. She pursed her lips as she inspected it.

"Does this match the one found with Nicole?" I said. "Luke told me Joey sent him to call the police, so Joey could have taken this when he was alone at the grave."

"Why am I not surprised you've talked to Luke Ward?" Christine gave me the look I'd seen parents give their misbehaving toddlers.

I crossed my arms. "I wanted to hear what my brother was like during his last days."

"Uh huh," Christine said.

"I really did," I said. "But tell me, is this like the other statue?"

"I'd say it's an exact match." Rob took the statue from Christine and turned it over. "It has the same maker mark on the bottom, but this has a number two on it. The one in the grave was marked number one, and it didn't have these dark splotches."

"This angel must be the murder weapon. Joey could

have tried to blackmail the killer." I could feel my pulse racing. "They must have murdered him to get it back, but he had already hidden it here."

"Let's not jump to conclusions, Sammy." Rob opened a plastic evidence bag and put the statue inside. "That might not even be blood on the statue. We'll try to match the dirt on this to the dirt on the angel buried underneath Nicole."

"Was there evidence in the boxes that suggested Joey was blackmailing someone? Or did he tell you that?" Christine said. "You didn't keep any information back from us, did you?"

"No to all your questions," I answered. "It's just that Jasper said Joey always had a plan or would come up with one at a moment's notice. I bet when he saw the angel statue in the grave, he thought it was worth some money."

Rob and Christine raised their eyebrows at each other. While I couldn't read their minds, I was pretty sure they were both thinking my theories had some merit.

"You found nothing else besides the boxes and the statue?" Rob looked inside the mausoleum.

"No. I didn't find his backpack or the tools."

"You know about the missing tools?" Christine closed the door to the tomb and studied the lock. "There are scratch marks, so he could have used the tools to open it. He didn't have a key, did he?"

"Not that I know of," I said. "Do you want my key?"

"That won't be necessary for now." Rob placed each shoebox into a separate bag. "We'll get the boxes back to you as soon as possible."

"I'd appreciate that. And I am sorry I didn't call before I opened the tomb." I stared at the ground.

"Mm-hmm," Christine said. "Benny, thanks for coming. Can you take this evidence to forensics?"

I looked up to see Officer Benny Stevens walking toward us with a large canvas bag in his hands. The first time was when Sissy tried to distract him while I snuck into a crime scene. The last time we met was at Hotel Jeanne after a murder and he escorted me out of the area, away from the media.

"Of course I can. Hello, Miss Richardson. Fancy meeting you at a crime scene." He raised his bushy eyebrows at me.

Well, there was no doubt that he considered me a magnet for crime. But he didn't give me a hard time. Instead, he said, "I am sorry for your loss. Did you want me to take Miss Richardson home as well, detectives?"

"No, we can do that," Rob said. "Thanks for helping."

Officer Stevens placed the boxes and the statue in the canvas bag. He tipped his hat toward me and then left. I walked back to the tomb and locked it. After putting the key back around my neck, I put my hand on my parents' name on the plaque. If there was an afterlife, I hoped they had welcomed my brother.

"Ready to go, Sammy?" Rob said.

"Yes, thanks." I followed him and Christine down the aisle. When we got to the end, Christine stopped.

"I'll meet you back at the station, Rob," Christine said. "I just need to check on something while I'm here."

"Say hi to Meemaw for me, Tina." Rob grinned. "Tell her I think the powder room is pretty now, too."

"You hush, or I'll tell her to haunt you." Christine shook a finger at Rob, but there was a sparkle in her eye. She winked at me and then left us.

"She actually believed Ruby when she said her grandmother talked to her the other day?" Christine didn't strike me as a believer in mediums and psychics, but then again, she was born and raised in New Orleans. I found the locals had a healthy respect for the paranormal and spiritual worlds.

"Maybe just a little, but paying respects to your ancestors is always a good idea." Rob grabbed my elbow when I stumbled over a broken brick on the path that I hadn't noticed. "I went to my granny's grave to tell her I was going to propose to Sissy."

"And what did she say?" I laughed.

"Nothing, but lightning didn't strike me, so I assumed she approved." Rob's whole body shook with laughter. "But honestly, Sammy, if you need someone to listen to you, come to your family's mausoleum. You could find the answers you're looking for."

I followed Rob through the gates of the cemetery. I might take his advice to talk to the dead later, but right now, I needed to talk to the living.

41

The living person I needed to speak with was right where I needed her — my home.

Rob drove me back, and when I entered the courtyard, I stopped at the sound of three people laughing. Verity, Ruby, and Papa sat together at the back table. The softness and joy in Ruby's laughter shocked me. Had I ever heard her laugh?

"Sammy, come join us!" Papa stood up and pulled out a chair for me. "We're looking at old photos. Wait until you see Verity's hair back in the day."

"Who's talking about whose hair?" Verity stabbed a finger on a photo in a photo album. "Look at Papa's hair."

"Papa had hair?" I couldn't help myself and I joined them at the table to check out the photo. I grinned at Papa. "I assumed you were always bald."

"After looking at the photo, you'll agree I'm better looking without the hair." Papa rubbed a hand over his smooth head.

"But those green snakes dyed in your hair were stunning." Verity snorted. "Marie Laveau would not have approved, no matter what you said."

Ruby covered her mouth with a hand, but it didn't stifle her giggles.

Papa closed the album. "Stupid me figured that hairdo would bring me money. Brought me nothing but embarrassment and a rash from that cheap hair dye."

I joined their laughter and almost forgot about the questions I needed to ask Verity. Part of me wanted to put it off for another day, to let her enjoy her time with Papa and Ruby. But Papa changed the subject.

"Sammy, I haven't had the chance to tell you in person I'm sorry for your loss." Papa put his hand on mine. "I lit a candle on my altar and at St. Louis Cathedral for you this morning."

"I'm sorry I didn't return your call last night, but I appreciate you thinking of me," I said.

"Any news today?" Verity asked.

"Actually, there is." I explained how, after speaking with Luke Ward, I checked my family tomb and found mementos. And how I also found an angel statue that appeared to match the one uncovered with Nicole's body. It looked like my brother took the statue while Luke called the police.

"So there was an angel buried with Nicole?" Verity's voice cracked.

"Yes," I said.

"Verity, what is wrong? Are you going to pass out?" Ruby put her arm around Verity's shoulders and, surprisingly, Verity didn't shake her mother off.

"It's time you tell us what happened, my dear." Papa pushed his chair back and carried it over next to Verity. "Your body and soul can only hold this secret for so long. Let it out. For you and for Nicole."

"Have you been trying to protect Nicole's reputation?" I asked. "Nothing you say will make Momo think less of Nicole or you."

Verity stood up and paced around the table. Nubi, Cleopatra, and Nefertiti appeared on top of the back wall and sat, their tails wagging in sync. Verity looked at them. "Are they here as the jury?"

"No one is here to judge you," Papa said. The glare Verity gave him said she didn't agree.

"The cats are here to offer you their support. Cats recognize when they are needed," Ruby said.

Again, Verity didn't appear to believe that either. But she stopped pacing and began talking.

"You need to remember that Nicole and I were only seventeen when we met Myles. He was older and treated us like we were cool like him." Verity closed her eyes, and I bet she imagined herself back in those days. "So when he asked if we wanted to have fun with him and Tabby, we jumped at the chance."

The cats hopped down from the wall and stretched out on the courtyard tiles as if they needed to be closer to hear Verity's story. I kept as still as possible, although I was dying to ask Verity a million questions. But I worried if interrupted her now, she wouldn't continue. Papa must have thought the same, as he placed his hand on Ruby's arm every time she opened her mouth.

"One night, we sneaked into Lafayette Cemetery with Myles and Tabby after midnight. With a bit of liquid courage, we climbed the walls and roamed the cemetery. We goofed around until Myles pointed at two marble urns and said we should take them."

Verity wiped the beads of sweat from her forehead. "Nicole and I laughed, thinking it was a joke."

But Myles was dead serious. He told the girls he had sold a few things to some of his dad's customers privately who wanted more. Tabby helped him, but if Nicole and Verity joined them, they could take bigger pieces. And that meant more money.

"He promised we would only pick stuff from abandoned tombs, so it was OK." Verity finally sat down at the table. "We were stupid and believed him. We went with him and Tabby to cemeteries around the city to steal stuff and then Myles sold them. Even Sutton peddled a couple of pieces to his clients."

Ruby let out an enormous sigh at Sutton's name.

"Yes, mother, you were right about Sutton. He did more than tarot card readings. He sold cemetery decorations along with fake predictions," Verity snapped. "But Myles started it and got in over his head."

Myles' customers asked for bigger items, like benches and crosses from the tops of tombs. One night, when the four of them tried to take a large cherub statue out of Metairie Cemetery, they discovered they weren't alone. A group of seasoned thieves were not amused to see Myles and the girls trying to muscle in on their territory.

"We left without the statue, but that wasn't enough for those thieves," Verity said. "They quickly figured out who Myles was and found him at the apartment building. Nicole and I were there when they showed up and they scared us. Myles too, but he acted like it was no big deal."

"Tabby and Sutton weren't there?" I interrupted Verity because I suspected she needed a moment to catch her breath. She walked over to the cats. Nubi meowed and reached a paw toward her. Verity rubbed the little white fur spot on his head before she answered.

"No, so they didn't see how serious those men were.

Myles convinced us to keep going, but we didn't go back to Metairie. We just scoured the city cemeteries. But Nicole and I soon realized how it was worse than we originally thought." Verity sat on the ground and continued to pet Nubi. "Those guys found us outside school a week later and told us we could work for them or they'd tell the cops about us."

"So that's when you and Nicole decided to leave," I said.

Verity nodded and stayed with the cats, not looking at any of the humans. Papa held Ruby's hand and at first, I assumed it was for moral support. But when he whispered under his breath, "Ruby, don't get up," I thought otherwise. He was either keeping her from going to comfort Verity or yell at her. From her clenched jaw and furious foot tapping, I was positive it was the latter.

"Yes. The last things we had stoled with Myles and Tabby were two angels statues. When we left the cemetery after that final robbery, we almost got caught by a security guard. Myles and Tabby ran off with statue and we went the other direction with the other," Verity said.

"That's why y'all had a statue," I said.

"Yes, When we told Myles about the threats from the other thieves, he said not to worry." Verity got up and came over to the table and sat down. " No matter what we said we couldn't convince them to stop stealing. So we left."

"But Nicole went back," I said.

"She said she'd give it to Myles. I gave her a note to leave for my mother after she saw him." Verity looked at Ruby, who didn't respond. "I put my charm bracelet on Nicole's wrist and told her to give it back to me when we met up in Seattle. She hugged me goodbye and went to see Myles. I left town."

"That's how Nicole ended up with your bracelet," Papa said.

"Yes, she always liked it and it was my way of saying thanks for dealing with Myles. I knew he would try to persuade us to stay. Nicole was stronger than me. She promised he wouldn't change her mind."

"So she took the angel and the letter to your mother and planned to drop them off before she left New Orleans," I said.

Verity nodded, but then turned toward the music that came from the house next door. The off-key saxophone notes added to the tense atmosphere in our courtyard. A soothing song wouldn't have helped. The more Verity talked, the more Ruby fidgeted in her chair and the harder Papa had to grasp her hand. I remained still, hoping that if I appeared calm on the outside, it would help Verity maintain her composure.

"Perhaps her pregnancy changed her mind then," I said.

"She would have left no matter what. Trust me, we both felt threatened by the other thieves," Verity said. "If she planned to keep the baby, she would have wanted to be far away from those guys."

"So you have no doubt her death is all about the pregnancy?"

"Yes. Myles or Sutton killed her when she said she was pregnant and leaving town," Verity said.

"What about Tabby?" I said. "If Nicole slept with Myles, she would have reason to kill her."

"Maybe." Verity tapped her fingers on the table. "She always struck me as the type of woman who would leave a man who cheated on her. That's probably why they're divorced."

I'd check that out, but for now, I dropped it. "So you

don't think Nicole's death had anything to do with the stealing business?" I said.

"No, but it doesn't matter why she died." Verity wiped away a tear. "We were in over our heads. And I just ran from it all and look what happened."

"Yes, look what happened." Ruby pulled her hand away from Papa and pushed back her chair. I shuddered at the screeching noise the chair made against the tiles. "I didn't raise you to be foolish and selfish. To steal from the dead and then leave your friend to fix it for you is appalling. I'll pray to the Goddess of Good for forgiveness for you."

"Don't bother." Verity stood up and grabbed her bag. "I've been searching for forgiveness since I left New Orleans and I haven't found it."

As Verity headed to the courtyard gate, Papa yelled, "Verity, where are you going?"

"Where I should have gone twenty-six years ago." Verity snapped her head around and her eyes were wet with tears. "The police."

Papa, Ruby, and I flinched as the courtyard gate banged loudly. The three cats were startled too and jumped into the water fountain that only held plants. Papa looked like he wanted to hide in there with them. The sadness in his face was undeniable. He stared at the gate, but he turned to Ruby, who slumped back in her chair.

"Ruby, shall we go inside?" He grasped her hand. "I can make us a cup of tea."

"Could you please give me a few minutes alone? I must speak with the Goddess of Good privately." Ruby let Papa help her up. "Samantha, would you check on Verity? Obviously, she won't want to talk to me for a while. If ever."

"Of course." I planned to track down Verity later, not just

for information, but she would need a friend after that revelation.

After Ruby returned to her apartment, I helped Papa gather the pictures on the table and put them back in the photo album. "Are you OK, Papa?"

"Me? Oh, I'm fine. I just feel bad for Ruby and Verity. They can't seem to get over the past."

"It's going to take more than looking over photos to mend decades of pain."

"An old man can dream, can't he?" Papa clutched the photo album to his chest. "I wish I had kept a closer eye on Verity back then. I could tell she was troubled."

"I hope she's not in trouble now."

Papa had been walking toward Ruby's door but stopped and turned around. "You don't think they'll arrest her for the thefts, do you?"

"I hope not, but I'm more concerned she's going to go ballistic on her old friends at Delmar Apartments." I rubbed my eyes. The drama of the past few days wore on me, but I couldn't rest yet. "I'll go check on her."

"Thank you, Sammy. Your help means the world to me and Ruby." Papa walked over to me and kissed me on the cheek. "But make sure you're taking care of yourself. Your problems are important, too, you know."

"I'll be OK. Keeping busy is helping." I kissed him back on the cheek and rushed out of the courtyard. Papa must have known I was lying about being fine, but didn't call me out. But being busy did help, especially if finding Nicole's killer led to my brother's killer.

42

"Yes, I waited for you." Verity leaned against the building, holding a smoldering cigarette in her hand.

"Did you want me to go to the police with you?" I said.

"I assumed you would follow me to make sure I went."

"Actually, your mother asked me to make sure you were all right."

Verity dropped her cigarette on the sidewalk and crushed it with the toe of her shoe. "I'd say you were lying, but you haven't lied to me so far."

"I'm not. She is worried, and so is Papa. You know your mother. She isn't the most tactful woman."

"But she was right." Verity squeezed her eyes shut. "I shouldn't have left Nicole by herself to deal with our mess."

"Nicole thought she could handle everything on her own. And you might have been buried under that fountain if you'd stayed." I put my hand on Verity's arm. "You can't go back and change things, but you can make sure her killer is arrested."

Verity opened her eyes. "Myles killed her."

"Why Myles and not Tabby? Or even Sutton?"

"Myles had the most to lose if it came out about his crime business. His father would have disowned him if he found out."

"But you two weren't planning on telling anyone, right? Do you think Nicole changed her mind?"

Verity shook her head. "What did the statue you found look like?" Verity started pacing back and forth in front of me, ignoring the curious looks from pedestrians walking by us.

"The angel was about ten inches tall and about fifteen pounds. I'm sorry, but there appeared to be dried blood on..."

"So that's what killed her." Verity stopped pacing. "Did it have a number on the bottom?"

"Yes, number two."

"That was ours."

"Most likely Nicole was returning the statue and Myles or Tabby hit her with it," I said. "Now that the police have both statues, it's evidence to corroborate your story."

"What do you mean, both statues?" Verity asked. "I thought there was just the one your brother took, the one Nicole was returning to Myles."

"The police kept that info to themselves. Another angel statue was buried with Nicole, and the detectives said it matched the one my brother stole."

Verity gripped my wrist. "Myles and Tabby stole the other statue, so it's proof they were there when she was buried. And it proves they killed Nicole!"

"You need to go see Rob and Christine now." I rubbed my wrist after Verity let go. "Tell them the truth, and that should be enough to question them."

Verity stared at the ground and didn't respond. I couldn't let her keep this information to herself.

"Listen, I realize this is difficult to talk about with the police..."

Verity put up her hand, and I stopped talking. She took a deep breath. "It is only because I'm ashamed. If I'd stayed, things might have been different. Or she might not have been missing for all these years if I came back when she didn't meet me."

While Verity didn't strike me as the hugging type, I did it anyway. She collapsed in my arms for a moment before pulling herself out of our embrace.

"You can't change the past, but you can help the police find out what happened. It might not be the forgiveness you've been searching for, but it's a start. I'm sure Nicole would want that for you," I said.

After wiping the tears from her eyes, she tightened her grip on her backpack. "Thanks, Sammy. I understand why you're the neighborhood busybody."

"Oh?" That wasn't the thanks I had expected after comforting her.

"Don't be offended." Verity laughed. "You let people talk and come to their own conclusions."

"I'll take it as a compliment then. But now you should really go to Rob and Christine. Do you want me to walk with you?"

"No. I need to ask you a favor."

"What do you need?" I said.

"Will you go to Momo? I don't want her hearing about what Nicole and I did with Myles and Tabby." Verity hung her head. "If the word gets out before I go see her, it will break her heart. And mine."

"Of course I will. Did you want me to tell her about the theft ring?" I asked because Verity raised her head and looked at me with pleading eyes. I didn't want to bring that news to Momo, but it might be easier hearing it from me. From the way Verity twisted her ponytail so tightly that she winced, I realized it would be easier on her, too, if I spoke to Momo.

"I know I should break the news, but if you want to, I wouldn't mind," Verity said.

"Momo will most likely realize I'm there for a reason," I said. "If so, I'll tell her, but otherwise, it should come from you."

"You're probably right." Verity sighed. "I didn't handle it well with my mother, so I can do better with Momo. But will you still go to her in case someone tries to tell her?"

"Yes, I will. Now it's time for you to go to the police."

I gave Verity another hug and nudged her down the street toward the police station. She held her head up high and moved quickly, so I knew she would head straight to Rob and Christine. It was time for me to see Momo.

I didn't lie when I told Papa that keeping busy helped with my grief, but I could use Momo's company. We could sit on her balcony and drink bourbon. Lady Clementine would lie at our feet as we quietly acknowledged our mutual sorrow for the family we lost.

43

As I walked to Momo's house, I tried to come up with a way to tell her gently about the theft ring, if necessary. Momo took pride in her family's tomb in St. Louis Cemetery No. 1, so I imagined she would be horrified that Nicole and Verity stole from mausoleums. Of course she would be furious they stole anything at all. But Momo's kindness would eclipse her anger. The truth might break Momo's heart, but seeing how happy Momo was that Verity was alive, I believed it would all be fine, eventually.

Delmar Apartments was coming up on the next block. Should I avoid it like Verity did the first night she was in town? I stood at the corner waiting for the traffic to go by as I decided if I was ready to pass by where my brother had been murdered. I couldn't avoid it forever, so I knew now was as good a time as any. Being across the street from it made it a little easier. But a chill ran down my spine as I stopped to stare at the building. It would be a while, if ever, that I would walk past here without thinking about Joey and Nicole.

Before my grief set in, I said a brief prayer for both of them and headed toward Momo's. But then I saw Sutton.

He came out of his apartment's front door with a red backpack in his hands. It might not have been my brother's, but what were the odds Sutton would have one? The bag looked out of place. It clashed with his faded black jeans, matching tank top, and a purple and silver chiffon scarf wrapped around his neck. He locked his apartment and put on a dark pair of sunglasses. I ducked behind a parked car, praying Sutton hadn't seen me.

I eased up from my hiding spot, hoping Sutton wasn't staring at me or, worse, coming across for me. He wasn't; Sutton plodded down the street as if he had to go somewhere against his will. His slow stride gave me time to cross over and follow him from a safe distance. A welcome breeze blew through the air, making Sutton's scarf fly behind him. Between his scarf and the red backpack, it was easy to track him. The crowds grew the farther we walked.

Sutton sustained a steady pace and, even with sidewalks full of people, I kept up with him. Where was he going? I waited for him to stop at a shop or at a home. Perhaps he was meeting someone on the street.

I pulled out my phone and snapped a few photos of the backpack. In case he got rid of it before I caught him, at least I'd have proof that he had it at one point. While Sutton was annoying and overbearing, I didn't see him as a killer. Even twenty-six years younger, I couldn't imagine him moving the fountain by himself, burying Nicole, and then returning the fountain to its original spot.

If he was Nicole's mysterious lover, why would Myles or Tabby help him cover up his crime? Maybe this was all about the theft ring. Sutton sold stolen goods according to Verity. If Nicole had changed her mind and planned to go to the police about the crimes, all three would have a reason to kill her.

Or he might be innocent and taking the backpack to the detectives.

But he wasn't.

Sutton knocked on the door to Delmar & Sons Antiques.

"Sutton!" I rushed up to him.

"Sammy?" Sutton stopped knocking on the door and turned around. "What a lovely surprise! Did you need another reading? By your face, it looks like you need spiritual guidance."

"The only thing I need from you is to know where you got that backpack."

"This? Tabby called me in a panic. She said she'd left a friend's backpack in her apartment and asked me to bring it here."

"I wouldn't call my brother her friend."

"This is Ray's backpack? The construction guy?" Sutton paled. "I still can't believe he was your brother."

"We can talk about that later." I snatched the backpack from him and unzipped it. Inside were the tools Luke Ward said he was missing, but there were also three wrapped pralines and photographs.

"Are you sure this was your brother's bag?" Sutton looked into the bag and plucked out a picture. "Oh, there's no doubt that this is you as a baby." He held up a picture of me sitting with Joey on a bench in Jackson Square with a box of pralines between us. My heart broke into a thousand pieces thinking of how just two days ago we reenacted that scene. My brother was sentimental to the end.

But I couldn't let emotions get the better of me. I needed to take this bag to the police. Along with Sutton.

"Sutton, we need to take this to the police now." I zipped the bag up and grabbed his arm.

"But I had nothing to do with your brother's murder." Sutton pulled away from me. "And I didn't kill Nicole."

"Are you telling the truth?"

"I am, Samantha." Sutton looked me dead in the eye and for the first time, I saw a real person behind the theatrical psychic persona. A seriousness and sadness covered his face. "Once Nicole was found, I should have gone to the police. But I needed to protect myself."

"Do Myles and Tabby have something on you?"

"Yes. Myles and the girls took stuff from the cemeteries and I sold some of it to my clients."

"Verity told me," I said. "She's telling the police about the theft ring right now."

"I knew this day would come. The spirits warned me I needed to atone for my foolish ways..."

"Listen, it will be all right if you tell the truth," I interrupted him. "I'll call one of the detectives and let him know we're on our way with the backpack. You can explain your side of the story."

Before I could get my phone out, Myles opened the shop's door. "Sutton, you're carrying the bag out in the open? How stupid can you be?"

"If I had known whose bag it was I wouldn't have brought it," Sutton sputtered. "Samantha and I are leaving."

"No, you're not," Tabby said.

Sutton and I turned around to find Tabby standing behind us. Her tight-lipped smile and clenched fists made my heart race. We needed to get away from the shop now. I moved, but Tabby pushed me into Sutton. Myles stepped out of the way as Sutton and I stumbled into the shop.

The clang of metal rang out as the backpack hit the floor. Sutton yelped as he landed on top of it. Or he could have been yelling because I came down on him.

"Lock the door, Myles," Tabby barked.

I rolled off Sutton, coughing from the dirt and dust on the floor. Sutton flipped over on his back and stared at me. My stomach dropped at the sound of the door being locked. Tabby reached out her hand to Sutton and pulled him off the floor.

"Sutton, I told you to put the backpack in a bag and bring it here." She brushed the dirt off his shoulders. "Why don't you ever listen to me? And now she's seen it." Tabby glared at me. "Your spirits aren't going to help you or her now."

44

I scrambled off the floor and grabbed the backpack. "It's too late, Tabby. The police know it was you and Myles who killed Nicole and my brother. The backpack is just another piece of evidence to convict you two."

"Exactly! I had nothing to do with any murders." Sutton puffed out his chest, but his attempt at bravado wasn't working on Tabby.

"But Sutton, you had the backpack." Tabby opened the drawer of the desk she stood next to and took out a what I assumed was a letter opener. That was until she took the blue velvet cover off the blade and the sharp tip of a dagger glinted off the chandelier lights. "If you killed Sammy's brother, you must have killed Nicole, too."

"I had nothing to do with either! You're setting me up!" Sutton growled.

He took a step toward the door, but Tabby jumped in front of him and put the dagger up to his throat. "I don't think so, Sutton." He tried to back away, but she grabbed his arm, keeping her weapon at his neck. "Let's go to the back room and talk this over. Myles, bring her back, too."

Myles lurched at me, but I sidestepped him, causing him to run into a side table. I raced to the door, but I stopped when Tabby called out to me.

"Samantha, if you leave now, I'll kill Sutton." Tabby towered over a trembling Sutton, with her arm wrapped around his neck, still pressing the dagger at him. "I'll frame him for your brother's murder and then frame you for his."

"No one would believe you." I bluffed, hoping my voice sounded stronger than my conviction. "You don't want to kill Sutton."

"There's a difference between want and need." Tabby smiled, pulling Sutton closer to her. "Are you willing to take that risk?"

As she pushed the dagger deeper in his neck, Sutton winced. He trembled and his eyes bored into me. I looked behind me to see Myles blocking the door, his arms crossed. But his stance was shaky as he shifted back and forth. I could rush him and get around him to the door. As I faced Tabby again, I realized I wouldn't make it out. Her grip on Sutton was tighter, but her face scared me more. She looked like someone who had nothing left to lose.

"Let's go talk in there, shall we?" Tabby tilted her head toward the door marked "private office."

Tabby acted as if she was a genteel hostess of a cocktail party instead of a murderer threatening to kill a hostage. And most likely she planned to kill me, too. I didn't want to go in that backroom, but I had no choice.

She pushed Sutton through the door, and I followed with Myles behind me. I slipped my hand in my pocket, hoping I could dial 911 without looking at the screen.

"Hands out of your pocket, Samantha. I don't mean to be rude, but I don't trust you." Tabby smiled. "You must have been reaching for your cell phone. Give it to Myles or he'll search you for it. And trust me, he would enjoy it."

Myles put his hand out without saying a word. His face was blank, so I didn't know if he was in shock or exhausted. No matter how he felt, he was letting Tabby take the lead. I gave my cell phone to him while Tabby took Sutton's cell phone.

"Why don't you and Sutton sit there for a moment while Myles and I chat?"

Tabby pointed to a pair of blue velvet wingback chairs in the corner of the room. The sign on the door said office, but it was more of a storage room. A floor-to-ceiling metal shelving unit covered the center of the back wall. Ceramic lamps and frayed lampshades filled the top shelf, chipped glassware and dented cocktail shakers made up the middle shelf, and the bottom shelf held boxes labeled china, silverware, and linens. The rest of the room was filled with mismatched chairs with broken legs or backs, side tables with cracked tops, and faded rugs rolled up against the walls. There was a door to the left of the shelving unit, but it was blocked by a large wooden china cabinet with broken glass doors.

Sutton and I maneuvered in and out of the furniture to the chairs. I sat down on the edge of the chair, needing to be ready to take my chance to grab Sutton and rush for the door. Myles and Tabby stood by it, but they hadn't locked it. That was our only way out.

Tabby and Myles huddled together, their whispers rising and falling in urgency and anger. I needed a plan to get out of here before they decided what to do with us. Hopefully Verity gave her information quickly to Rob and Christine and they were already looking for Myles and Tabby. Until they showed up, I needed to get Myles and Tabby away from the door. And the best way was to keep them fighting with each other so they would be distracted.

Looking at them, it should be easy. They were still in each other's faces, their voices now growing louder with each minute.

"Sutton." I elbowed him to get him to sit up. "We have to get them away from the door, so we can get out of here."

"Are you sure? Maybe they'll just lock us in and they'll leave." Sutton twisted the ends of his scarf in his hands. "Let me reach out to the spirits to see what we should do."

"You don't need your tarot cards or the spirits to see we're in trouble," I snapped. "Tabby and Myles are killers! If they were going to leave us, they would have done it already. We need to take care of ourselves. Or I'll just take care of me."

"No, don't leave me with them," Sutton pleaded. "Tabby obviously was going to frame me for the murders. I don't want to go to jail. Or die."

"Then follow my lead."

45

"Tabby, Myles, the police know about the angel statues and the theft ring, in case that affects whatever y'all are discussing," I said after coughing loudly to get their attention.

"What?" Myles lost all color in his face and leaned back against the storeroom door. Great. That wasn't the position I wanted him to move into. But Tabby took the bait.

"I have no idea what you're talking about, Samantha." She stepped toward the center of the room, about ten feet away from me and Sutton. "Even if they found a statue with Nicole, they can't tie it to us."

I nudged Sutton, hoping he would get the hint to follow my lead, as I had said.

"I'm going to confess to the police to cleanse my soul." Sutton sat up tall and straightened the scarf around his neck. "I will accept my punishment and throw myself at the mercy of the court and the spirits."

"You've never done anything that would put yourself in harm's way, Sutton." Tabby flipped her hair over her shoulder. "You won't go to the cops. No one will believe a fake fortune teller and a girl who ran away twenty-six years ago over two upstanding New Orleans business owners."

"Verity's with the police right now and she's telling them about the statues." I studied Tabby's and Myles' faces. She didn't react, but Myles looked down at the floor. "Actually, there were two statues in the grave. One was underneath Nicole's body. My brother stole the other statue with the bloodstains."

I didn't know if the stains on the statue were blood, but I thought it was worth the risk. My gamble paid off.

"Myles? What is she talking about?" Tabby spun on her heels to face Myles. "You told me you sold the other angel."

"Tabby, shut up." Myles moved away from the door and stepped next to her. "Let's go. We'll just leave them here."

"Myles, did you kill Nicole because she was going to leave town with your baby?" I asked. "Did you put the other statue in the grave because you regretted killing her? By the look on your face, I'd say you cared for her, maybe even loved her."

"I didn't know she was pregnant until the police told me," Myles said. "Tabby, did you know Nicole was pregnant when she was alive?"

"No! I told you, she came to your apartment while you were out and threatened to go to the police," Tabby insisted, but there was a shakiness to her voice. "We fought, and she fell against the fireplace. It was an accident."

"Myles, if you had talked to Verity, you would have known they weren't going to the police. Nicole was leaving town. She just wanted to give you the angel statue and start a new life," I said. "But Tabby killed her and you helped her cover up her crime."

"Tell me the truth, Tabby!" he growled. "You knew she

was pregnant, didn't you? Is that the real reason you killed her?"

Tabby hesitated, but then her face fell in apparent resignation. "Yes, I was jealous. You would have left me for her." She grabbed Myles' hands, but he pulled away so hard she stumbled backward and lost her balance. Tabby pushed herself up off the floor and stood up.

If looks could kill, Tabby would have been dead on the spot. Twenty-six years ago, Myles must have thought his world was collapsing when he came home to find Nicole dead. But he and Tabby covered it up and their thefts were never discovered.

In the end, they had lost each other and Myles had lost his chance at being a father. I remembered how sad he looked when he said they hadn't been blessed with children. Now Nicole was unburied, along with their crimes and the lies Tabby told.

Myles' rage came out as a burst of expletives at Tabby and then turned into violence. He grasped her neck with both hands and screamed at her. Tabby scratched at his hands, trying to pull them off as she kicked at his shins.

Sutton tugged my arm. "Samantha, we can run now."

"You can go, but I have to stop this."

He shook his head. "A gentleman never leaves a lady."

I did a double-take. I expected Sutton to seize the first chance to save himself, especially when I gave him an out.

"Stop, Myles!" I screamed and jumped out of the chair. I took a few steps closer to them, but not within arm's reach. "You don't want to be a killer like Tabby!"

Myles released his grip from around Tabby's neck and took a step back. Tabby rubbed her throat and inhaled and exhaled deeply. She then pointed at Myles and let out a laugh that chilled me to the bone.

"Samantha, Myles *is* a killer," Tabby snickered. "Who do you think murdered your brother?"

"Is that true?" I took a step toward Myles, but Sutton stood up and grasped my hand. He squeezed it gently and when I looked into his eyes, I saw his concern. He was right to be; we now were in a room with two murderers.

"Yes, I killed Ray, or whatever your brother's real name was." Myles pinched the bridge of his nose and squeezed his eyes shut for a moment. "Do you really care what happened to him? He was a killer."

"Yes, he was like you and Tabby," I said. "But even though he was a murderer, he was my family. I want to know what happened."

"Tell her, Myles." Tabby rubbed her neck. The confidence had returned to her voice.

"Your brother was always too quiet, sneaking around." Myles frowned. "We didn't realize he was squatting at Mrs. Riggins' place. After Nicole was found, we were speaking by the stairs to her apartment when he opened the door with a grin on his face."

I imagined the scene. Joey must have thought he hit the jackpot — blackmail money from Tabby and Myles would be worth more than what he'd get at an antique shop for the angel statue.

"He called us inside and he hit me up for money, but I hit him with a hammer laying by his backpack," Myles said. "We thought his backpack would lead us to the statue, but you got to it first."

"Myles had to do it. There was no other way out," Tabby said.

To Tabby's and Myles' confusion, I gave a hollow laugh. I couldn't help it; that's just what Joey told me when he explained why he murdered two people before trying to kill me. Some might see this as poetic justice, but after I stopped laughing, the heartache of it all crashed down on me.

"You should have paid him. You had a way out besides murder," I said.

Myles shook his head. "I couldn't pay him. I'm broke. Why else do you think I sold the apartment building? I'm about to lose my business, too."

"The shop?" Tabby screeched. "I divorced you because I thought you'd pull yourself together if you actually lost me! Instead, you dated those bimbos from the casinos and your business tanked."

"Tabby, you divorced me to save your precious little boutique," Myles snapped. "You saw a sinking ship, and you left. I'm broke and now I'm going to jail. And you're going with me."

Tabby and Myles got in each others faces and I waited for a repeat of their earlier fight. Instead, they just yelled at each other, their words so jumbled together that I couldn't understand them. I doubted they understood each other.

"Sutton, now it's time to go." I gripped his hand and tugged him toward the door. I flung it open and Sutton followed me. He slammed it shut and locked it.

"Help me with this." I picked up one end of Myles' desk and Sutton took the other end. We pushed it against the door. I stacked a few chairs on top for good measure, but neither Tabby nor Myles tried to escape. I didn't care what they were doing inside the storeroom as long as they stayed in there until the police arrived.

"We need to call 911." I scanned the store for a telephone.

"No need." Sutton pointed to the front of the shop. Rob

banged on the front door. Christine peered in through the left window and Verity looked through the other one.

"Before we let them in, I must tell you something." Sutton said.

"Now, Sutton?"

"Just one quick thing. After all this, you need my spiritual guidance classes. I can offer you an even better discount since you saved my life." Sutton clasped his hands together. "You still have much to deal with regarding your past."

"Let's just focus on the present and get out of this mess." I put my arm through Sutton's and dragged him to the door. He must never miss a chance to promote his services, but he wasn't wrong. I needed to face my past — by putting my brother to rest.

46

With the turn of the key, I buried my brother.

Verity had kept her word and told Rob and Christine about the cemetery theft ring. They immediately looked for Tabby and Myles with Verity suggesting they search the antique shop first. Ruby claimed Verity's spiritual gift had led her to the store, but Verity dismissed it. But not too much.

When the detectives let Tabby and Myles out of the storeroom, Tabby had denied any wrongdoing in Nicole's and Joey's murders. Whatever they had screamed about when I locked them in, it had taken a toll on Myles. He confessed to everything. Now that they were in jail, I heard Tabby was considering a plea deal along with Myles. For Verity's and Momo's sake, I hoped they would. And for mine, too. I wanted Joey's funeral to be the end of this saga.

Sissy and Aunt Charlene arranged the burial for my brother since I was at a loss of what to do. Sissy's parish priest gave a quick but thoughtful service, and even Aunt Charlene said a few pleasant words. Jasper might have had something to do with it, but the gesture was kind all the same.

Connor stood by my side from the moment I came home from the antique shop until the funeral. Could I have handled this by myself? Sure, I was a strong woman, but I didn't have to go through this alone. Having a boyfriend who let me process my grief on my own terms was something I would never take for granted.

After locking my family's tomb, I turned to face everyone who came. Jasper had his arm around his mother, who leaned her head against him. Neal and Rose held hands as they spoke softly to Andrew and Beau. Sissy stood off to the side with Christine and Rob.

Connor shook hands with Mr. Hugo before he returned to his post to begin his shift. William, Libby, and Frankie waved as they left. They were organizing brunch in the apartment's courtyard after the service. Second line celebrations were common after a funeral in New Orleans, but I decided against it. The first part of a second line is a somber walk with a brass band playing solemn music. It then turns into a celebration of the deceased's life with upbeat music and dancing. It wasn't appropriate for a murderer.

But he had been my brother, and burying him in the family tomb was the right thing to do. Our parents meant the world to him, and I wouldn't deny him being with them in the afterlife.

"Thank y'all for coming this morning. Joey hurt all of you in different ways..." I couldn't finish my sentence. The first tears of the day spilled out. Crying at a funeral was normal, but when the deceased was a killer, it felt wrong to mourn him with such emotion.

My friends stepped toward me, but Andrew reached me before the others. He embraced me and said, "Funerals are not just to pay respects to the dead. They are also to support the living. And we are all here for you, my dear."

Connor stayed with me while everyone else waited by the cemetery's front gate. I faced the tomb and ran my hand over my brother's name, Samuel Joseph St. Martin. My adopted name was taken from his, as Sam was the only word the two-year old child separated from her family in a hurricane could say.

"Sammy, Momo and Verity are here." Connor placed a hand gently on my shoulder.

I turned around to see them coming up to the tomb. While I still saw a sadness in Momo's eye, her physical presence was stronger than before.

"My darling, I'm sorry we missed the service." Momo kissed my cheek. "The darn airline took forever and a day to add Verity to my flight."

"We're going to New York for Nicole's funeral," Verity said. "Her father insisted on burying her there."

"I'm sorry, Momo. I know you wanted her buried in the family tomb here," I said.

"It's out of my hands." Momo shrugged. "Nothing I can do, but at least I'll have Verity with me. That reminds me. We need to pick up more bourbon before we go."

"Momo, they have bourbon in New York." Verity laughed.

"Fine, let's get sweet tea then. I know they don't have that." Momo hugged me and said, "Thank you for everything you did for me and Nicole. She can rest in peace finally."

"Momo, I want to talk to Sammy for a moment," Verity said. "Connor, will you walk Momo out?"

Connor nodded, and even though Momo insisted she didn't need help, she took Connor's arm. They stopped at the end of the row as Ruby and Papa walked up. To my surprise, the two women kissed each other on the cheek and then went their respective ways.

"Would you look at that?" Verity's entire face lit up. "There appears to be hope for them."

Ruby, in one of her long black chiffon dresses, came up to me. "I needed to speak with several spirits, so they delayed me for your brother's funeral," Ruby said. "Verity, stop at Marie Laveau's tomb before you leave. She will have much to say to you."

"Oh, I bet she does." Verity rolled her eyes, but she smiled. "I need to ask Papa something before he leaves."

"Let's talk over here, Verity. I'll be back, Ruby." Papa and Verity strolled over to another mausoleum about thirty feet away.

This felt like a set-up. Ruby stepped over to my family's tomb and put her hand on my birth parents' names. "Your parents, both sets, want the best for you."

"Did they contact you?" I didn't believe my adoptive parents or birth parents would reach out to Ruby from beyond the grave.

"No. Their spirits aren't here. But I don't need to talk to them. All parents wish for their children to be happy." Ruby looked at Verity with a softness in her eyes. "Even if their path is different from what you hoped."

"Thank you." And I meant it. This was the kindest thing Ruby had said to me. I took it as her way of thanking me for helping her with Verity. Was this the start of a kinder, gentler Ruby?

Apparently not.

"Verity, come on. If you stay too long, you'll have a spirit attach itself to you. And Samantha tends to attract negative spirits," Ruby called out and started toward her daughter.

"Mother..." Verity sighed as she walked over to me. She hugged me and whispered, "See, she likes you."

"I wouldn't go that far." I smiled. "I hope you'll come back to visit your mother and Momo. And me."

"I will come back. It'll be hard to be here without Nicole, but the French Quarter has a way of drawing you back in." Verity glanced around the cemetery. "The past and present somehow work together here."

"I couldn't agree more." I hugged Verity again.

"Verity, come on, the spirits are getting restless around Samantha," Ruby called out.

"I better go. Thanks for everything, Nancy Drew. I owe you." Verity rushed over to her mother and they left, arguing about which spirits should be in this cemetery.

I kept my laughter to myself as Verity and Ruby walked out of my sight. To someone else, it might seem crazy, but I was glad Ruby was still going to berate me for my ability to attract negative spirits. While I hoped we understood each other better, I actually enjoyed the back-and-forth nature of our relationship.

One thing I learned so far from living in New Orleans was that I had to accept the bad with the good. While I buried part of my past today, it would always be with me. And that was all right. I could live with it even if it meant trouble followed me. Or was I inviting it in? As I left my family's tomb to join my Thibodeaux Mansion family, I decided to just wait to see what happened next.

THE END

Sammy's New Orleans adventures continue in
The Dead End Tour

ACKNOWLEDGMENTS

The image of a writer is usually one of a person bent over a laptop by themselves at home or at a coffee shop. While this is me much of the time when I'm writing, I am lucky to have the help of my family and friends.

I wouldn't have started this writing journey or continued it without the love and encouragement of my husband, Dave. Whether it's listening to my crazy story ideas, making time for me to write, or sending me off to New Orleans by myself, he always supports me. I love you.

And to my children who are growing up so fast, you make me so proud. I'm sorry for all the takeout dinners this year, but you always understand when I need to write. I love you and you'll always be my babies.

Thanks to the new kittens for the joy you've brought to our family's life. Now if I could just teach you not to walk on my keyboard.

Dad and Wanda, four books in and you're still willing to read the rough drafts! Thanks for your help, as always. Love y'all.

Amanda, Amelia, and Doug, even with our crazy schedules, our critique group keeps chugging along. Thank you for your constructive criticism and your friendship over the years.

Thanks for being a beta-reader once again, Jenna. Your feedback is invaluable and always spot-on. Thank you for helping me grow as a writer, and for your friendship.

Katy, you're a beta-reader, therapist, friend, and so much more to me. Thank you for all you do for me and my family.

Leann, you came back for more! Thanks for being a great beta-reader again and for helping me in some many ways.

Susan, thanks for joining the beta-reader crew and giving me one of the greatest friends I've ever had. I hope we'll meet in person someday soon.

Chrystal, I'm glad to have you as a beta-reader and as a neighbor. Thanks for being both.

And as always, thank you to my family, friends, and readers. Your continued support and encouragement help more than you know.

ALSO BY JEN PITTS

The French Quarter Mystery Series:

Coffee, a Scone, and a Place to Call Home - a Short Story Prequel

The Key to Murder

The Gates to the Afterlife

A Deadly Check-In

Bury the Past

The Dead End Tour

A Corpse in the Cafe

Happy Homicide

The Witches of the French Quarter Series:

Mardi Gras and Magic

Red Beans and Rituals

ABOUT THE AUTHOR

Jen Pitts is a lifelong mystery reader who turned her obsession into writing cozy mysteries of her own. When she isn't plotting fictional murder, she's chugging coffee, traveling, reading, and enjoying life with her husband, children, and two cats in the Pacific Northwest.

Learn more about Jen through her newsletter. A free short story prequel is available exclusively for newsletter members. Sign up at www.jenpittsauthor.com

And keep up daily with Jen on Facebook where she shares her books, her cats, and her love of New Orleans.

You can also find Jen on the following social media sites:

- **f** facebook.com/jenpittsmysteryauthor
- **⊙** instagram.com/jenpittsmysterywriter
- **g** goodreads.com/jenpitts
- **a** amazon.com/author/jenpitts
- **BB** bookbub.com/authors/jen-pitts